From a Distance

Larry Baker

Ice Cube Press, LLC
North Liberty, Iowa

For

G

Ellie: I Am Born

I kissed a page for him. After I finally found him. I knew it was him because he knew who I was. I told him I was somebody else. But he knew. He gave me the name I never knew I wanted. And he is pretty. I have never seen a boy so pretty. He thinks I am older. I am. But he knows the real me. And he is tiny. I can look down at him. He's like a giant pretty boy doll.

I was at the dirty bookstore, the one next to SJB. You can see the dust in the air. The light hits the dust, lines in the air. Like that poem I read a hundred times. I had seen him there lots, he never saw me. But he caught me stealing a book today. He never caught me before. I thought I was safe again. It was in my purse and I was almost safe. I heard his voice. He has a proper voice. I stood still. I can be invisible when I want to be. I can go away. But he still saw me. For that first second I was scared, like I am when it happens to me at home, when I cannot escape. But he did not growl at me. He just asked me if I needed any help.

— Are you looking for anything in particular?

I said no. I was fine. But then I looked up and directly at him. He was so pretty. I wanted to cry. But he was on to me.

—Perhaps that book in your purse needs a regular store bag? So proper. I was caught. More than perhaps.

I was wrong. He had always seen me. The other times. He must have seen me stealing before. But he did not talk about that. He just asked what I liked to read. I told him Nancy Drew, like the book in my purse. I told him that I liked books about smart girls. He smiled at me and held out his hand. I knew what he wanted. I handed him the book. He asked if I wanted to pay for it. I told him that I had no money. And then he did something that made me almost faint. He looked at me but tilted his head. As if it was me that was crooked and he had to adjust his sight to that. And then he handed the book back to me. Told me to keep it.

—A gift from me.

He could have hurt me, but he gave me a book. He introduced himself, but I did not like his name. I know about his father and mother. They are important. I am not. I did not want him to be their son. Then the most wonderful thing happened. He turned his back to me for a second and I saw the paperback book sticking out of his pocket. It was a dirty book. I had seen it at my house. And when he turned around he realized that I had discovered a secret about him. I had power over him. He had been reading *Peyton Place*. He told me his real name, but I told him that I was going to call him Peyton. That was his name from me, our secret. He turned red. I have never seen any man turn that color from embarrassment. From other things, yes. Anger or other things, but never a real blush. He laughed. Tried not to, but he laughed. And he asked who I was.

He did not know me. I could be anybody I wanted with him. I could be who I was at home, or I could be one of the others.

I chose my favorite. I told him my name was Elizabeth Elliott. He could call me Liz. But he shook his head.

—Liz is not your name. Your name is Ellie

And that was the moment I knew he was the one. I had never known I was Ellie until he named me. He saw the one true me before I did.

We sat for an hour at his desk in the corner near the big window. He was so young compared to the old people who worked there. They were old and wrinkly and smelled leathery, like the store. I wish I could remember what we talked about. He did most of the talking. I just wanted to look at him. He is so pretty. He asked when I would come back. I was mean to him. I told him I was never coming back. He just looked at me.

— I want you to come see me again.

I stopped teasing. How could I not see him again, ever. I wanted him to hold my hand. But he was still trapped in his old name, his real name. He was still his parents son, but I knew, I knew in my stomach, that he was going to be mine. I took the lipstick out of my purse and rubbed it across my lips. I knew he could not turn away. I asked for his book. I kissed the first page for him. It was a promise. Then I turned to the last blank page. Used my lipstick. I wrote a big red letter . . . *E*. I know what a whore is. I am a whore. They tell me that. Peyton knows Ellie, not the whore. I handed the book back to him and told him that I would be back tomorrow. I did not tell him that I had no choice. I was going to be his Ellie forever.

As he walked me to the front door, with the old people looking at us, he asked where I went to school. I told him it did not matter. We would never meet at school. We were from different sides of Broad Street. He told me that he was a junior.

Me too, I said. He said he was sixteen. Me too. How could I tell him that I was only thirteen. How could I tell him that he would never be as old as me.

This is my new story. All the pages I have written for the past four years . . . I am burning them tonight. I was born today.

Almost the End

Suicide would have been an understandable gesture, if everyone knew the truth, but Bobby Beaumont had a secret, so he told the Germans to go to hell. Not in those words, of course, because they would have seen such honesty as mere confirmation of his ego. No, Beaumont had a secret, so he had simply refused to move out of his office when everyone else vacated the building. He would wait until the very last moment. He had spent twenty years in the corner of the 22nd floor, had looked toward Broadway a hundred times a day for those twenty years, and had decided that even though the Germans owned the company he would not follow them to their new building. He had seen the plans. Mausoleums had more charm; prisons, more character, not to mention architectural imagination. And, besides, the new building was intended to be smoke-free. How insane was that?

The Germans had sought Beaumont's agreement, hoping that his example would ease the pain and misgivings of his people. The head German, the tall one, would say to them, "See, Bobby is making the change. If he can do it, so can you." The head German was a confident man, a man of assumptions. He assumed that Beaumont had agreed to the move. A nod to the German was a contract, like blood on a page. Soon enough, the paper pages could be signed and notarized. For Beaumont, however, a nod was a sign of thought. *I will give it some thought*, his nod said, but he never shook hands with the German, and he never offered his own blood. As soon as the Germans revealed their plans for a new building, Beaumont announced his retirement from publishing.

Beaumont cared about his people, even loved a few, but he had not told them the truth either. He had spent the last year making contacts for them with other publishers, but most of his people had told him, in the beginning, that they preferred to go with him to the new building. If he was not going, however, all bets were off. Sally Graham, his assistant, had insisted that *the soul of Windsor was not in bricks and glass, but in who we are.* She had then put her finger in her mouth and feigned a gag. But Beaumont knew she had believed what she said.

Sally was his favorite, and he would miss her the most, but he had not even told her about his lungs, although the coughing and fatigue were more obvious, and his heart had never fully recovered from its first attack five years earlier. Nor had he used the Windsor insurance to pay his bills and thus leave a paper trail. He had lots of unused money, and money bought him privacy. Even at the beginning, when the news was most harsh, and his grief most painful, Beaumont was already keeping it all to himself. He had controlled his life, why not his death? Of all his staff, he assumed that Sally had figured it out, the finality of it, but she kept it to herself, another reason that he trusted her.

Sally was the best of his people, and his only regret now was that he had not listened to her when he should have, when he got the call from Harry Windsor's son. How could he have missed the obvious? In hindsight, too many coincidences. He had never gotten over the death of someone he loved years earlier, then his own symptoms, and then the phone call from the son telling him that he and the other Windsor son had decided to sell the Windsor name and business. The Germans would make Windsor even more successful, right? All that money to buy new books and lure established writers. The buzz had been instantaneous: *BOBBY AND THE HUNS—WINDSOR TO RIVAL RANDOM?*—the headline in *Variety*. The *New York Observer* was more subtle—*WILL WINDSOR HOUSE REMAIN A BOUTIQUE?*

The Germans arrived as a Trojan Horse, disguised as money, and Beaumont had missed the obvious hollow sound. His medical diagnosis had been a distraction when he had talked to Windsor's son. A month after that conversation, the Germans bought Windsor. More than Windsor House, they also bought the building in which Windsor had lived since its creation in 1979. As any accountant would say: *Books can make money, but real estate makes a profit.*

The Germans had bought Windsor House, the building, and the people, or so they assumed. As soon as the rumors began, which always preceded the gossip, the Germans had been adamant: The sale was contingent on Bobby Beaumont staying as head of Windsor. *Credibility and Continuity* was their daily message. *We want the Crown Jewel of American publishing, but we do not want to change anything.* All the other Houses knew the truth. Windsor was merely the diamond wedge into the American market. Editors took their deck chairs and began shuffling. Confidential inquiries, cocktail party hushed conversations, late lunch drinks and "what if" games. The Kabuki Dance of self-preservation. A stew of metaphors, but Beaumont did not care. He had heard the rumors long before anyone else, and he was already coughing blood.

The tall German had made a personal appearance, and his English was impeccable. "Tell us what it would take to keep you here and happy," he had said, humble and sincere.

Beaumont had already begun the process of not caring. "I want what I already have. I want my salary, my people, and complete editorial autonomy." The German nodded, and Beaumont began playing games, "And I want a bonus for all my editors and all my department heads." The German nodded again, but slower. Beaumont tested him, "Fifty thousand per person ..."

The German twitched, but he was more prepared than Beaumont had expected, "Including you? If not, then we're talking about just twelve people, correct?"

Beaumont had to count in his head. For some reason, he had thought there were more, but the German was right. "No, not me, just the twelve," he sighed. Windsor had always been a small House, but it had the biggest names. "And put it in writing." Beaumont had made a career out of handshakes, but he wanted the German signatures in triplicate. A nod was not a handshake. A handshake was not a signature, not this time.

The German nodded. Beaumont was thinking about his failing lungs and his broken heart at the moment, or else he would have been suspicious of the smile in front of him. He had gotten everything he asked for, but he neglected to ask for budget autonomy in addition to editorial autonomy. It was all the Germans needed in the long run. Sally made sure that

Beaumont understood that, but too late. "I thought you were the smartest damn man in publishing, Bobby. So how come this slipped by you?" She was one of the few who were allowed to lecture him.

Beaumont understood why Sally was upset, but he assured her that it did not matter. She and the others could go to another House. He would retire and die in peace, he told himself. Or, if he could recoup some of his waning energy, perhaps he could take the Germans head-on and rescue Windsor from the dark side of the publishing world, the bottom-line crowd, the *publishing is just another business* crowd. But, then again, perhaps they were right. It had always been an overly romanticized business. He was too tired to really care anymore.

Perhaps—it was a seductive word. But Beaumont had been wrong. With less time came less energy. Then the drawings for the new building crossed his desk, and he realized that he had lost. He had failed Sally and the others, but, just as suicide became a serious final option, his last act of self-control, he called Sally and read to her the first line of a final project: *I kissed a page for him.*

Those pages had arrived six weeks ago. Tonight, Windsor was still alive, but Beaumont would finish this day without his usual ritual. On any other night in the past, he would close his office door and then stand in the dark, looking toward Broadway and then up toward the distant spire of the Empire State Building, watch the lights blink in thousands of windows around him, absorb the beauty of stone and electricity, think about his day, smoke a final cigarette, and then go downstairs to his Windsor Building apartment. In the past, before the others had vacated their own offices, he was usually not the last to leave. His assistant editor, whoever she was, was always at her desk, usually flanked by stacks of manuscripts or correspondence. She would wave as he passed, and say, as her role in the ritual, "See you tomorrow, Bobby." Every assistant he had ever had went on to become a senior editor at some other House, an ascension implicit the day she was hired, and it was always a she. Sally was the last assistant he had hired, but she never left.

Tonight was different. Beaumont was alone in his office, as usual. New York City, an hour after sunset in August. The Windsor Building was empty and dark, disemboweled, stripped like a corpse ready for cremation, Beaumont's office and apartment were the exceptions. Somewhere else in the City, everyone was assured, his new apartment waited, with new furnishings, for a new life. Tomorrow, the demolition engineers would begin prepping Windsor for its implosion, but he wanted one last cigarette in his office, one last look down. Beaumont played with the word *last*. To come in last. To last, to endure. Then he lit a cigarette in the dark. Not the last of his life, he knew, but damn close.

The Germans were already in their new building. Windsor House had been boxed up and carted out of the Windsor Building weeks ago. The best of Beaumont's people had dispersed to the other Houses, taking their talent and their best writers with them, but Beaumont knew that his replacement would eventually re-create Windsor in his own image, as he himself had first created it over twenty years ago. The Germans had made a smart choice, he admitted, and would re-coup their investment soon enough. He just wished he would live long enough to see what they did after they had restocked Windsor's stable.

Beaumont coughed. There was a grim pleasure in the thought of being alive to see the future. But, he decided, not enough reason to stretch out his own life.

The dazzling outside light cast shadows off every object in the dark office. Beaumont had insisted that nothing be removed until the last minute, and the Germans had agreed. Even as the building itself was being emptied, his office was untouched. It was part of his secret. He was taking only one thing with him tonight, a gift to Sally, a seventeenth century map, matted and framed and the first thing he had taken to his, then new, office back in 1979. Everything else would fall into the Windsor Building rubble that was going to be created in a few days. His full bookshelves, the desk and chair, gifts from a hundred writers, the framed magazine covers, the pictures of him and his people at major and minor awards programs, dozens of original manuscripts of books published years ago, all of Bobby's sentimental favorites. The party pictures. His material history would feel the first shudder beneath it as the dynamite explosions rippled along the lower steel skeleton. For a moment, Bobby closed his eyes, dizzy, imagining himself in his office as its floor disintegrated, his body and professional life falling to the ground, walls and windows tumbling down after them. It was almost comforting.

Bobby knew that he felt something like love for this building. He had always assumed that it would last forever. Surely, longer than him. He took one last look at the city below him, went to his desk in the dark, picked up the map, walked through the bare outer offices to the elevator, and did not look back. Tonight, he was headed to a Plaza Hotel suite, his temporary home until he left for a much-discussed vacation to Europe. He had made sure that everyone knew his plans.

On the ground floor, he paused to say goodnight to the black doorman, the first man that he had hired when Windsor House was formed, older than Bobby back then, but not looking much different this night. The doorman had also lived in the Windsor Building, and he had locked the front door thousands of times. With the building soon to be history, Bobby had made arrangements for the doorman to retire, to go back to his home in Louisiana and live comfortably. The old man was not part of the German plan. Tonight was his last night in his Windsor apartment.

"Only a few more days, Mr. Beaumont," the doorman said as he held the door open.

"Just a few, perhaps two weeks, that is right," Bobby said. "Do you plan on being here for the demolition?"

"Oh, no sir, that would grieve me too much. I'll be sitting on a porch back in the Ninth Ward."

"Going home is a good thing, no doubt."

The old man did not reply, just nodded, and then Beaumont said, "Those arrangements I asked of you…about the lock and keys…you are comfortable with that?"

The old man nodded again, saying, "It's a small task. I'll be glad to do it."

"And the couch in my office. You will move that?"

"Yessir. The dolly is already up there."

Bobby's relief was obvious, "Good, I have always depended on you. And you will always have my gratitude. So, now, how about your future, your plans?"

"I'm gonna write that book I always said I was gonna write."

"Well, it is my hope that you make me look good, and be sure to get a copy to Sally. She will help you."

The old man was too respectful to laugh, but Bobby could still appreciate the mirth in his voice. "Oh no, sir. This book's about me, not you. I've done a lot, seen a lot. Things my family in New Orleans might want to know. No, my book's about me, my time here, and a few pages about them too, all the things that happened."

"As it should be," Beaumont said, pausing in the doorway, warm evening air to his back, cool lobby air flowing past his face. Power to the entire building would be shut off the next day. After that, yellow tape x-ing all the doors and a chain link fence around the building would appear. As he was about to step on to the street, he paused and asked one more question, "Say, I was wondering, do you remember Harry Windsor?"

"Of course, Mr. Beaumont. That man would be hard to forget."

"You would recognize him if you ever saw him again?"

The older man furrowed his brow and squinted, but he did not rush to answer. The question made no sense, but he could see that an answer was required. "Been dead a long time, surely that's the truth, sir. You and me and his bookkeeping man, and your young lady friend, we spread the ashes. A godly beautiful morning, as I recall. That's who you mean, right?"

"Yes, that is he."

"Well, sir, I would be taking it as a bad sign if I was seeing a dead man."

Beaumont smiled and nodded, "Of course, but how about talking to a dead man?"

The old man brightened, "Oh, sir, I do that all the time, speak to the dead. Sometimes they talk back, most often not, but the words pass between us."

Beaumont sighed and reached over to pat the old man on his shoulder, "So, this is it. Good night."

"And good night to you too, sir. A good night, indeed. Please give my regards to my friends at the Plaza."

Ellie: Peter and Paul

They don't know about Peyton. Don't know about me either. I wish he had been reading a different book when I found him. It would have been so cool to see the mockingbird book in his pocket, and I would have known he was Atticus, but I always knew that Atticus was not real. I am okay with Peyton. A name with secrets. I bet my Peyton has secrets. I would have liked to be Scout. She is like me without a mother, and she did have Atticus, but she is not real either. People like her do not exist. Peyton is right. I am Ellie. I exist.

Ellie does not live here. She is at that musty bookstore. But I am here now, waiting for Peter and Paul to find me. Peter and Paul. Peter and Paul, down the hall, Peter and Paul behind the wall. But they only let me talk to them at SJB. They only listen at SJB. Their lips are sealed there, sealed in glass, silent shepherds. And if I had not found them at SJB, how would I have found Peyton, so close all that time. All I had to do was go from their muteness (is that a word?) to the store with old books and young Peyton. Maybe Father is right. There is a divine plan. All the parts make sense? I found Peyton's place? His place is my place? His face is...perfect.

We'll go on walks in the park. We'll hold hands. We have all the time in the world. I will only be Ellie with him. He will never know about the others. They do not exist. He will want to tell me about his other family, the father and mother I do not have. Perhaps I will let him use his other name, maybe not. Doesn't matter. Down deep, he knows he is Peyton and that I named him. We will talk about the future, our secret future. He will be a famous writer and I will be his subject. The heroine who saves little girls from the Peter and Paul who live with me, not at SJB. Catcher in the sty, catch her in the sky, catcher from the lie. Fuck them all, short and tall, make them crawl, kill them all!

My other life is all burned to ashes now, gone in smoke. Peyton will only know the new me, the true me, not the blue me. I should be a poet but I hate rhymes. No, I want Peyton to tell my story, to make everyone weep when I die. If I had never met him I might have been an Emily. I like her a lot. I understand her. She wrote about somebody standing in a corner like a loaded gun. I bet we could talk. She would understand me because I understand her. But Peyton will do. Perfect Peyton and his perfect face, living in his perfect big home...I've seen it from the outside...with his perfect parents. I don't think he will understand me as well as Emily would, but he will love me. That's enough. That is more than I deserve. Whores don't deserve anything. But Ellie deserves Peyton.

I think I hear Peter coming. His boots always give him away. He's a sad man. He always buys me gifts. Paul is the mad man, the bad man. But Paul is generous. He shares me with the other apostles and saints. Peter is selfish. He wants the whore for himself. I prefer Paul.

Will he smell the leftover smoke? Will he smell the end of the past? I am surprised by how little is left after you burn paper. I really wanted to save some ashes, but what was left simply fluttered into something that could not be held in my hand. All that is left is the spiral wire of the notebook. Blackened brittle spiral wires, I have ten of them. I could make a bracelet out of each one, or string two together for a necklace? Peter and Paul would never know what they were, never know how they had held the past together, page after day after page after day, all that was left of the other person I was. From now on...only Ellie. The others are a story I am not in. The black wires are too flexible even now. I wish the burning had made them into new steel. One could have been a sword. Two together could have been a cross. I know all about vampires.

Peter will want me to play the piano. He bought it for me when I was ten. He even paid a woman to teach me how to play. Had not had my first growth spurt. My feet barely reached the pedals, but soon enough I was the right size. And I kept growing like a beanstalk, like a weed he said. He knows I am not very good. But I can do complete songs. He has his favorites, and I hate them. But I do not tell him that I have my own. Someday I will play those for Peyton. I like the new groups but their songs are too good to hear just on the piano. Those songs need guitars too. I will ask Peyton about his favorites and then we will find a music store and I will perform for him. I will use one of their pianos. I am sure his house has one of those giant grand pianos, not like my upright, but we cannot go to his house. He cannot come here. We will find a store and I will play for him and a million strangers. And then when we are older we will have our own private piano. I will play about flying to the moon or paper roses, whatever we like. He will think I am brilliant and talented, because I am...I will be for him.

Peter is tapping on the door. I always ignore him, so he will start knocking. I will ignore him, but he is used to that. It is our ritual. He will tap, and then knock, and then he will whisper my other name. I always open the door. I mean, she does.

A Manuscript?

"Bobby, you look like death eatin' a cracker."

Sally had walked into his office and found him in his usual stance...his *usual trance*, she would tell herself...looking out the window. When he turned around, she wondered if he had had another sleepless night. That was his usual excuse, lack of sleep, and it was plausible enough to be believed. The German advance even had her tossing and turning at night.

"And there are those who ask why I like you," Bobby said softly and smiled, pointing her to the old couch in front of his desk. Sally had heard the same line more and more in the past year, and she wondered if, perhaps, she had indeed become less likeable in that time. *Lord knows,* she thought, *I have the potential.*

Everyone at Windsor had been edgy ever since capitulation to the Germans had become inevitable. When Bobby was not in the office, the others would vent more openly. Sally was the referee in his absence, trying to be as calm as Bobby seemed. She had been with Windsor for a long time, but almost everyone else had been there longer. Still, she sometimes felt like she was the housemother at a fraternity. The maternal dust-mop and cook, tending to the needs of others, she was also known for snapping. But everyone else also knew that she and Bobby had their own history, and she was granted immunity from being the cause of hurt feelings. When the others began asking her if Bobby was ill, or merely depressed, Sally assured them that he was merely stressed about publishing in general, Windsor in particular, and probably, on some cosmic level, *the entire goddam universe, so back the fuck off!*

She did not tell the others the truth. She knew something was wrong with Bobby, but it was up to him to tell her, not for her to ask him. Their own rules. Unwritten, unspoken, but obeyed.

Bruce Tucker, Windsor's head of Publicity and Promotion, had been teasing her for a long time. "You and him are like an old married couple, finishing each other's sentences, reading each other's mind, even the same body language sometimes."

Sally had not been impressed with his insight, "If I'm his so-called long-time wife in your world, then I must be every husband's dream, with me and Bobby having the most open marriage in town, since he never seems to lack for a date with young pretty women."

Bruce had not backed off, "You know what I mean, Sally."

She did know, and, although she would not admit it to Bruce or anyone else, she did not mind the comparison.

Sitting across from Beaumont this morning, Sally noted the difference between his face and his voice. The face was tired, but the voice was excited. She had heard the same voice many times, always when he first mentioned a new book he liked. His enthusiasm was infectious, and at the Windsor sales meetings, when reps were presented with the upcoming catalog, Bobby's love of a book was obvious and motivational. If Bobby liked it, it must be good. "Let the Word go out," Sally had whispered to Bruce, nudging his elbow, the first time she had seen Bobby's pitch to his sales reps.

His voice this morning was youthful, but noticeably quiet. "This is the story I told you about last night, that first line I read to you. I want you to handle it."

"So you really like it?" she asked, assuming the answer was obvious, but Bobby surprised her.

"I believe it has much potential. But it is not in any form to be published. Just a series of scenes. You can perhaps imagine a plot, but it is still not a book yet."

Sally was suspicious. "Potential? So why am I confused? I thought you…"

"I think you should handle this. I have known this writer for a long time, so I am not going to be objective. I want you to handle this, and I want you to not let anybody else know it exists, not even the rest of the people here. If you like it, the writer will make any changes you want. Anything at all."

Seeing Sally about to interrupt, Bobby stopped her with a raised hand, "And if you like it, can somehow make it make sense, then I want you to take it to your new job, make it your first selection for them. Will you do that for me?"

Will you do that for me? As if I could now say no, Sally thought as she spoke, "Anything else? Soup or salad as an appetizer? You got any laundry for me to pick up?"

Bobby laughed, as she knew he would, and shoved the thick grey manuscript box across his desk toward her. "One last thing. Can you get this edited and copy ready in six weeks, regardless of when it gets published? I would like to see the final version, if such a thing is possible, before we get evicted from here. Six weeks, okay?"

Sally did not respond. The comment about six weeks was another reminder of the unavoidable future. Everyone else thought she was merely angry about the German takeover, and she had been honest with everyone about those feelings. But she was more than angry. She had been depressed for almost a year, had even gone to a therapist. But that professional, once he ruled out a chemical cause and therefore chemical relief, had pointed out the obvious: *Sally, you have no control over this. Your environment is changing, not you. You need to share this with the others who are suffering that same change. You can help each other more than I can help you.* She knew he was right, but he had also figured out her other emotional fault-line: *When you're ready to talk about your feelings for your boss, come back and see me. My door is always open, ten to three, by appointment. Come talk to me.*

Sally opened the manuscript box, as she had done a thousand times. No title page, no author name. She looked up at Bobby, "The title?"

"To be determined," he said, turning to look out the window. "But, let us see if it is a book first, and then you can worry about a title. Okay? And not to discourage you, but there is another box the same size. A lot of handwritten pages."

"Bobby, you hate me, don't you. You want me to hate you, right? Two boxes of typed and handwritten pages, and six weeks to turn them into a silk purse? Need anything else? How about one of my kidneys?"

Beaumont did not answer.

More silence, until Sally stood and went to the door,

manuscript box under her arm. She knew what was about to happen, as it happened more and more to her in private lately, a spasm of uncharacteristic and uncontrollable sentimentality. "Bobby, you know, I loved working here. I really did. There's no other place like it." Beaumont did not answer, nor did he turn back to face her when she continued, "Sometimes I think it's not real, this place, that it's only an ideal."

That turned him around. He arched his eyebrows and then waved at her, acting like he was a busy man, "You are right, we are not real. You and I are characters in a sad story. But, that being true, darling, you need to scoot back to work anyway. Get out of here before I shoot you and call God tomorrow to tell him you are dead."

"And how many times have I heard *that*," Sally answered, but the line still had its intended effect, especially since she knew that he only said it to her, his fellow Southern expatriate. She was soon back to her un-sentimental self. "One more thing. Stephen Malloy called and asked if he could come see you this week. I told him it was okay. You've usually got time after lunch. Was I wrong?"

Beaumont's face went from fatigue to confusion, and then to pleasure. "Steve? I wonder…but it does not matter. It has been a long time. It will be good to see him."

Sally was relieved. She knew the story about the two men. *Everybody* knew *the* story. New York might be a big city, but publishing was a small town.

Ellie and Peyton

Another day with Peyton. How many now? A hundred? Less? I lost count. He is totally mine for sure, but I do not think he thinks I am his yet. I would do anything he wants, but all he wants to do is talk. I wonder if he really notices that I do not talk. I nod a lot. I always agree with him. I laugh when he is funny, but he is funny in odd ways. He does not tell jokes, but he is funny. I am not sure what that means. He makes me laugh, and I make him smile. And he holds my hand as we walk in WPG.

That is my...our...favorite place. But we only have two places anyway. WPG or the smelly store where he works. That is where we meet, and the prehistoric people who work with him no longer stare at me. I am just another old book to them. I should ask him why he is the only live person there. Wrap the others in cotton, they would be mummies. But I see how they treat him. As if he was their boss. The real boss is a ghost, never seen by other ghosts like me. Peyton talks about him, but I have never seen him.

There are ghosts in WPG too. I don't see them, but they are

there. I told Peyton about Stephen Bonnet hanging from a tree, but he already knew that story. He seems to know so much about Charleston, but he says that is because his father knows so much. He loves his father, I understand that, but when he talks about his mother it is different. He does not hear his own voice when he talks about her. After I die, when he tells people about me, I want his voice to sound like it does when he talks to me about his mother. He worships her. That's what I hear. More than love. I want to hear that voice when he talks about me.

His house is bigger than a hotel. It's like a mansion or a palace or a castle. I have seen it even though he has never taken me there. He lives south of Broad. Not me, I live here in North Chuck. I told him that and for a split second I saw him stop being Peyton. As if I had just told him that I came from goddam Mars. But then he was right back to being Peyton. Just gone a second, and I felt a different future. But then he just tilted his head and smiled.

—That's okay.

I was okay again? I was forgiven? I was explained? No, I was thrilled. I stepped toward him and hugged him with all my might, letting him feel my broken heart heal. I did not have the words then...about a broken heart healing. I usually think of the right words later. We did not talk for awhile. All I did was blubber snot all over his shoulder. I have been sitting here for hours re-living that moment, searching for those three words—broken heart healing. And here they are now, on paper, and they don't come close. And the other feeling? Inside my body, as I pressed myself against him. It was not my heart. I understand my heart. But I do not understand this other feeling. I want him to grow up and be taller than me. I want him to kiss me with his perfect mouth. But he is still just a boy.

Other than holding hands, it was the first time our bodies ever touched. I did not let go, but neither did he. We were in WPG, standing in the gazebo. It was like a stage. I think he would have been embarrassed to be seen like that, if we kept hugging like that. I am sure his perfect parents would not have approved. But I wish my mama and daddy had been there...to see me in love.

I told Peyton the truth about my parents on our very first walk in the park. They are not Ellie's parents, because Peyton created Ellie, but my parents loved me a lot. I have seen pictures of my father holding his only daughter in his arms, seen him in his Marine dress uniform. A very handsome man. But I do not remember him as a person. He died. End of story. But I remember a lot about my mother, how she smelled, the perfumes and soaps, the smell of our kitchen being her smell too. The starch of her blouses. But she was gone when I was eight. I remember the smell of her dying at home. That's the strongest.

I will tell Peyton more about my parents. I have to be ready because he will want to know. He will ask me. And I will tell him the truth. About everything that was my past life up until she died, I will tell him. I will even tell him my mother re-married after my father died. But I will not tell him that she married Peter, and that Paul is his brother. Peter and Paul do not exist in WPG.

This is stupid. STUPID!!! Stupid Stupid Stupid! How could I be so stupid?? It's been a year and he has never once told me that he loved me. Doesn't matter that I have not told him that I loved him. He should know how I feel. I know he loves me, but he will not say it. Fuck, even the old woman at the bookstore knows he loves me. I sit there today as he goes to look for some stupid book and this old witch from the back of the store, where they must keep all the sorcery books, she comes to the desk looking for Peyton and finds me, the pathetic puppy who hangs around.

—So you and the boy are going steady?

Going steady? Do old people even know how lame that is? Going steady? I wanted to yell at her that hell no we are not going steady we are already married with twins on the way. I wanted to say that, but I did not. Because, I sort of thought, she was just being nice. She said it like she was happy for us. If I had a grandmother, she would have been perfect.

And then she says the perfect thing.

—You make him very happy, you know. He is always asking if you came to see him when he was not here.

How could I not forgive her? It was me, not her. I was the problem, but then I realized that it was Peyton too.

A year, and we have never done more than kiss good-bye? A year and he has not taken me to meet his parents? How stupid am I? Why is it that a simple thing he tells me yesterday should have been the goddam siren of my life. I have always known about his house on State Street, but then he just ever so casually drops that they have a maid and a butler! Two negroes in uniforms for sure. Probably wear white gloves to open the doors. He had to see the look on my face when he told me that, right? Why not just plant cotton in the back yard I asked him, but he did not understand. And when he did not understand I just wanted to hurt him more. I wanted to say something about where he went to school, that tea-sipping Porter-Gaud Academy. You go to a school with boys only? I asked Peter about Porter-Gaud and he told me it was a school for upper crust fairies. Is that you, Peyton? Is that why you have never wanted to do more than kiss me? I wanted to scream at him, but I shut up. He held my hand until I stopped shaking. That was when I decided, just out of nowhere, to tell him that I was not seventeen like him. I was only fourteen.

I think that I am pretty. Peter and Paul tell me that all the time but how would they know? And why should I care what they think. I can look in the mirror and see somebody there. I think she is pretty. I put make-up on her face, powder and lipstick, eye-liner, the best that Revlon can buy. My hair is getting longer. I am doing that because Peyton said he wondered what I would look like with longer hair. He said it before I told him how old I really was. But that was a long time ago. When he still loved me.

I wish I could go back and keep lying to him. But the truth was a lie too. I told him that I was fourteen, which is how old she was. But I am actually older. I mean Ellie is older. I want all this to make sense, and sometimes it does. I met Peyton. He found me. I am Ellie. But then somebody else told him that I was fourteen. What a joke. Would any fourteen year old girl be me? She would kill herself for sure. And Peyton would not love a fourteen year old girl. How could he love a girl so young?

So he said that he had to stop seeing me, or Ellie, or whoever the hell I was.

—It is not right. You should have friends your own age.

Friends my own age? But here's what I know now, my darling gallant Peyton...you love me, you love Ellie, and whatever bullshit Southern gentleman code your perfect parents taught you is total crazy crap. You gave yourself away when I asked you what your favorite love story was. I thought you were going to say some sugary something like Romeo and stupid Juliet, but you slipped up and told the truth. And you didn't think I would go get a copy and read it myself. You didn't know that any book or poem you ever said you liked I would go look for it too. Did you think I would have to get it from that book tomb you work in, and give myself away? Did you think I had stopped stealing? Fuck that. I am the Princess of Theft. I am too young for you Peyton? Too young for you? You think that us not seeing each other for almost a year now is going to make me old enough? How many pages have I written to you since then? But you will never see them, this one or any of the others. But mark this first day of 1970, Peyton Finch (yes, I gave you your true last name too)...you love me. If I have a soul, it knows you love me. And yours knows it too.

Oh, fuck, not again...they keep coming back, as if she still lived here. I should tell them that she went away to be with Peyton, but then they would know about him.

The Beaumonts

Robert Lee Beaumont was an only child, born and raised in Charleston, son of Forrest Haywood Beaumont and Margaret Virginia Lee, the frailest of the Lee sisters. In Charleston society, the young Beaumont benefited from what was commonly known as a *good background*. His family credentials were impeccable. As he was reminded by his mother, beginning while still in her womb, no doubt, he was a direct descendant of Lankford Charles Beaumont, himself an only child.

A West Point graduate of 1855, but one of the first Confederate heroes, Lankford Beaumont had used his West Point training to assist in the rubbling of Fort Sumter; after which, he had walked to his parents' home a few blocks from the site of his shore battery. In The War of Southern Redemption, as Beaumont himself called it in one of his few letters home, he had acquitted himself with honor, killing Unionists and writing poetry. But the War was not impressed with honor, it seemed, as Beaumont spent the last two years of his service in a Union prison with walls more stout than Sumter's. He returned to Charleston in 1867, his parents dead, his estate intact, his fortune dwindling but mysteriously augmented by thousands of northern dollars in his valise, for which he offered no explanation.

Beaumont was a changed man, all agreed, older in more than years, scarred in more places than his face, reclusive in society and silent about his past. *That damned conflagration*, he spoke at a party honoring his new bride in 1870, casting a pall over everyone except that bride, who had endured darker thoughts in private and still accepted his proposal, *killed more than men and my country. And anyone who thinks otherwise is a fool.*

Lankford Beaumont built a wall around himself and his bride, literally. With his name and his money, he exploited the misery of those around him, newly free black and recently poor white, whose land was not productive enough to both feed families and pay taxes. Ten cents on the dollar, he bought cheap but did not sell. Still, if there was a vestige of that honor for which he had praised himself years earlier, it was manifested only in his effort to hire for his new ventures those displaced souls who were foolish enough to have believed in the inevitable junction of hard work and opportunity, the American Dream that would not even exist as a social trope until the next century. Beaumont believed in land first, opportunity later, and money that worked hard around the clock. In his world, growing cotton and rice was a road to nowhere. But his honor, as he once tried to explain to a skeptical rival, also required him to hire blacks and whites and pay them the same. For that equanimity, more than his ruthless acquisitions, he was shunned by his former friends and acquaintances.

The only time he ever had to borrow money, he explained his vision to a Charleston banker who saw the same future for the South. Beaumont staked his fortune and the bank's loan on textile mills and grain processing. The first workers hired were those he had rendered homeless. The bank was paid back in five years, and Lankford Beaumont became a father.

Textile money begat more money for more land, and Beaumont built his home on the outskirts of Charleston, a scandal of a house because it was New England clapboard and shutters, two stories high, gabled seven times, more than big enough for his family but still much too small, too Northern, for the land upon which it sat, a full five acres surrounded by a stone wall which was broken only by the entrance directly in line with the front door a hundred yards away.

At his funeral, Beaumont was mourned by his widow and three sons, who, upon their mother's death, rancored each other about their presumed fair shares. But Lankford Beaumont charted their future as much in death as he had done in life. His widow had merely followed his instructions: the bulk of his established wealth to his eldest son, a hundred acres of undeveloped land and a pittance of money to the others. In life, he had not favored his eldest son more than the others, so his final gesture had to be interpreted as more symbolic than vindictive. Those who thought they had known Lankford Beaumont in life all agreed: *Charleston had sent a favored son to the War, but the War had returned a stranger, and not a very likeable stranger at that.*

Abraham, that eldest son of Beaumont, had a knack for making more money than his father, but spawned fewer sons. His two boys were night and day, emotionally black and white, but Abraham Beaumont refused to hear any comparison to Cain and Abel. The boys still grew up with the story of their grandfather's legacy as part of the humid Carolina air they breathed, and, as much as their father assured them that *their* shares would be equal, the poison between them had no antidote.

Abraham did provide his sons with something that his own father had denied him. As soon as his mother died, Abraham moved away from the walled estate of his father. He returned the Beaumont family to live on State Street, south of Broad, in downtown Charleston, described by a future Carolina writer as the *Secret Maginot Line* of Charleston culture. These were the *South of Broad* families. The very oldest families inhabited the largest mansions below Broad Street, and Abraham Beaumont wanted to live there, not on the fringes of society. Astute observers of the Beaumont family spoke in whispers about Lankford tossing in his crypt, and how Abraham's mother was channeled through her son. She might have loved her husband, but her own family knew of her bitterness about being isolated from the world in which she had been raised.

Abraham then did his younger son Rutledge another favor. Lacking proof of his own valor in comparison to his father's, seeking validation of his courage, and thus constantly clouded by his father's shadow, Abraham went to Cuba to fight the Spanish and died of dysentery. The older son then did little brother Rutledge a much bigger favor in 1910. He went swimming and disappeared, his nude and bloated body surfacing a day later and a mile away from his last known breath. Although still a boy at the Porter Military Academy, Rutledge was charged with preserving and perpetuating the Beaumont line. Still, he was always sensitive to the perception of those around him, never spoken but always sensed, that his older brother's death had been very convenient. In 1925, Rutledge begat Forrest Haywood. He had intended to sire a dozen children and split his estate into a dozen pieces; indeed, had made that public declaration many times, pledging that his children would not be cursed as he was with both wealth and suspicion. To facilitate his children's future poverty, he began selling land and investing in the most worthless Yankee stocks he could find. His wife discreetly left him, Forrest still in diapers. She secured professional help, and had Rutledge committed before he could do more damage. She did not have to convince anyone of her husband's insanity. The Beaumont estate was preserved for posterity, embodied in Forrest Haywood Beaumont, and Charleston society waited to see how much of the father was in the son.

When news of the Crash of 29 reached him in his sanitarium suite, Rutledge calmly told his doctor that "the work" was finished, his own and the doctor's. The doctor nodded and made a note in Beaumont's file. An hour later, Beaumont stood in his third floor window, spread his arms as if acknowledging the warm applause of an audience, then leaned forward and joined his father and older brother.

Charleston society was disappointed in Rutledge's son. Forrest Beaumont would turn out to be depressingly sane and well-adjusted, marred only by an inexplicable support of the civil rights movement. He married well, to a woman he had loved since he was ten and who had loved him in return. Forrest was unabashedly happy with his life, for which his mother and wife were given much credit, and his son Bobby adored him.

Ellie Smokes

Sometimes they make me laugh. I mean, they don't see how absurd they are. How stupid. They found my cigarettes. I am surprised it took them so long because I had stopped hiding them months ago. Why bother. I don't care anymore. And I am surprised they never noticed the smell. I am a walking talking fucking Virginia Slim. Peyton noticed it the first time we ever got away from that smelly store of his, out in the air of WPG, he asked me if I smoked. No use lying to him. I confessed and he does the classic Peyton thing.

—It is bad for you, and you are too pretty to spoil yourself that way.

So of course I stop immediately, but then he stops seeing me so why bother anymore. I like to smoke but if Peyton wanted me to quit breathing I would do that too. Oh gag me, stupid lines, how I make fun of him. Of us. He is right. I should be an actress.

Peter found them while I was sleeping, and he yells.

—What are these, what are these?

So I smart off to him like I am getting used to doing. He

can't stop me anymore. And he slaps me. But he slaps like a girl. He never hurts me. But then he tells Paul and I know I am in trouble. Paul comes to the house and yells at me too. But I do not provoke him. I made that mistake too many times. Even when they both start saying crazy stuff like the only girls who smoke are sluts. I can ignore that. I can live with slut. But then Paul says that smoking is bad for my health is when I almost lose it and start screaming...You and your friends and your brother are FUCKING me and you are concerned about my goddam HEALTH!!!!! And then Peter sees the lighter on the dresser table, the only one I have ever used, the one with a palmetto tree on one side and a Rebel flag on the other, and he demands to know where I got it and I do scream this time...It's my mama's. Do you remember her?

I scream and scream. And then Peter sets me free. He sets me free. He is a rage, so much I even thought Paul was afraid of him, and that was never true before. He starts tearing my mama's pictures off the walls. He goes for the only family album I have left and he starts ripping pages out and tearing them up, pictures and all. I will never un-see him as he took away all the pictures of his dead wife and left me with...okay, my freedom. Not sure what I mean here, but as he and Paul calmed down and shut the door to my bedroom and turned back to face me...I knew that I was finally Ellie again. And Ellie was not afraid of them.

Robert Lee Beaumont

Bobby never heard himself referred to as Robert unless his father was angry with him, which was rare. Bobby was a youthful name, and his mother almost made it sound like *Bubby*. As he grew older there might have been a time when Bobby became Robert or even Bob, but Bobby Beaumont stopped growing at the height of five feet seven inches. He was a short man, and never seemed to flesh out or up. Always slim, and unnaturally handsome, almost beautiful, even as a child. Dark wavy hair, dark eyes, and a mouth that women eventually desired to touch with their own lips. Only when he went to New York did the line between Bobby and Bob have a professional as well as social meaning. Permission was implicitly required to call him Bobby. Some sort of intimacy had to be established, perhaps only an acknowledgement by him that the other person had talent.

His mother's constant refrain, when asked why she and her husband had only the one child, was that, "Bobby is much too perfect for me and Forrest to chance having another child who would pale in comparison. He is my darling, and more than enough to fill my heart." His mother talked like that a lot.

His father, of course, told him the truth. In his study, where all things male were shared, a glass of bourbon in his hand, Forrest Beaumont explained, "You were a very difficult birth, Bobby. The labor was long, almost thirty hours, and your mother was in much pain. Much terrible, terrible pain." His voice had softened and his eyes looked away from his son, "And I was much concerned for her. So we agreed months later, after she finally admitted that she did not want to endure that again, we agreed that you were to be our only child."

Bobby was about to start high school when he heard this story. His adolescent radar for perceived adult hypocrisy was beginning to assert itself. "But those stories about me being too perfect, and all that other crap, that was just crap, is that it? It was not about me at all was it, it was all about her."

Forrest Beaumont's face had tightened and he set his bourbon aside, freeing his right hand to point directly at his son. "You are not to talk about your mother that way ever. Do you understand me, Robert Beaumont? You have said something very hurtful, and you are to apologize."

Bobby protested, "*She* did not hear me! *She* is taking another of her naps."

"The apology is for me, Robert." His father had stood.

"So what am I supposed to believe? You both act like we live in some damn fairy tale…"

"Robert!"

"And so now you tell me that pain explains everything. What kind of truth is that?"

"Do you honestly believe that your mother is not telling the truth when she says you are perfect and that you fill her heart, that you are the darling of her life? Is that what you believe, Robert, that she is untruthful? Disabuse yourself of that thought, if it is your true feeling. For your mother, and myself, you are the soul of our heart."

Bobby Beaumont had wanted to cry, but he was not going to do it in front of his father. He was fifteen. Many years from that moment, looking out the window of his New York office early in the morning, his home in Charleston sealed, furniture draped in sheets, his parents alive only in the pictures on the walls, Bobby imagined telling his father, *I was so foolish*, and his father would reply, *You were young, so you were allowed to be foolish*, and the Bobby at that moment in the future knew that if his father were alive, they would both laugh about the past.

Of all the stories about Bobby Beaumont the Editor, amid rumors of his homosexuality (how else to explain his long-time bachelorhood?), his mysterious facial scar, his unerring knack of seeing talent before anyone else, his ability to keep the same staff with him year after year, despite his infrequent but volcanic anger, everyone, even the media in every profile ever written about him, always mentioned two things: his voice and his manners. His voice was most often low, but his South Carolina accent was what set him apart, an accent compounded by constant formality. He never lost it. Not even after thirty years in New York City. Of course, those New Yorkers never saw him when he went back to visit Charleston, when that accent was even more pronounced, when some sort of restraint was lifted, some professional requirement that northerners understand him so his inflection and articulation were much more precise. Back home, Bobby sounded like his mother and father. His only slippage in New York was when he talked with the Southern writers he published. An outsider hearing those conversations would sometimes need a translator because Southern metaphors were often a foreign language to the uninitiated.

His manners came from his parents as well. When visitors came to his apartment they were greeted by him and helped out of their overcoats. He held the door open for everyone and let them pass through first. He never ate or drank in company unless someone else started first. He rarely interrupted, often to the regret of his assistant editor, who would sit with him as some writer or agent sucked the air out of an office. If he really wanted to inject himself into the conversation, he would very slowly raise his hand a few inches off his lap and subtly raise a finger, like making a silent bid at an auction. In conversations about Bobby Beaumont, one word came up over and over, and if someone had been searching for the right word they would nod in quick agreement when someone else lit the bulb for them: Bobby Beaumont was the most *gracious* man in New York City.

Growing up with his parents, Bobby had no choice. Forrest and Margaret Beaumont insisted on their son having the right *background*. The first lesson was that adults were not simply big playmates. A child was not their equal. Deference must be paid. Their black maid Ruby was still an adult. Their black gardener Bailey was still an adult. Age, not race or social class, made the difference. In fact, a true sign of that nebulous trait called *class* was that a person with class might be superior to lesser men and women, but that superiority came with obligations, and anyone who overtly condescended toward a perceived lower class was in actuality of that class themselves. Bobby's father was more succinct after enough bourbon: *Too many damn snobs in this town to suit me. Too damn many.*

The second lesson was that restraint was a sign of maturity, especially restraint in a world of seven deadly sins. As Bobby grew up, his father refined the lesson about restraint. It was not synonymous with abstinence. *Pleasure is a gift from God,* Forrest Beaumont would say as he and his son took their daily walk. Bobby's father had many worldly pleasures, bourbon in the evening being among the foremost, but rich and exotic food a close second. Season tickets and regular attendance at museums and symphonies might have been seen as patronage by others, but the elder Beaumont loved to call them indulgences. He had forsaken only one pleasure in his life, he had told his son as they walked one sultry summer evening. *Your mother insisted that I quit smoking before she would marry me.* Forrest had then stopped in mid-step and mimicked the act of smoking, imaginary cigar between middle and forefinger raised to his lips, a slow inhalation and release, and then he had flicked the invisible cigar off into an immense distance, doing a final mock wave good-bye with his empty hand, and spoke to himself while his son played the mute audience, *The smartest thing I ever did in my life.*

In any conversation describing his parents, Bobby always had to overcome his listener's skepticism. Surely, they would insist, your childhood was not *that* happy. Bobby could describe all sorts of traumas and disappointments, but his parents were never the cause. He might have resented having to dress formally for dinner every night, but that was balanced by raucous mornings of breakfast in his pajamas with his parents still in theirs as well, the maid Ruby allowed to feign disgust with their coming to the table with hair uncombed, and Ruby was genuinely appalled by his father's effort to gargle pineapple juice before swallowing, a routine done at least once a week, which always brought protests from his mother before she would succumb to his charm. *Your father*, she would tell Bobby at the kitchen table, with her husband next to her, *is not a mature man, but he does, so very much, make me laugh.*

Even as a child, Bobby understood that his parents lived in two different worlds. One was adult, the other was populated only by the three of them, with Ruby and Bailey as discreet silent witnesses. Lavish parties were held at the Beaumont house, but the very young Bobby was not invited. The gardener Bailey, with appropriate wardrobe, would be promoted to doorman for those nights, the maid Ruby would have extra help, and Bobby would be introduced to the guests but then led upstairs, where he was allowed, like a scene in a hundred movies, to sit on the top step and look down at Charleston society moving in slow motion below. His mother and father were always the most handsome couple, and his father a gracious host. When he described those scenes to Sally Graham years later, she put into words what he had always felt, "Jesus Christ, Bobby, they sound like Scott and Zelda without all the baggage."

When Bobby was a teenager, he was allowed to stay downstairs as long as he dressed as a version of his father, more directly absorbing the rules of hospitality from his parents. Standing next to his father those evenings, he slowly learned the difference between wit and humor. Forrest Beaumont would never gargle pineapple juice in front of this crowd for sure, Bobby knew, and they would not believe him if he told them about his father's other comic habits, such as his predictable response upon receiving the bill after a restaurant meal, a response that always forced his mother to blush. Forrest Beaumont would take the check, stare at it, blink furiously, and then his arm would start shaking so hard the bill would almost fly out of his hand as he muttered "My lord, we are going to have to wash dishes." Charleston society never met that man. The Forrest Beaumont of their circle was urbane, a bit too liberal, and witty enough to provoke smiles but seldom laughter.

Your daddy's rich and your mama's good looking, so hush little baby and don't you cry. Bobby's father would play his Gershwin records and sing along, and his mother would serve sweet mint tea to Bobby on the veranda and juleps to her husband. Describing that to Sally at her first Windsor New Years Eve party, Bobby was almost embarrassed, but he laughed at her response: "You're shitting me, aren't you? Forget Scott and Zelda. You were raised by the Confederate Ken and Barbie." Sally had been drunk. She was the only person at Windsor allowed to talk to Beaumont like that about his parents. But he had his usual retort for her: "At least I was not raised by George and Martha."

Hearing about the academic couple from *Who's Afraid of Virginia Woolf* for what seemed like the hundredth time, Sally had almost slapped him. "You fucker. My parents loved each other and they loved me as much as yours loved you. And they were not drunks." To which Bobby reminded her, "But you will admit that they were... rather...loud, or so you tell me. And they did argue, am I not right?"

Sally had corrected him, "My mother was loud, and my mother was always on my daddy's case, but, dammit, they loved each other. I never doubted that. And yes, my daddy was a bit of a drinker, but I never saw him drunk." As she slurred her words, she had wondered if there was any mistletoe at the party.

Other than Bobby himself, Sally was the only Windsor person who had been born and raised anywhere south of Maryland.

He had not told anyone, not even her, but that was one of the reasons he hired her. Within a few months, however, he realized that they had come from two different versions of the South... *Old* versus *New*. He was not disappointed. She was still the best assistant editor he ever had, and would eventually be his best friend, but she had not filled the void he felt. Something he had lost by moving North, and had not even known it for a decade. Sally understood it, finally put it into words for him, and then mocked him for it. "Bobby, you seem to come from the South that the South wants to believe in. As if you could ignore the slavery and the hillbillies and the gun-toting pick-up driving bubbas and lousy schools. Your South is all white gauzy and *noblesse oblige* and them darkies is all happy to picks our cotton....no, I'm sorry...*that* part's not you. But here's the best I can make out...your world was genteel, and southern gentility was built on a lot of bad stuff. My parents had no illusions about that stuff. But you were raised different than me. Your parents raised a gentleman. My parents did not raise a lady. They raised me. They were educated people, but they sure as hell weren't genteel."

Ellie Goes Back

I went to see him. I was right.

I wish everyone was me. I wish everyone was as happy as me. I was right. He never stopped loving me. I think I have lived every day of my past just to see the look on his face yesterday. I went to the store but he was not there yet. But all the old people they hugged me and held me and rubbed my shoulders, like I was some sort of lost kid of their own. They had missed me. Especially the oldest woman who should have been my grandmother.

—He'll be back soon, back soon, so you must hide.

And then that little bell rang, the one that rang every time the front door opened and the old woman said—hide hide—and I think she grabbed me and pushed me behind a shelf. He was back.

How did they know what to do? He sat at his desk and they all gathered around him like a wall so I could sneak over behind them without him seeing me. And just at the perfect moment the old woman stepped aside and Peyton looked up and there I was. I was not there and then I was there. He had not seen me in a year, and he had never stopped seeing me. I thought to myself that he had stopped being pretty, but he was now almost handsome. He is almost eighteen. He sat there looking up at me, and we were surrounded by a million old books that nobody ever read I was sure and with the three old people as our witnesses. I am sure they saw what I saw, how he did not speak, just his eyes getting wet and his still perfect lips forming a single word not said.

Hello, Peyton, I said, and he looked down and then up and then stood and did not move. I felt the old woman nudge me in the back.

Go Go—I am sure she was thinking, so I went over to him and put my arms around him and whispered in his ear as I felt him trembling, or it might have been me, as I whispered I love you. And before I could finish the thought I was thinking that I love you with all my heart and soul and will always love you but I will die if you do not...

And then he whispered back.

—I love you too, Ellie.

I do not think the old people heard us, but we heard each other.

I almost laughed for a dumb reason, as he held on to me. I saw the future for us, but as I stood there wrapped around him I realized that even though it had been a year he had not grown any taller. I was not a giant, but I was still much taller than him, and that's when I almost laughed because I realized I would always be taller than him. Always. And our children would be taller than him, even the girls, but that was okay. In fact that was perfect. We were exactly like we were when he caught me stealing a book. Our future was right there at the beginning.

Does that make sense? It makes sense to me. We were meant for each other from that first moment. His age and my height made us one person. I know this is the truth. See? I am him. He is me. That's the love story he waited for me to understand.

The old people were fluttering.

—Go go away, go be by yourselves we will watch the store. Go away. Fly.

Peyton began nodding and smiling and turned to arrange a stack of books on his desk while I thought how so typically Peyton. Still keeping his world in order all neat and arranged. We should go to the park I thought first, but then I knew where we had to go first. I wanted him to see Peter and Paul.

No no, not them. He will never meet THEM. I wanted him to meet Peter and Paul at SJB, my friends. I wanted our world to get bigger than the store and WPG. Peyton deserves that. How many times have I gone there before or after seeing him? Almost every time? How many times have I gone there in the past year, so very close to him but never getting closer? We had...have...all the time in the world. We walked slowly, holding hands, and I let him tell me about his future. He is a senior at Potty-Guard...he hates when I say it that way but he laughs...so he and his parents are deciding where to go to college. He might stay or he might not. Everything is up in the air. I did not care. I knew that even if he went away we were still in love and I would see him all the time and then when I was eighteen, I would go anywhere he was.

You never told me that you were Catholic—he said as we entered.

Oh, Peyton, you do not have to be Catholic to come inside here.

It was so much fun yesterday, the best day of my life, seeing him again and then taking him to my church. Thursday in the afternoon it is almost always empty and so cool and so quiet. I told him to whisper because the sound of our voices would whirl around and rise up to heaven and then come back to us in a different language. He told me that was odd. His word—odd. And I also told him that we could not hold hands because it was against the rules.

—Whose rules?

My rules I said.

I told him to sit and wait while I did what I always did. He was still new to my world, but he was gracious. I walked through all the pews on the east side looking for missals and hymnals that were not in their slots on the back of the pews, and I put them in their proper places. People are so careless and messy sometimes. I knew he was watching me. Did a bell ring? I wanted it to ring. It is one of my favorite sounds. I lit a candle and then I came to sit next to him. Somewhere in the back we could hear the front doors open and close.

—But you are not Catholic.

Quiet, I told him. We are safe here.

He is right. I am not Catholic. I am white-trash Methodist. He is Episcopalian. I already knew that. And Episcopalians are sort of like Catholics, so I knew he was not really upset with me. Then it was time to introduce him to Peter and Paul.

You know how a baby learns to swim? You hold it in the water so it gets comfortable there with your hands under it, and then as the baby starts to kick and float you slowly slip your hands out from under. That was me and Peyton. I told him to lay down in the pew, full stretched out, and to rest his head in my lap. He shook his head, but then he looked all around to see if anybody was watching. Then he twisted his body, and then the back of his head was on my thigh. I looked down to see his perfect face looking up at me. I wanted to close my eyes and just stop time because I did not expect that feeling to come back from the first time we hugged but there it was...his weight pressing into my flesh and the center of me was a fever. I could see it in him too, the feeling in me. He wanted to talk but I put my finger on his lips and sssshhed him. Look up...no, higher... not the big windows along the sides. Above them, the smaller windows across the top. See those two. I pointed and he looked in the right direction, but I could see that he was not really seeing so I told him to focus on the two stained glass windows... right there...and I saw him squint and then open up wide as he saw Peter and Paul. There, I told him, look under their feet and you can see their names.

They are my Peter and Paul. I tell him and they hear all my sins and they always forgive me.

—Your sins?

I felt the back of his head start shifting in my lap, and then as I looked down I knew why that day was different. He rolled over enough to...he actually did...press his lips against my thigh and kiss me through my skirt so deep that I lost my breath and looked up to thank Peter and Paul. I touched the back of his hair until he raised up and sat close beside me with his arm around me and we waited for...I don't know. I don't know. Something was waiting for us. You know? Something more than the future.

We had two directions to go when we left SJB. North and South. The whole day made sense. All it took was for me to go see him. All it took was for us to see each other again after a year. But Peyton had one thing for me that I did not expect, but it was the last piece of the puzzle or the picture or whatever has pieces. He was not the same Peyton he was a year ago. We walked out into the sunshine again, and I think I was talking to myself, and I said something like I would kill Jesus for a cigarette right then. I shut my mouth as soon as I realized what I had done, but he did not scold me.

—Do you smoke the same brand as you did before?

I knew it then. Peyton is finally me.

Books

The first book he had ever read? A question he could not answer when he was asked by *Esquire,* when he was the most famous editor in New York. But, the first book that mattered? Bobby knew the answer to that question, and his reasoning was simple: it was the first book he ever read twice. And when he fell in love for the first time as a young man, with a girl he could not tell his parents about, he read it again. How to explain a teenage boy's fascination with passion and rage wrapped around masochism? *Wuthering Heights* was too personal. He gave the reporter a different book title for the magazine profile. He kept the truth private.

Bobby had grown up surrounded by books, first his father's, then the public library's, and finally those he sold. As wealthy as Forrest Beaumont was, he made it clear to his son that if he wanted money he would have to earn it. Bobby resisted the temptation to point out to his father that *he* had never been required to work for a dime. Indeed, work had never been a necessity for either of his parents, but Bobby let the contradiction slide. He had known for years where he wanted to work anyway, known because he had spent time there every week after school ever since his freshman year at Porter-Gaud. A half-mile from his State Street home, the Palmetto Bookstore was Bobby's other home. Like the movie theatre next to it, the Palmetto was gone now, both replaced by larger, yet lesser, buildings.

Bobby had walked into the store as a young boy and asked for a job, but the owner, Sam Simon, turned him away. *Kid can't be serious,* he told himself. Bobby came back, and was turned down again. Forrest Beaumont then came to the store by himself the following week. Bobby's father had a hundred Simon books in his State Street study. In an elliptical conversation, the elder Beaumont inquired about Simon's business, any new acquisitions, the humidity, a host of the usual small talk topics, and then he asked Simon if any of his customers had ever requested a book to be delivered to their home rather than having them come to the store. Simon allowed that he had often mailed books to his local customers, and that seemed like an equitable arrangement for those not inclined to venture out in the Charleston heat. Forrest Beaumont persisted, *But, of course, a book hand-delivered to their door seems so much more gracious, you would agree? So much more personal. And books, after all, are a personal thing, it seems to me.* Bobby was never mentioned. A month later, he went to the store and sought out old man Simon. "My father wishes to purchase any copy of *Gulliver's Travels* in your possession and for me to deliver it to a Professor Conroy over at The Citadel." Seated at his desk strewn with books to be shelved, Simon had closed one eye and looked up at the persistent applicant, as if to smell a conspiracy.

"Your father does, does he?"

Bobby had nodded without a hint of collusion. The boy,

Simon knew, was unaware of the strings still tying him to his father. And so, Simon, understanding Forrest Beaumont's prior intentions, asked Bobby, "You know your way around Charleston, I am to understand, so perhaps you might be interested in a regular courier position with me, perhaps a few times a week, a flat fee per delivery, no salary, and perhaps that might lead to a more significant position later?" Bobby's face was proof of his innocence.

Unlike Sam Simon and the other employees, Bobby was not that enthralled with the age or scarcity of a particular book, but he loved the store. Known for its rare book collection, the Palmetto changed little in the fifty years of Sam Simon's ownership. Only grudgingly did he let Bobby convince him to offer a small selection of new titles. Those new books were relegated to a spot closest to the only window in the storefront, thus the brightest spot in the store, but an area that could not accommodate more than a few hundred new books, all chosen by Bobby. Recently published mingled with others that Bobby, with his father's input, thought worth making available. Magazines, however, were strictly forbidden by Sam Simon.

As sales clerk and new book buyer, Bobby began a lifetime of reading *Publishers Weekly* and *Kirkus* and a dozen other review periodicals. He also read as many of the actual new books as possible. He even read reviews of books he had already read, and he eventually knew which reviewers were to be trusted so he could recommend a book on their judgment, without himself having read it. Over time, he could lure customers to his corner and match title to individual. The other employees at first sniffed derisively at those new customers who never went past Bobby's corner and who never seemed interested in the classics. Soon enough, and a surprise to Sam Simon, those employees would venture over to Bobby and ask his opinion about what they *might buy for ourselves or a friend, something new, you know, something popular, but still good, you know.* Only a teenager, Bobby was adopted by the older souls around him. After him, the youngest employee was forty-three.

Sam Simon had been Bobby's first conquest, but the last to admit it. Simon's own children had gone north years earlier, and his wife died a decade before Bobby was born. In time, one of Simon's secret pleasures was getting a call and being asked a question about some book published after 1950, usually a best-seller, and telling the caller *you'll have to talk to Bobby about that,* and listening as Bobby always had an answer. Simon considered Bobby's knowledge to be, ultimately, of no value other than commercial, but he was impressed nonetheless.

Bobby loved the old leathery smell of the Palmetto, the feel of it, the darkness of it, the dusty labyrinth stacks, and he loved the daily adventure of finding a requested rare title. Sam Simon's filing system was infamous among rare book dealers. Longevity of employment was the key to understanding the Simon system, and since Bobby was the youngest and newest of anyone there in its last few years, he knew it would take years to break the code. Not alphabetical or chronological, Simon filed by association. One book reminded him of another and was shelved next to it. Or, one author reminded him of another, and the two were bonded in Simon's mind, as if the book were the author himself and Simon could say to it, *Hello Mr. Goldsmith, I'd like to introduce you to Miss Austen. I think the two of you will get along famously.* Within weeks of working at the Palmetto, however, Bobby understood the basic problem: Sam Simon was slowly losing fifty years of memory. Even *he* could not find books that he had filed. Long time employees were necessary for retrieval, especially those employees who had worked there so long that they had absorbed Simon's mind as their own. No customer ever came in off the street and found the book he wanted. A title submitted, the customer was usually asked for a phone number. *We'll call as soon as we know if we have it.* Inefficient for sure, and sales were often lost even though a book was found, but Simon did not care. In a suspicious but reflective mood sometimes, Bobby concluded that Simon wanted to keep his books, not sell them. Only when Simon died did Bobby find out how old he was. A year away from his centennial, Simon went to sleep with a copy of *Pilgrims Progress* next to his bed, an edition bought by his own grandfather as a young man, and the only book that Simon never took to his store.

The Palmetto eventually withered, but it was not strangled by the intrusion of a mega chain store nearby. It simply died when its owner did. Bobby came to work a week after the funeral and the doors were locked. He and the other employees had expected changes after Simon died, but not so soon, not so final. But Sam Simon's estate was being divided among distant heirs who cared nothing about antiquated books and loyal employees, some of whom had worked there for their entire adult life. Those heirs even contested Simon's final bequest to his employees, that they be allowed to have any ten books they wanted from the stock before it was liquidated. Simon's heirs might not have understood the value of words, but they understood the value of rare books and signed first editions of limited first printings. Any ten books could have been worth thousands of dollars. *That*, they understood. Their New York lawyer, however, did not understand the Charleston lawyer that Bobby's father hired to protect the employees. *Damn Yankees*, Forrest Beaumont had laughed when he heard about the dispute. *Do they understand how slow things can move down here, that the concept of a New York minute does not apply here, especially when Tracy Calhoun applies his mind to some deeper meanings of the law and life in front of Judge Clemens downtown?*

The litigation was settled as soon as the Charleston lawyer made it clear to the New York lawyer that if the employees were not allowed their rightful legacy from Sam Simon, then the New York Simons could expect to be in South Carolina courts for at least five years, and as Mr. Calhoun explained, *You, sir, will be on the clock of fee remuneration, while I will be offering my services to these poor folks down here merely for the love of their cause. Not to mention your folks up there having to wait for years to dispose of any other asset, such as land and building, because you can be assured that I will have those properties sequestered more tightly than a virgin bride before deflowerment.* Calhoun only talked like that to Northerners.

Bobby had asked his father to intervene, knowing that his father would relish the cultural jousting, but the truth was that Bobby himself was not interested in the ten-book inheritance. It was the principle of the matter, and his father certainly understood that. Father and son had both been offended by the Simon heirs.

Bobby had joined the other employees for their own memorial service to Simon, held in the Palmetto the first morning they were allowed back in the store to claim their ten books. Everyone else knew exactly what they wanted, but Bobby's only choice was a collection of maps from the seventeenth century, bound by hand between hard leather covers. His interest was not geography or history. He just thought they were gorgeous drawings, and the colors were still vivid. He envisioned them on a wall of some future office. Even more inexplicable, Bobby had requested the second floor couch to be set aside for him. The aged couch had no value, thus there was no objection to his request.

The small group stayed for an hour, knowing that the settlement between New York and Charleston lawyers required them to make their choices within that time, after which, everything else was to be packed and shipped to a dealer in New York for sorting and disposition. The Palmetto would be empty soon enough. As the others began their scavenger hunt, Bobby went for his maps, and then he waited. Hour over, the four women and three men who had been his work-mates met him at the front counter, a dark oaken plane, older than Sam Simon himself, and they said their good-byes to each other. The oldest person among them, a woman who had worked there forty-five years, called for everyone's attention, and made a ceremony of handing Bobby a gift from Simon himself, a gift mandated by him to her, with instructions to wait until this final scene. Simon, everyone agreed, had a flair for the dramatic. None of them understood his gift, a first edition of *Wuthering Heights*, but Bobby held the book in his hands like it was the robe of Christ.

Speech, speech! ... his co-workers implored, all of whom had only slowly accepted him into their midst, having seen him as too young when Simon had hired him. But they all knew they would miss him, that *his* life was only beginning. They were puzzled by Simon's gift, so Bobby confessed, "I had always asked Mr. Simon if he had a copy, but he always said..." and Bobby made them all laugh with his imitation of Sam Simon's raspy but effeminate voice, *Well, I think I have one but I don't recall where it is, but you can have it if you find it.* "And I looked and looked for it and never did." So he asked the woman where Simon had kept it, and when she told him it was next to *The Great Gatsby* he nodded and smiled as if he clearly understood the connection, too embarrassed to admit that he had not read *Gatsby* yet. "Of course, that makes perfect sense now," he said, not understanding at all.

Bobby went home that night and found a copy of *Gatsby* in his father's library. He was still too young to understand, but his father seemed pleased at his interest in Fitzgerald. *It is one of those perfect books, Bobby, not a word wasted, not a word too many. But this copy is mine. You will have to find your own. You can borrow mine for now, but not possess. Fair enough?* Bobby acquiesced, wishing he had known enough to take a copy from the Palmetto when he had the chance.

Years later, many readings later, Bobby finally understood the mind of Sam Simon. *Too bad*, he told himself, *that I did not understand life better when I was young. I think that Mr. Simon had more secrets than he led us to believe.*

Ellie Plays the Piano

This is not going to work. Me and Peyton. He is going away. I knew that was going to happen. But I was going with him. I told him that and he did not disagree. I was even willing to wait until I turned eighteen and escaped Peter and Paul. It would work. But today was like a giant damn light bulb. More. A giant exploding light bulb. It was supposed to be just the opposite. I had practiced and practiced to get ready. I had even fooled Peter about why I was practicing so much. And he figured out that it was important to me so he took it away from me. He put a fucking lock on it. Who does THAT? A lock on the lid over the keyboard? But he knew he had what I wanted, so he made me give him more of what he wanted. And I did it. She did it. We both did it for Peyton. Me and her and them and the whole fucking world. For Peyton.

I told Peyton that I wanted to play the piano for him. I practiced and practiced a song just for him. All he had to do was find a piano. I just so wanted to remind him that I knew he had a piano at his house, but why bother? We weren't going there. But he knew a place, a place even older than the old store he worked in.

King and Broad, I think. I got lost as we walked there, but when we walked through the door I thought we were back in the bookstore. That old smell. Not leather and paper, but old wood for sure, and Peyton told me all about the music store being the oldest in America, going back to the 1800's. It might as well have been when dinosaurs roamed the earth. He laughed when I said that. Is anything new in this town? I said that and he thought that was funny too. Then all the old people showed up, just like the old people at the bookstore. They all knew Peyton. A man named Reynolds rushes over and I swear that he bowed to Peyton. Then Peyton introduces me to the owner, a man named Mr. S, and I got nervous. I think they had heard about me before we arrived. Peyton had arranged my recital. And for some reason I kept thinking that the store inside was getting bigger and bigger and that I was smaller and smaller. And it was so quiet. A room full of beautiful stuff but the most beautiful was the grandest piano near the front window. I had seen pictures of pianos like that, but never the real thing. I whispered to Peyton that my piano at home was like an ugly duckling compared to this one. An ugly ducking to a swan. I did not tell him that my life was an ugly duckling. But I knew it was hopeless. I was never going to be a swan. Peyton is a swan.

I wanted to run away. I wanted to die. But Peyton took my hand and led me to the piano bench. Mr. S asked if I had brought my music with me. I felt better. No, I told him. I knew it by heart. But before I could even take a breath to hold, Reynolds tapped me on the shoulder and held up one finger, stopping me. He motioned me to lean back and then he ran his finger across every key. None of the notes sounded like my piano back home. The notes in Mr. S's store were...???...real music? Reynolds nodded to himself. Was he hearing what I was hearing? Then he nodded to me and stepped back. I closed my eyes and touched the keyboard as my feet found the pedals. You should have heard me. I had never played better in my entire life. I did not miss a note, did not miss a beat, did not make a mistake. When I finished I knew I would never play as good again ever in my life, but I had done it for Peyton. I kept looking down at the keys, my right hand still there, but the store was completely silent. I was afraid to look up, look around. Not a sound, but I could still hear the notes in my head. Peyton was standing behind me, finally taller than me, and I felt his hands on my shoulders, and then he kissed the top of my head and whispered.

—That was so lovely.

And he kissed me again. I was turning to mush. I swear. I started to cry and he pulled me up off the bench and we hugged. It was so nice. I thanked him and thanked him and thanked him. And I was thinking that this moment was important because he was showing the world, his world, that I existed. All of the world could see how much he loved me, not just the bookstore world.

But I was wrong. All the other music store people were not there. They had made arrangements for Peyton and then they had vanished. Peyton had been my only audience, and he would be the only person in the world who had heard how good I had been. That is okay. Peyton had been my audience, Peyton and God, they were enough.

We talked and talked, and he told me all about the music store. I knew that he played the piano, but he had never told me that this was where he had lessons, twice a week since he was eight. I had just assumed that he had them at home.

—No no, lessons here and practice at home. And see that piano over there, not so grand as this one, but that is the one that Gershwin used when he was composing Porgy and Bess.

I knew about that music. Knew who Gershwin was, but I could not remember hearing any of it before. But I must have, right? But it was like the Civil War to me, a relic, ancient history. Everybody in this town seems to still be living that war, especially Peter and Paul, but not me. Peyton spoke as if it was all new, still happening.

The Gershwin, he said, was not to be sold. And he told me the story about how Mr. S's grandfather had kept the store open during the Great Shitty War by making drums for the Confederacy. Who cares, I wanted to say, but he cared, so I told myself that I should care too.

Soon enough, all the others returned. They congratulated me, but I knew they were just being nice. They had not heard me. But they were nice.

And then it all began to fall apart for me. Why did I think it wouldn't? It had to fall apart. Mr. S told Peyton he had some bad news for him. I did not hear the news, but I saw Peyton's face. Death. They were whispering and I looked at the others. They already knew.

The store was closing. The building was to be sold. The Gershwin would have to find another home. I knew the real lesson. You could get old, but you couldn't stay old forever. You had to die. Everything died. I felt bad for all the old people around me, they were going to die, but then Peyton killed me too. He turned and spoke to Reynolds and the others. News of his own. The ghosty owner of the bookstore had died. The bookstore would be closing too.

Crying is sad, but old people crying is worse. I was surrounded by crying adults, but I was angry. He had not told me first. Why had he shut me out? I was really angry. I hated the world. But then I thought of the old people at the bookstore, who loved me, the old woman who should have been my grandmother. I started to cry.

But that was not the revealing thing. (Revelation?) Being angry and disappointed was easy for me. But I was still in love with Peyton, and I know he loves me. It seemed so innocent, an innocent request from Mr. S to Peyton, but when it was over we were a million miles apart. A billion. A universe. Mr. S asked Peyton to play the piano for him and the other old people. Why had it not dawned on me? Of course he could play. Lessons and practice, remember?

He said no, thanking them, but they insisted, and I stared at him, right into his eyes, and he looked away.

—What would you like to hear?

All of them had a suggestion, but Mr. S told him to wait, and then he disappeared through a curtain and then came back to the showroom with five other old people. The entire store had stopped everything. Peyton was going to play the piano. It was a big deal. I was getting smaller and smaller.

Moonlight sonata, and Gershwin. I had heard the sonata a million times, but never like Peyton played it. And I would never hear again better. I want the words but they are not here or there or anywhere. Nobody I had ever heard played as well as he did. So absolutely effortlessly. Like a piano in heaven.

And then, just for Mr. S and his own father, Peyton said—

Summertime.

How had I never heard that before? It was so Peyton. And the words? Rich daddies and good looking mamas. His world. Some of the old people could not stop themselves. They were singing softly along with Peyton as he played. Yes, that was Peyton's world. And there I was on the outside. I was not in the circle. Perfection surrounded by adoration...those are the words I was feeling but only understood when I got back home and looked for them. And I saw the future.

I was always going to be a small ugly duckling. Peyton was always going to be a swan.

The Weight of History

Bobby Beaumont learned everything he knew about his family from his father. Forrest Beaumont let other men manage his money while he devoted substantial hours every week to his wife and son, and then in descending lesser amounts of time to his walks, his charities, and to the Charleston Historical Society. The Beaumont home became its unofficial headquarters, with members visiting and boxes of documents coming and going. Forrest was often called to speak at clubs and schools, and he contributed a monthly column to *The Post and Courier* about Charleston history. Until he was twenty, Bobby Beaumont thought he knew everything about his own past, from Lankford to Rutledge, but his father saved one fact until he was close to graduating from Porter-Gaud Academy, delivered to him at the same time he was falling in love for the first time, a time when he perceived himself at one of those poetic diverging roads, and a fact which had the effect of altering history and thus altering the present and future.

Forrest told his son, "I looked at the picture, and I read the letter, and it was like standing in front of a famous painting for the first time, a painting that I had seen in a dozen coffee table books or in a hundred other reproductions, but seeing the original for the first time was like *really* seeing it for the first time, seeing the lines and color and texture I missed before. Bobby, son, does that make sense?"

With time and distance from that moment, Bobby would describe that scene to Sally with precision, even imitating his father's wonderfully animated face, his pleasure, as if the revelation had been the last piece of a genealogical puzzle on which he had toiled for years.

His father's hand gestured for Bobby to sit beside him, there in their State Street mansion, in his book-lined study, protected by mahogany walls, with the smell of old leather, in the afternoon absolute quietness, as if the earth itself was motionless. The father's wink and smile initiated a bond to be shared between him and his son and possibly a future Beaumont as yet un-conceived in mind or body. "You have to promise me, Bobby, to keep this between me and you. Your mother need not know it. You know how she is, and the Lee family. They tend to take these things much too seriously, right?"

But at that moment, still a teenager, Bobby merely blinked and nodded, the future famous editor at a loss for words. He was about to learn that God did not exist.

The sepia-toned daguerreotype was straightforward enough. Two soldiers, one in rags, the other in a dingy but distinctly Union uniform. Side by side, but the man in rags was rail-thin and staring past the photographer into some grim future. The Union soldier was merely grim at that moment. The man in rags was shackled, and the Union soldier had his own arm entwined with his prisoner, supporting the frailer man.

"Bobby, this is the only picture in existence of your history. Your great-great-grandfather," his father said. "From whom all our blessings flow."

Bobby had heard the Lankford Beaumont stories from the moment he was born, but all he had ever seen was a portrait painted late in the man's life, wife beside him, sullen sons on the floor at their feet, a portrait that Bobby passed every morning as he left for school. The pride of Charleston, native son gone to war and returned from prison, the dark Lankford of legend.

Bobby looked at the photo, at the death look in the ragged man's eyes, and the stories made sense. Who would not brood, would not see the worst of humanity, and thus return home and isolate himself. Bobby was fascinated by the vision in his ancestor's eyes. After a studied look, Bobby turned, looking for traces of Lankford in his father's face, as well as trying to remember his own face in the mirror that morning. The result was confusion. Forrest Beaumont, from his son's perspective, was a man without a worry in the world, and that optimism must surely spring from some internal dynamic of his blood, not from the external world of his wealth. Perhaps the genetic dance was as Bobby had learned, that traits can skip generations, recessed only to flower later. If so, how much of Lankford was in himself?

Bobby hesitated before speaking. It was obvious that his father wanted to hear his impression of the picture, but it was also obvious that this was to be one of those moments that Forrest so loved having with his son. As he had told Bobby many times in the past when he sought his son's opinion, *This is surely something upon which we should reflect.*

Affecting his father's own speech, Bobby said, "He is much

as I imagined. I can only wonder that he did not end his life, rather than return to a land that was as ruined as he. But your concern about mother's feelings, I am not sure of your intent. Would she be *that* grieved by this image?"

Forrest Beaumont had walked to the liquor cabinet and returned with two tumblers of bourbon. It was the first time he had ever offered Bobby a drink, to be shared as part of some more profound initiation.

"A toast, Bobby, to our past," he said as he sat down, handing the glass to his son.

Bobby was even more confused. He knew his father well enough to recognize his ironic tone.

"Is this not Lankford Beaumont?" Bobby asked tentatively, not yet sipping his drink.

His father smiled, and then looked down at his own drink, and his chest seemed to heave quickly as he stifled his more natural reaction. Forrest Beaumont was trying not to laugh.

"No, no, that tortured and wasted soul is indeed Lankford Charles Beaumont…"

And Bobby felt it coming before his father even finished the revelation.

"…but he is not your great-great-grandfather nor my great-grandfather. That honor, source of our seed, belongs to the other man. The victor, not the vanquished."

Bobby took his first sip of his father's bourbon. He pondered a response, but he was also fascinated by what seemed his father's pleasure at the knowledge of the Beaumont moorings being rendered adrift. Father and son drank in silence for a minute, and when it was obvious to Bobby that his father was waiting on him to speak, he finally said, "There is more to this story, is there not? More, of course?"

His father beamed, "Of...course." He was an amateur historian, and for him *The Tale of Two Beaumont's* was a treasure.

Ellie Sees The Stairway

I can't wait any longer. But, where?

Home. I am his first. It was yesterday. I am finally rested. He thinks he is my first. I should definitely be an actress. I was probably rehearsing long before I met him.

I wish it were somewhere else. I wanted it to be in his bed at his home, but that was still Mars for me. I wanted him to be on bottom, looking up at me as I sat on him, so he could see me and then look around his room and forever that room would have us in it, our ghosts, and even if I died he could never go back to that room without seeing me. I would forever be in the famous Peyton House.

I was running out of time. The store was closing. He told me that he had decided to stay in Charleston for college but I knew that wherever that was, he could not let me be part of it. We had always had the bookstore and WPG and SJB, but the bookstore was headed for demolition just like the music store. Torn down or blown up, who knows, but gone. Our world was shrinking.

It had to be the bookstore.

I told him I wanted to see him late at night. I wanted to see him in the dark, but with candles. He laughed, something about the store being a fire trap for sure, but he did not say no. I wonder if he knew what I was really thinking? Doesn't matter now. We would have a picnic I told him. I would bring candles and food. We could use the big table near his desk or we could spread a blanket on the floor. But I already knew where I wanted to do it. The big couch on the second floor. Old and stuffed and worn at the seams. Perfect.

I was so smart I thought, and when Peyton agreed I floated all that day long waiting, but who was I kidding? Did I really forget who I was and where I lived? I could just pack a lunch and waltz out the door at midnight, right? Peter would just wave ta-ta at me and hold the door, right? I made the rules, right? And if I did manage to sneak out, what would happen if Peter came to my room later, like he had done in the past, wake me up and I would not know what time it was but only that it was time again. If I was not there, he would call Paul, and they would both be waiting for me when I returned. But when I needed to leave to see Peyton, I was not scared of Peter and Paul anymore. My house was still lit up but I knew Peter was asleep. The floors creaked, but who cared. I was gone. I was never coming back.

Charleston at midnight was spookier than I imagined. Little Red Riding Hood. Little Red Riding Hood. I knew I must have looked silly, wearing my red skirt and carrying a basket. Sneaking through Charleston chased by wolves named Peter and Paul. I was starring in my own goddam fairy tale. But when I got to the corner where the bookstore was, Peyton was waiting for me outside the front door. And I could see the red tip of his cigarette. He saw me and waved. Even under that dim streetlight, I could see that he was dressed up, not for a picnic, but more like for church. He was wearing his PG dark blazer and slacks, white dress shirt and tie, smoking one of his stupid Marlboros. How much more proof did I need to have to convince me that he was perfect for me? Perfectly perfect.

I stopped walking and waved back. But neither of us moved. I wanted to yell at him that I loved him more than God. But I yelled out the line we both hated from the book we both hated. A line that always led to gagging fits and then laughter.

Just remember, Oliver, love means never having to say you're sorry...My line.

Drop dead, Jenny...His line.

We could do it in our sleep. But there we were on King Street at midnight. I lit my own cigarette and walked across the street as he opened the door for me. An hour later he was inside of me.

No need for details. I do not need to write them down to remember them. Besides, how to describe it? The difference. I never let Peter or Paul kiss me on the mouth. Rule one for all whores. Only Peyton, the only person who would ever kiss me. And with him inside me we did not stop kissing. He was so tender to begin with, and I knew I should tell him that he wasn't hurting me, but I had to make him believe I was a virgin. He had to believe it was not good for me, the first time, or else he would know it was not the first, or the hundredth. And he came too soon, but we did not stop kissing and I would not let him off of me. I held him close, there on that couch in a (dying?) dark bookstore, and we began again and there was no reason to pretend I was a virgin anymore. Neither of us. And it

78

was all I wanted. I was his first. He was mine. When we finally stopped, there was only one more thing I had to do. His eyes were closed and he was breathing deeply as I slipped off the couch and walked naked to the bathroom downstairs. I made myself bleed. I did it quickly, and then I went back upstairs and lay down beside Peyton again. He was my first. My blood was on that couch.

But here's the thing. The important thing about that night. It WAS my first, but not for sex, for something more important.

How late was it? (Five?) We were both still wide awake, deflowered (his word) many times over. But I knew I had to get back to my house. I was no longer Red Riding Hood. I was Cinderella, and had to sneak back into my house before the sun came up. But as Peyton was locking the front door he turned me into a stone.

—Would you like to see my home?

How could I breathe after that? All I could do was blink, and nod, and cry, but I could not talk. He had been planning it all along. It was going to be his picnic surprise, but my surprise for him put his plans off schedule. His parents were gone. He had the house to himself. But we had to hurry. The maid was coming at seven o'clock. We lit our cigarettes and started walking, almost running, to the Peyton House.

And there it was, the outside I had seen a hundred times. White and columned and not my house. A block wide? Seemed to be. Peyton became the tour guide, like he had been at the bookstore years ago and I had been at SJB before. I stood just inside the front door and froze again. It looked bigger on the inside than I had imagined from the outside. And all the sheer curtained windows were letting the morning sun come in, filling the house up with golden light first and then white. Every room had a history, all the portraits on the walls had a history. I don't think there was a piece of furniture from the twentieth century anywhere in the house. The thing that Peyton did not seem to understand was why I had to touch everything. I wanted to see if it was real. He wanted to know why I was staring so much. How could I tell him that I had never seen anything so clean and so...so orderly...before in my entire life. I'm glad I didn't tell that my first thought was that he lived in a museum, that all his world was simply a showroom but that real people could not live there. Then I thought it was not the room or the furniture that were so pristine and orderly. It was him, his parents, this was not an empty showroom. It was them. It was their real world. And I was running out of time. I had only seen the first floor. I told him I had to leave and he insisted that he go with me, to make sure I got home safely. How could I let him do that, after seeing his home? How could I let him see where Peter and Paul lived with me? I grabbed him and kissed him truly madly deeply and was about to escape when I looked back and saw the most beautiful part of the house. How did I not see it from that first moment of walking through the front door? Had I been that overwhelmed?

The wide and winding spiral stairway to the second floor. Carpeted deep red and leading to Peyton's bedroom. He saw me stop and stare and he told me a story about that stairway being the place his father first saw his mother, when they were children. I looked at him, but he was staring at the stairway, as if remembering a story he had been told a thousand times. He knew it by heart. And he was smiling at the memory, as if it had happened to him.

I let go of his hand and ran away. Dropping stones all the way back to my mother's house. Stones that used to play in my head, like the song says, but smaller and smaller and then gone, like me.

The Tale of Two Beaumonts

Both men in the photo were Beaumonts, kin to each other, but from alien families. Lankford fought for the South. His cousin Jones Beaumont fought for survival. The two men had met as children, a family gathering forgotten by Lankford but etched in Jones, a constant reminder of his family's status in the Beaumont chain. Fifteen years after that gathering, Fate sent a defeated and captured Lankford to Camp Douglas in Chicago, a rancid and rat-infested prison, the Northern answer to Andersonville, pridefully named after the Little Giant Stephen Douglas. Camp Douglas had welcomed and then buried thousands of Confederate prisoners, none of whom died of old age. Since history was written, and taught, by the winners, the Northern shame was little known for most people. But it had been a point of inquiry by Forrest Beaumont as he prepared a monograph on the history of his family. A polite letter to the Douglas Archives, and then a phone call in 1970: *Would it be possible to visit your offices and peruse any files relevant to Charleston prisoners?* The Douglas staff had been accommodating to a fault. They invited Forrest to Chicago, and he had returned with a case of letters and photos in his possession, secured by his word that he would return them at his convenience, but definitely return them. Months passed, there seemed to be no hurry, and Forrest found the picture first. He did not recognize the ragged man, but the prison guard looked familiar, not so familiar that the eventual truth was obvious, but...*familiar.* The letter from Jones Beaumont was in a separate box, and the penmanship was less than fluid, but the substance was clear, and the logic was compelling. Forrest Beaumont intuited the mind of the writer when he realized that what he held in his hand was merely a first draft of another letter that would be polished and submitted for consideration. It was a request for money, addressed to a Mr. Raeburn at a Chicago bank. Jones was a Beaumont of lesser means, from a poor family of rice farmers, a family that was embittered against the gentry Beaumonts, a family whose Carolina loyalty was tempered by their Carolina class. When the Great War came and volunteers were solicited, Jones went North. He never considered himself a traitor, merely an entrepreneur. That first draft was the clue and key to further searching by Forrest. Calls were made to the bank, with no result, but then a call to the descendants of the letter's recipient. Tedious work, more letters from Jones to others were found, but slowly the evidence was accumulated.

Jones Beaumont had recognized his cousin as soon as he saw him in shackles, but he did not identify himself at first. Too much perverse pleasure in seeing the mighty rendered weak. But a grain of unfamiliar empathy forced itself into the Union

Beaumont's heart, where it flowered into compassion. At first.

Jones took Lankford as his charge, providing extra food and protecting him from the indiscriminate abuse suffered by others less fortunately connected. This was the narrative that Bobby's father surmised, with a twist that all such stories require. As Lankford Beaumont regained his health and strength, his pride was also revived. An early offer by him—*When this is over, you must return with me to your own country, and we will work the land together. You will be my brother, not my cousin, and we will prosper*—evolved into—*When this is over, you are always welcome in my home. I will speak well of you to others, and doors of opportunity will open for you*—which devolved into—*There will always be a job for you in Charleston. I will need many good men.*

"Those words were Lankford's?" Bobby asked his father in mid-story.

"Close enough," his father said. "Certainly the spirit, if not the letter, of the truth, and as best I can determine from one of Jones' letters to his wife back in Chicago."

Bobby shook his head and blinked, "Wife?"

"What would come to be known as common-law, and evidently a very understanding woman."

"I am confused," Bobby said, immediately realizing that *confused* was an understatement.

"Finish your drink," Forrest said. "From a distance, all things are understandable."

Jones came to realize that his cousin no longer regarded his benevolence as *compassion*, but rather as an *obligation* owed an upper Beaumont from a lesser Beaumont, so his heart hardened within while his overt behavior was deference personified. Lankford was casual in his conversation, oblivious to Jones' studied interest in all names and places and other assorted details, including the petty gossip, of Lankford's Charleston life. Jones was not sure of his eventual goal, all he knew was that he was indeed going back to Charleston. He would rival his cousin in some form.

Lankford's final transgression against the charity of his cousin was his conspiracy with other prisoners to escape, to leave Jones behind and secure his own freedom. That escape was thwarted by the famed Allan Pinkerton, and Lankford returned in shackles. He was greeted by dysentery, smallpox, and a hostile kin. His decline was precipitous. His death was less than noble. He was buried in a mass grave, his name recorded on the prison ledger, a courtesy not granted to thousands of nameless others buried with him, and then his remains were re-buried under the *Confederate Mound* monument in the Oak Wood Cemetery in 1867. Jones Beaumont survived the War, survived a steamboat explosion after the War, survived pneumonia, secured his borrowed money, and went to Charleston. Lankford was home.

"Do you now see the forest from which you come?" Bobby's father asked him, pleased at his own pun.

"Daddy, you seem to be unfazed by all this, or am I missing something?" Bobby was feeling the effects of bourbon and history. "I mean, if I can piece this together, I mean, use the word, this means that our *background* is not that of a true Charleston family. Rather, we are... ," and he hesitated, slowly being infected by his father's pleasure, "...we are the...," and he smiled, albeit resistant to the inevitable conclusion, "...we are the legacy of a..."

His father raised his left hand, motioning for Bobby to let him say it, and then uttered the word at the same moment he raised the tumbler in his right hand and tipped it slightly toward his son, "...carpetbagger."

Bobby nodded.

"And now, son, I think it's time for a refill."

Ellie Goes to the Past and Sees Her Future

How many pages have I thrown away? I write them and burn them. I only want to write about Peyton. How perfect it has been. For so many months and times. Each time is better and better. He cannot stop wanting to see me. We do it in the store and WPG. He even took me to a hotel. I had never seen such a big bed and the room was actually two rooms. He just wanted to look at me. I told him he could do anything he wanted with me but he did not believe me. He does not know. He still does not know that I will do anything for him.

But I still live with Peter and Paul, with the men who Paul brings to fuck me. Thank god for rubbers, right? Or else I would be a walking pestilence. Everything I write lately comes back to them, so I burn it. When I write, I think. I want to think only about Peyton but sooner or later I have to think about them and I write about them and it gets mixed up with writing about Peyton. How can Peyton not notice that? I lie to him all the time. I must be good at it. I am afraid that if he knew he would not love me. So I lie. And I think about him only in my head, not by writing. But today is too much. I am too happy. I want to write what I am hoping.

I want Peter to die. I want somebody to kill him. I want God to kill him. If he were gone I could escape. I am almost old enough to live by myself. I think I am. I have a job now, a shitty job, and I lie to Peter about how much I make. He takes some every week, to pay for my upkeep, he says I should pay for some of my upkeep. What a dumb word...upkeep. I want to scream at him that he ought to be paying me for my pussy or my mouth. I can use those words when I think of Peter, but not Peyton. I would never talk like that to him even though sometimes we need to use dirty words to talk about what we are doing. But when we are actually doing those things we don't even need to talk. He is so much better the more we do it. He knows what I want without me talking. Me too, I know what he wants. And how is it possible that he kisses so good? One time we just kissed for an hour, and then more. Every sex thing I ever did before Peyton does not count. But it all comes back to Peter and Paul. Before Peyton I never understood why they bothered with me. I never thought they were having a good time. But who can I tell what I know now? How I know what they want because I know how much Peyton loves to be inside me, and all the other things I do for him. With Peter and Paul I am somewhere else. With Peyton I am with only him at that exact time. I only feel with him. I want to understand this. This difference. How Peyton makes me alive when he touches me, and they make me dead.

Fuck, it is happening again. I was only going to think about Peyton but here I am trapped in the shit-hole of Peter and Paul.

I want them to die. Peter should go first. But I want Paul dead too. I wish I was brave enough to do it myself. I know where they keep their guns. I know where the biggest knives are. I think about what I would say to each one right before I killed them. It is the same thing I think to myself as they are doing me. The same words. The same speech over and over. I once thought that I could ask Peyton to kill them for me. For about a half a second. Because to kill them he would have to know about them and I can never let that happen. And if I don't write about them they don't exist.

This was such a happy day for me. Peyton and I took the tour boat out to the Fort. We were just another couple of tourists. The tall witty and beautiful woman that was me and her shorter beautiful husband who spoke such proper English. Among complete strangers, we had always been older. I talked old. He acted old. He has manners. And manners are old. We were bundled. It was too cold for most everybody else. That worried me. I feel safer with him in public if we are part of a crowd. The bigger the crowd, the more invisible we were.

I have lived here sixteen years and I had never been to the Fort, not even on some stupid school trip. Peyton must have been there a hundred times because he knew so much more than the ranger guide. He knew all the names. Anderson and Double-something and he knew all the Confederate names too, his saintly ancestors back here in town shooting at the Fort. I asked him about that, his past, but he did something strange. We were standing in the middle of the grounds, the walls around us blown to crap in 1861. It was me and the others, even the ranger guide had been listening to him. The ranger guide knew all about Peyton's ancestors and when I asked Peyton to tell the rest of us too...because of all the things he and I had ever talked about, he never talked about that distant past...which is odd because I thought that people like him and his mother and father, those kind of people, that they always lived in the past. But there was that blush again, like the time I saw his book and named him Peyton three years ago. (that long??!!) He just shook his head. He said something about it being a long time ago, not something to be so proud of today. THAT really set off the ranger guide, who acted like he was Jefferson Davis's brother or somebody like that. Peyton had just pissed in church you would have thought. The other tourists must have been Yankees. But Peyton smiled his Peyton smile. The guide wanted to argue. Peyton remained silent. I wanted the guide and the tourists to disappear at that moment because I wanted...Peyton inside me. I had never been so turned on in my entire life. Never. And he had not even touched me. I had to settle for a quick kiss as we dropped out of the group and found a corner out of sight. I asked him if we could go find a private place when we got back. He told me that he already had that hotel room reserved again.

It was the hotel with the giant mirror facing the bed, floor to almost ceiling. The mirror in which I had seen our children. He saw them too. He liked to watch me look at myself. I was beautiful. Ellie or me or whoever, I did not care. I had never seen that person until he watched me look at her. The first time he was standing behind me and I could watch his hands on me. But then it was clear. We were both looking at our doubles in the mirror, but he was looking only at my face and I was looking only at his face and we were so close that our faces were side by side. And I saw our children. He did too. Our two faces together got blended. We became an "us"...a single thing. This is hard to write, the thing that we both saw. He explained it to me. He and I were in love. We were part of each other. Something about halves united. An old myth I had read about but did not understand until then. I was crying because I really understood. I remembered my parents' faces from their old pictures and I looked at my face and I saw them. I was them. Peyton must have been seeing his own mother and father... himself as their love. And that was how he explained it to me. My face and his so close together right there in front of us and we knew that the only way to ever really see the thing that was ...us...was to have a child. He or she would be a mirror. That's what Peyton said. I was totally naked and his arms were wrapped around me, but I saw our child. I have written and re-written this a hundred times and all I see is Peyton's face next to mine, we were one face.

A Loss of Place

The knowledge of his true family history did more than momentarily confuse Bobby Beaumont. Unlike his father, who seemed to relish the truth, Bobby was unmoored. The impact was not obvious to him at the beginning. But he was a thoughtful young man, thoughtful in terms of being considerate and well-mannered, but also thoughtful in that he was capable of thinking. Bobby became the only heir to the Beaumont history, that forbidden knowledge which he was sworn by his father to reveal only to the first male heir to the Beaumont name and fortune. *Never to the women*, his father had said, and then sealed the male bond with a tap of his bourbon tumbler against that of his son, *Never to the women*.

Bobby kept his word for almost twenty-five years, until it was obvious that he was to be the last male Beaumont; indeed, the last Beaumont at all. He did not tell the woman with whom he was in love when he was a teenager. Nor any other woman, certainly not to his mother, who survived his father by many years. Not until it was obvious that he was the end of the line, his own death not only inevitable, but imminent, did he find a repository for the *Tale of Two Beaumonts*, a tale which began with his father's research and was then augmented by Bobby's own archival work in Chicago after his father died. That repository was a woman.

Sally Graham had eventually become his priest, a twist of wit that she did not appreciate at first, but which she eventually resigned herself to being. "You just have to hear my confessions," Bobby had told her many years after she started working for him, late in the afternoon after he had come back from another visit to his doctor. "You do not have to grant me any dispensations or assign me any penance. Will you do that for me? Just hear my confession?"

"It is after six o'clock, right?" Bobby had smiled at their private joke, but she still saw his pain. If she was to be his priest, she assumed that he would explain why he was beginning to look different, to feel more tired than usual, that he would finally tell her his life story. "And you'll answer any question I ask you?"

"Of course not," he told her. "You are my priest, not my grand inquisitor."

Over ten years together, and only a single time, a night for which he had apologized, a moment of weakness induced by their mutual alcohol and his private stress, and never repeated, never mentioned again, their own secret. His apology had made her angry, and she wanted to quit, not as a bargaining chip for a commitment, but simply because she thought she could no longer be around a man she loved but who did not love her.

Sure, call me Sister Graham, celibate pathetic loser, your friend, your sexless goddam buddy, she wanted to say that and even more to him, *how about I be your priestess, not priest, sounds a bit pagan to me, and more fun,* but instead she told him another truth,

"Sure, I'll listen, no strings attached."

It was after six o'clock. She was allowed to drink at the office.

"Do you mind if I smoke?" Over the years, he had smoked less, and he tried to avoid it around her in particular, her distaste for that vice of his, a distaste which was repressed in the beginning but released with familiarity, that distaste had become too obvious.

"You smoke. I'll drink. It's after six, another day at the office, right?"

Sally did take a selfish pleasure out of one part of Bobby's smoking. Her first Christmas present to him had been a silver cigarette case, monogrammed with his initials, and which he kept with him at all times. When he would open it, take out a cigarette, close the case, and tap the cigarette against the lid… Sally enjoyed witnessing that every time it happened. Even at award ceremonies or parties, she would wait for the moment when he reached for a cigarette, perhaps even offering one to a woman who was with him on that occasion. And, best of all, if by chance he happened to see her looking in his direction, the case in his hand, he would arch his eyebrows at her and smile, acknowledging her contribution, making her complicit in the act. She always wondered if he ever saw her own initials at the edge of the case. His *RLB* was in bold relief on the cover. Her *SG* was etched in the smallest script she could get the jeweler to do, script too small for a casual eye to notice, tiny letters, her only claim. She never told Bobby, and he never told her he ever saw them.

Her with a glass of wine, him with a cigarette, her sitting on the old couch in his office, him pacing back and forth, he told her the *Tale of Two Beaumonts*. The actual facts were interesting enough, hardly controversial to Sally, but it was Bobby's self-analysis of the *Tale's* effect on him, the consequences to come that he did not see at the moment when he first heard about Jones Beaumont. Bobby's hindsight was the important revelation to Sally.

"My father was a complete man when he found out. I think that was the difference. He was fully formed. I was not. He accepted the past because the present, his own place in Charleston, my mother, his entire life, was settled. He knew who he was. Being merely young, I, of course, knowing everything, as young men assume they know everything, thought I was settled too. I was a Beaumont from Charleston. I had come from a long line of Charleston Beaumonts. So why did it matter? Up to that point I had always assumed that since Charleston was my past, it would also be my future. Continuity assumed, right?"

Sally wanted to interrupt, to tell him, *You and that Old South thing of yours, Bobby. You gotta get over that.* But she remained in character, Beaumont's priest.

"And there were other factors, of course, things I could not tell my parents at the time. I was falling in love, but not to a woman of whom they would approve…"

Sally listened more intently.

"… and, as much as I knew they would want me to be happy, as much as they understood love, twined around each other as much as they were, I did not feel they would approve of this woman." He noticed Sally leaning forward. "It was a long time ago. I was young. She is gone now, if that is what you want to ask. But my point is this… the story of Jones Beaumont did not allow my allegiance to Charleston to harden, as it had for my parents. I was not in college at the time. My parents felt no need for me to commit to anything. I had all the time in the world to find myself, their words, to find myself. In an odd way, I came to feel like an outsider in Charleston, a bit of a fraud, a role my father accepted for himself with good humor, but unsettling to me. Many things were unsettled for me then. I began to wonder if the person that I was, or was to become, could not, would not, be found in Charleston. I actually thought about moving to Chicago, but my father, a bit too accommodating of his only son…as he was told by his friends, he told me later…my father said that if I was going to seek my fame and fortune, and how he smiled when he said that, I must wade into the belly of the biggest beast of all." He paused to light another cigarette "I must go to New York City. You are too young to remember this, but New York in the early seventies was not a model city."

Sally shook her head at that, laughing out loud, "Unlike today, you mean."

"Like I said, you are too young. Back then, New York was dirtier, more crime-ridden, and worst of all, in my father's eyes, it was financially bankrupt. He had a simple and consistent motto: *If you cannot manage your money, pay somebody to do it for you.* It was, as I was told, the embodiment of everything wrong with the North. But, see, in my mind back then, it was what I needed. It was not Charleston. I needed to get away from Charleston, away from a life I had inherited under false pretenses, a life I did not deserve because I was also doing something about which my parents, and my friends, would not approve."

Sally frowned at him. "Did you *really* believe all that?"

"I still do, mostly. They did not approve, and if I stayed there my mother would have eventually found out. I still believe that. It was mostly the woman… she was not… not… well, my mother would have been concerned about my choices... but there was always the bigger question of who I was supposed to be. From my vantage now, it seems like I was actually going through a phase at eighteen that I should have gone through when I was sixteen. I was rebelling. It was a damn silly rebellion, I suppose. I left Charleston, and I came here after a few months skipping around the country. Before he died, my old boss at the Palmetto Bookstore had always told me to go see his friend Harry Windsor if I ever got to New York. I told my parents I wanted to be on my own for a while. There had been a bit of a dust-up between me and my father about the young woman, which we kept to ourselves. That collusion against my mother required us to both maintain a lie to explain some rather graphic evidence of the truth."

Sally was about to interrupt, but Bobby stopped her. "*That* is a story for later. For now, the important story is my exit. To their credit, even my mother, they encouraged me, but only my father really understood. He offered me a thousand dollars traveling money, a lot more then than it is now, and I left Charleston."

Sally did not speak for a minute, and Bobby seemed to have finished. She wondered about his first love, and all the ones that must have followed, some of whom she had seen in person over the years, others about whom she had heard gossip even before she went to work for Windsor. Finally, she risked an awkward question, about something more important than his infamous and mysterious love life, "So where's your home, Bobby?"

"Charleston," he said, turning to face her, "It was always Charleston."

Ellie Exiled

Peter is dead. I killed him. God killed him, but I made it happen.

Peyton is gone. I will never see him again.

They are coming for me tomorrow. They said I could write some more soon, but I had to get better first. I had to do what they told me and then I would get better. I told them that there was nothing wrong with me. All I needed was Peyton. But they took him away from me. They said he was not safe with me. They are liars. But so am I. I know that. But they are telling the truth. Peyton is not safe with me.

I went home after seeing Peyton. Paul was waiting for me. On the front porch. I could smell him as I got closer. The stinky chaw and stinky whiskey. Peter did not smell like that. Peter was always soapy smelling. I saw Paul and slowed down. I knew what he was there for. What he was always there for. I was just glad that he was alone. My stomach was getting sick when I saw him. I had just had a perfect day at WPG with Peyton. But there was Paul. I stopped, thinking he might not have seen me.

He yelled at me, yelled to get over there. And then I heard it in his voice and closer saw it in his eyes. He was crying. He was a baby crying.

—Your father's dead. Your father's dead.

I knew that, I told him, but he kept screaming.

—Pete is dead. Pete is dead.

I stood there. Peter is not my father. My father died a long time ago. But then I understood. And I started to walk backwards, looking right at Paul, but he was up and off the porch and ran toward me and grabbed me and held on to me and I could feel him shaking.

—Pete is dead, Pete is dead!

It was sad, him so shook up that way. As if he was human. All I could do was look at the house in front of me as he kept hugging and slobbering all over me, look at the only house I had ever known. Peter had been alive when I went to see Peyton. Peter was dead now. All the mumbo-jumbo that Paul was saying added up to a simple thing. I had been wrong about God. He had been listening to me. I was a sparrow. I had wished Peter to be dead and God made it happen. It was all so simple.

—Where have you been? Where have you been?—Your father went looking for you and he must have run a light and he is dead now. He was worried about you and went looking for you and he is dead now.

I kept looking at my house. My house. I was free. I could ask Peyton to come see me now. I would wash it a hundred times, scrub everything a hundred times, and Peyton could come see me. I was free. Ellie, me, free. It was like winning a prize or something. My name is called. I won. Win an election, win a prize, just win. And you could die at that moment and you would have experienced some sort of high that most people never feel. I won. I was free. Peter was dead. Ding goddam dong the witch is dead. I started to laugh right there in Paul's arms. I tried to laugh inside me, but it was too much. I laughed out loud. I wanted to scream a laugh. I wanted to run into my house and lock the doors and laugh forever. Most of all, I wanted to see Peyton.

Paul slapped me. I kept laughing. He pushed me away and held on to me and then slapped me again. He couldn't hurt me. I was sure. My lip was bleeding but he could not hurt me. And then God died.

—You bitch. You bitch. He died because of you.

Paul screamed at me and hit me. Then he killed me

—You think this is funny! You think this is funny? You go in and get your stuff. You are coming to live with me. Pete made it in writing. I was your guardian if something happened to him. You're all mine now. I'll sell this pit and you'll live with me.

I just kept looking at my house, looking as he screamed about him owning it now and going to sell it now. I was his. He was shaking me as I watched my house disappear. And I vomited. I puked all over him and I felt myself start to shit in my pants. I was emptying myself all over him there as we stood on that sidewalk. People were stopping to stare at us. I was bleeding and puking and shitting. Some negro man ran over and grabbed Paul. That must have been Paul's worst nightmare. For a colored man to put his hands on him. His pride rose up and turned away from me to attack my savior. And then I disappeared. I was free of Paul and I ran away. I ran and ran and ran and ran all the way back to the bookstore where I would be safe. Peyton was waiting for me. I was sure. But he was not there, and the bookstore was closed. How could I forget that? The store was closed. Peyton was not there. I slowed down and stood still. I ran to the music store. It was closed. I only had one place to go, but I knew it would be the end of us. I ran to Peyton's house. He had been waiting for me. He must have been waiting because when I got closer I saw him on his beautiful wide front porch looking for me. He saw me and came down to my level. Blood and shit and piss and puke all over me, but he ran straight for me and wrapped his arms around me as if I was his holy something, something lost and found. And I told him the truth. Every lie was gone. I told him about Peter and Paul and all the things they had done to me since I was ten years old. I confessed everything to him. And he hugged me closer. I told him about Peter dying because I asked God to kill him. I told him about Paul waiting for me back at my house. I told him everything.

—You will come to live with me and my parents.

Did I hear that right?

—You will come here. We will take care of you. I will go with you now to your house and we will get your things and you will come back here.

He ran back into his house. I stood on the sidewalk. I had won again. A horn honked and there he was in a giant black car next to the sidewalk motioning for me to get in. It was not his car. I was embarrassed. I would ruin the inside of that car if I got in. He jumped out from behind the wheel and came around to open the door and nudge me inside to sit beside him. We slowly drove and he did not talk. He knew no haste. That was something I read somewhere. He knew no haste. How did he know where to go? I had never told him exactly where I lived. But he knew how to get there. How did he know that?

Paul was waiting for us. Sitting on the porch. Drinking from a can of beer. The look on his face as we walked toward the front steps? Wonder and awe and rage? I knew the rage look. But the other looks told me that I really had totally kept Ellie a secret from him. And Peyton. We walked to the foot of the steps and Peyton told him that we were coming for my things, that Paul had better stay out of our way. Peyton had seen what Paul had done to me a few hours earlier. He must have known what Paul could do, but he took my hand and helped me up the steps and into the house as Paul let us pass.

I was shamed again. Peyton was seeing the inside of my house before I had a chance to clean it. The filth was everywhere. The stink was everywhere. But he did not notice. I only had one suitcase. It was my mother's. It still had her clothes in it. I was crying again. I told Peyton that there was nothing I wanted to keep except what was already in the suitcase. He said okay, we could buy all sorts of new things for me later. I looked around the room one more time. Remembering where the pictures of my mother and father had once hung on the walls. I looked up the ceiling and saw the water stains and peeling paint. How many times had I focused on that space above me as I lay on that bed, shutting out Peter and Paul, looking over their shoulders. I was very tired all at once. I wanted to sleep forever.

Paul was waiting for us when we went downstairs. Peyton was holding my bag and he stepped in front of me and told Paul to get out of the way. I was taller than Peyton. Paul was taller than me. I knew things about Paul that Peyton could not imagine. I wanted to tell Peyton that people like Paul did not exist in his world, but Paul did not give me time.

—Leave her be, you pretty faggot boy. Go back home.

Peyton was perfect at that moment, all I ever thought he was, he was perfect. He was brave and he fought for me. But he is a boy. Paul was a man. We all three heard the sirens at the same time and Paul seemed distracted as Peyton started to lead me out the door but then Paul was on us and I saw the little can opener in his hand swing into Peyton's face and the blood was everywhere and Peyton fell and Paul was kicking him over and over. I flew at Paul but I was empty and weightless and he threw me off and I felt my chest crack as I fell beside Peyton on the floor. His eyes were closed and I could not see half his face so I tried to pull him toward me but I lost my breath as Paul kicked me in my heart. I was sure Peyton was dead. I closed my eyes and tried to hear him breathe but all I heard was men shouting and the door busting. I opened my eyes. Peyton's face was not the same. Paul was screaming but not near us anymore. I sat up, seeing two sheriffs beating him with clubs and dragging him away. Peyton and I were alone and we were dead. I started to crawl toward him but then I was stopped by a giant hand. A giant man was in the room with us, dressed in a white suit. It was Peyton, a giant Peyton wearing black framed glasses. An older Gregory Peck handsome taller Peyton who looked down at me and smiled. It was Peyton's smile. But there was something else in that face. I knew the Bible. It was a Bible face. It was wrath. He was smiling and he was angry. Peyton? I must have whispered to that face. And God responded.

—Help will be here soon—You must not move—You are safe now.

More sirens, more men coming into the house. Crowding around me and Peyton. Trouble in the voices. I looked for the giant man in white. He was in the corner. Standing aside to let smaller men tend to Peyton. He was not looking at them. He was staring at me. Peyton? Are you Peyton? I had seen a picture of him somewhere before. I was confused. He shook his head.

—I am his father. He told me all about you. I am here to take my son home. You and I will talk later.

They are coming to get me tomorrow. I do not care. God took Peyton away from me.

Into the Belly of the Beast

Bobby arrived in New York City at midnight, a young man from the provinces. His train was late, and he had been sleeping as it finally pulled into Grand Central Station. He had two bags, a copy of *Fodor's*, a list of names and addresses supplied by his father, and a hundred dollars in cash. As he would tell Sally later, "This was back when gasoline was thirty cents a gallon."

Arriving so late, and having been asleep, he had not been able to see the City from a distance, to descend slowly into the *belly* of his father's metaphorical beast. Even though late, there would have still been the spectacle of the lights from afar if only he had been awake, but he went to sleep in Pennsylvania and awoke in Manhattan.

Off the train into the bowels of the Station, bags in tow, he stepped into a disappointment. He did not yet know the history of the building, the earlier loss of Penn Central, the lawsuits to save Grand Central from the same fate, the reprieves. He would eventually contribute a hundred thousand dollars to its restoration and see it re-dedicated in 1998. But his first night was merely confirmation of his father's bleak expectations for the entire city. The roof leaked, stonework was crumbling, steel was rusted. Pollution and dirt had stained the walls and floors. The symbols of American commerce, like the Kodak sign and the Newsweek clock, blocked out natural light. There was not much *grand* about the station, but Bobby was undeterred. He looked around, lifted his bags, and walked out to 42nd Street.

The street seemed to be teeming with people, unlike midnight in downtown Charleston. And the lights? The immensity and height of the buildings? For the first few minutes, Bobby realized soon after, he must have looked like the proverbial tourist, the yokel who was not local. His father had warned him about the proper posture for the city: erect, self-confident, and never stare up for longer than a few seconds. But his first vision of New York was both dark and electric, almost pulsating, and dotted with what seemed a million illuminated windows.

After a cab ride to the hotel where he thought he had a reservation, Bobby was re-initiated, his expectations overturned. Since he had arrived so late, and the reservation had not been guaranteed, and it being a Friday night, there was no room for the young man from Carolina. In the otherwise empty lobby of the hotel, feeling himself the center of attention and the object of derision from the hired help surrounding him, a clerk and a bellman, Bobby stood mute. His friends had warned him about the rude and abrasively callous nature of New Yorkers, and he felt his spine stiffening. The reality was different. The Persian clerk apologized and then started making calls to nearby hotels for him. A Negro bellman appeared with a cup of coffee for him and suggested that he sit in one of the Queen Anne lobby chairs while the clerk sought another room. Beaumont recognized the black man's accent, a strong thread of south Louisiana. Already wide awake, the coffee made him even more alert.

A new room secured a few blocks away, Beaumont was further surprised when the clerk suggested that the bellman accompany him. He insisted that he could find the hotel all by himself. *Go out the door and turn right, go two blocks, and there it is, isn't that what you said?* The clerk had smiled at the bellman, who arched his eyebrows, a smile and an arch between wizened men who had assumed responsibility for a babe in the woods. *No problem, sir.* The clerk was deferentially insistent. *I can certainly spare Taylor for a few minutes. He can carry your bags and be back here without me missing him. Right, Taylor? We think it would be better if you were assisted, and escorted.* A nod from the older black man sealed the pact.

Less than five minutes later, Bobby was standing in front of his new hotel. He thanked his escort and was about to turn back into the building, but his man Taylor did not budge. Bobby was momentarily confused, but quickly realized, *Of course, the protocols.* He handed the man a five-dollar bill, the smallest he had, and thanked him.

Taylor stepped around Bobby and opened the glass door for him. *No, thank you, sir. And welcome to New York.*

Bobby was awake for the next twenty-four hours. Caffeine augmented by adrenalin, he wanted the sun to rise much sooner than the laws of physics would allow. He had much to see. Until the morning, however, he sat in his room and wrote letters to his parents, one for each. Each letter was uniquely tailored for its audience.

With the new day, he began walking, and, as he jostled his

way through streets full of people indifferent to his existence but all seemingly intent on overcoming a collective tardiness, he made his way down West 55th to Fifth Avenue, turned left, and there it was, towering even from a distance, the Empire State Building. In a letter back to his father that night, he told him that he finally understood the sensation that the elder Beaumont had described upon first seeing the photographs and letters of Jones Beaumont.

It was like standing in front of a famous painting for the first time, a painting that I had seen in a dozen coffee table books or in a hundred other reproductions, but seeing the original for the first time was like really seeing it for the first time, seeing the lines and color and texture I missed before, his father had said, and Bobby understood. No film or television image, no postcard or newspaper picture… nothing conveyed the reality of the original, the overwhelming awe of the first real confrontation.

Twelve hours more, and then the whole next day, Bobby postponed the contacts he had scheduled for himself. Saturday night, he found Broadway and Times Square, tacky and gaudy, perverse and seductive. He was not in Charleston anymore.

With Sunday, he went to St. Patrick's for the 11:00 mass. He was not Catholic. He just wanted to sit in the church where Bobby Kennedy had been eulogized by his brother a few years earlier. And, besides, his mother would be pleased to hear that he had gone to *any* church that morning. Her view of New York City was not as forgiving as that of her husband, and her Episcopalian faith would certainly endorse Catholicism even if it only provided a temporary refuge against the sins of the city.

Sunday afternoon, he strolled through Central Park, wondering if he might see somebody famous, perhaps even

Jackie Kennedy? He did not imagine that twenty years later she would grace one of his famous parties. The simple truth was that at that moment Bobby Beaumont had no plans for his future. He had no career goals, no timetable for success, no measurement of happiness. He only had a Sunday afternoon to fill in Central Park before he went to find Harry Windsor.

Ellie and the Doctor

You seem like a nice man, and you have a kind voice. I wonder if that is the real you, or is that how you were trained? You must have known a lot of people like me, and you had to keep your distance, right? You must also be a patient man. As soon as you told me your name I hung up on you. All I needed to hear was your name. You called back. I hung up. You sent a letter. Yes, words on a page made you safer to me. Then you called back and I listened a little more. You are patient. I am your patient. You say you read all the files on me at the hospital, all the other doctor reports, but, excuse me, you could not anticipate me being a little...just a goddam little...put off when you told me that your name was Peter.

But you are right. I need to start using real names. Peter was not my stepfather. But if you had told me that your middle name was Paul then all bets were off for sure. Too much damn karma. I asked you and you had two seconds, but you kindly said your middle name was Wayne, as if it was no big deal. Your soft voice said Wayne and I exhaled. I even liked your last name, so solid, but I am going to change it to Rock. You are PWR.

Hello, Mr. PWR. Should I call you doctor? I'm sorry, but I don't remember meeting you while I was at the hospital although you said you had met me. Of course, I don't remember a lot about that time anyway. Some stuff I can tell you, if you are really interested. But you read the reports, right? And they did release me. The right pills, I turn eighteen, I was a productive free white woman again. With a few minor restrictions. A court order, a requirement to regularly report back with the clinic to prove I was not a homicidal baby-killer and that I was a good patient who took her medication, just like a common criminal on parole, all perfectly legal. Everything under control. As long as I never saw another certain person, I could stay free. Free, and dead. Because the only person who makes me not crazy, who makes me alive, is the only person I can never see again.

But you know all that because you read the files. The top secret Ellie files. You admitted that right up front. You know all about me. What took you so long? But you seem like a nice person. You want to meet me. Of course, I am so damn interesting, surely for someone like you. But you want to do it differently. You want to talk on the phone. You want me to write to you. But you do not want to read what I write. You said you would be my audience in print, and we might meet in person, but I never had to show you any of this. Get the thoughts out of myself, put them at a distance. I thought you were silly, but you said the magic words.

—You need to stop talking to yourself. You need someone outside yourself. Let that other person be me.

You said I should look at this as a first draft. Clever you. You knew I understood that. You knew all about my obsession with writing. You read everything, didn't you. All the pages I wrote up until I died when his father saved him.

You asked if I had written more since I was released. I could have lied and said a million pages, but you knew me too well. I could already see that. But your voice was kind...and respectful. You said that every day was like a rough draft of the day to follow. I liked that. And it was okay to re-read and re-write first drafts, but paper first drafts were different than life first drafts. Life first drafts could not be changed, only understood in hindsight. Paper first drafts could be changed, made better, made clearer, so I could see what I was trying to say and failing. Do not let this go to your head, Doctor PWR, but the only reason I am doing this now is because you are the first doctor I might...might...might just tell the truth. But I might not. But I liked your idea of going back to all the things I had written earlier. The other doctors wanted to keep those pages away from me, but not you. But I'm not sure I can do what you said... read those pages as if written by someone else. That girl was me, but she is not me now. You said that, that girl was past tense, remember? But I like your idea. Read them again. My idea is better though...make them what I really wanted to say but could not. I had no control then. Words would gush out, as if they were choking me inside and I had to get rid of them. They were like poison. Except when I wrote about Peyton.

Sure, real names now, except for Peyton. I know you know his real name, and I am not crazy. I know his real name too. I know where he is. I know he still loves me even if he is silent. I know we will meet again when he is ready. Not me, it has to be him.

The other doctors before you? Assholes and fools. And they hated me. They think that the medicine cured me. Of what?

My energy? Success. I can barely get through a day without a lot of naps. If I had a real job instead of the crap one I have now, I would probably get fired. My looks? Oh sure, cured of that too. Fifty extra pounds will do that. My mood swings? I'm as calm and cool and comatose as a cucumber. My writing? Yes, they cured me of that too. A giant void is all I have of the past few years. But, as I told you. Why not? A void because nothing is there. I am cured.

You, Doctor PWR? (I think I have to write your name a lot to make it not be the other Peter who is not really named Peter.) You want me to write things to you that you will never read, and then you want to talk eventually. Is all this more first draft exercising so I can tell you the same things later face to face but more in control of them. I know about your profession. Drugs for sure, but also force the patient to talk to you because the real audience is the patient herself. She has to hear herself out loud. She has to confront herself. You are merely the pump, right? But I know you are different. The other doctors thought I had cheated on all the tests they gave me. I cheated! I cheated? I cheated on an IQ test? No way, I heard them talk among themselves, no way I was that smart. I wasn't a genius, but higher than they would have predicted? The verbal tests, I cheated? Peyton would have laughed at them. He could have told them like he told me. I was the smartest girl, the smartest person he had ever met. More than your parents? I had teased him. I remember how he blushed. Parents are different he had stammered. Yes, I remember him...stammering. But he was right. I know that now, although all I could say to him then was something like... I wouldn't know.

I learned to read before I was three. I sort of have a memory of my father reading to me, but I might be wrong. My mother read to me all the time, and then as she got sick I read to her all the time, for hours, her books, not mine. We had those condensed novels by Reader's Digest. I read those and she would help me. I read the newspaper and the comics to her. I read magazines to her. I read poetry to her after I had read it to myself. I memorized poems and performed for her. I could do that for Peyton too, perform poetry for him and the other old people in the bookstore. I was the center of attention. Peyton and I would do dramatic readings from plays for them too. I loved him for trying, but he was an awful actor. Sometimes I would make him sit down and I would do all the parts, changing voices with each character. And they would applaud me as I bowed.

When P&P (sorry, decompression is slow sometimes) took my life away from me at home, they made me read for them too. I was a little talking puppet for them. Too soon for these details, Doctor PWR? Too soon to tell you about me being twelve years old and standing naked in front of them as I read from a book they gave me, a book about fucking and sucking, making me walk around the room after they had both jacked off on my flat chest? Too soon? Was that story in my files too? Probably not. The really good stories, the ones I knew they wanted to hear, I never told those other doctors.

So, Doctor PWR, you think I am smart and you want to study me. How wonderful is that idea...to study me. But I do not feel so smart now, as smart as I was with Peyton. Can you make me that smart again? You say that you want to "reconsider" my diagnosis. Possible new treatments but first the diagnosis has to be right, right? I like that word...reconsider. I want to be reconsidered. Most of all, I want off these goddam drugs, or get me better drugs, the right drugs for the love of Jesus. I want to be pretty again. I want to be smart again. You can study me from now until hell says hello to my uncle. You can study me forever, just as long as you make me okay for when Peyton comes to get me.

Harry Windsor

Sam Simon had told Bobby much about Harry Windsor, his old friend in the city. Simon's history of Windsor, Bobby would discover after meeting Windsor, was incomplete. But, then again, Windsor had many histories, some of which contradicted the others. Aware of his own impending death at the end of the twentieth century, Bobby made a list of regrets. On that list was his failure to get a unified truth about Harry Windsor's life. Of the three older men who shaped him...his own father, Simon, and Windsor...the New York Jew was the most elusive.

New York Jew was Windsor's own description of himself, repeated too often, as if forcing his listener, especially new acquaintances, to pigeonhole him in a cliché already ingrained in their mind...*I'm just a New York Jew. You should expect me to be something else?...* but a cliché used as a shield, to stop further analysis. *New York Jew* explained everything, right? In one of their rare arguments, Bobby had snapped at him, *New York Jews deserve a better example, a better symbol than you, Harry Windsor.* The cause of the argument? Forgotten soon enough. But Windsor always liked to remind Bobby of his heated comment, especially when Bobby expressed some exasperation about another Windsor venture. *I'm just doing my best to be the best New York Jew in New York*, and the two men would laugh at each other.

His first Sunday in New York, Bobby had taken a cab to the Windsor Building, instructing the cabbie to drop him off a block away so that he could consider it from a distance. Sam Simon's story was true. The Windsor Building was a knock-off of the Flatiron Building. The language of architectural design... *Flatiron's ornate but restrained facade is composed of stone and terra-cotta panels whose forms simulate the effects of rustication...* described Windsor as well. In fact, the entire façade of the Flatiron was stolen by Harry Windsor. His building looked different in only two major ways. The Windsor Building was a traditional square structure, and although it was advertised as having twenty-one stories, just like the Flatiron, it was actually one story taller. As Daniel Burnham had filled the triangle lot afforded him, Harry Windsor only filled half of the block he owned. When Windsor had told his contractor to copy the Flatiron in every detail except shape and height, the contractor at first had thought that Windsor was not serious. *Goddam right I'm serious*, Windsor had insisted. *I love that building on 23rd. You make me one like it. I want the corners rounded too. I worked with the god Burnham. I hauled stone for his vision. I was there to set the cornerstone and I was there when it opened in 02. I was there.*

That was not true, but Windsor repeated it enough so that it entered the minds of some who repeated it to others. Windsor said it to Bobby the first time they met, but Bobby was immediately suspicious. *Mr. Windsor, that would mean you are at least a hundred years old today, which you do not seem to be, or else you were an infant when you were hauling stone.*

Goddam it, young man, it's just a story, Windsor had railed back at him. *True or not, it's my story. You get your own.*

When it was finished in 1930, the Windsor Building had one other deviation from its Flatiron inspiration. Shape and height were in the public domain, but its core was Windsor's personal touch. The four sides surrounded a vast inner courtyard. The building itself was composed of outer offices and apartments, each with a view to the outside world of city streets, and inner apartments and offices, each with a view of the courtyard. Rent for those spaces was much higher. In the courtyard was a playground. Slides and monkey-bars, merry-go-rounds and teeter-totters, a park with rides and shade trees.

Separating the inner and outer halves of the Windsor Building on each floor was a continuous hallway. Harry Windsor had insisted to his contractor: *I want a complete unobstructed circuit. I want to be able to walk completely around the inside of my building without having to open a door. I want to be able to walk around those halls from point A back to point A and I want to be able to do it in my sleep if I have to. You figure out how to do it, put the support beams where you have to. But I want it done that way.* Asked why by the contractor, Windsor had been adamant. *Goddam it, it's my building, and that's the way I want it. You want answers, you go to St. Patrick's. You want to get paid, you do what I want.*

In their last conversation, on a bench in the Windsor courtyard, Harry told Bobby why he had liked him within a few minutes of their first meeting decades earlier. *You saw through me from the very beginning, Bobby. You knew I was full of shit and hot air, and you weren't afraid to call me on it, even back then, even though you were only a kid of twenty... twenty, right?... but you were always a gentleman about it. Sam was right about you. You were a gentleman. I couldn't bluff you. You mother and father raised you right. But you shoulda been my son too, instead of the ones I have, the ones who got all my hot air but none of my charm, right?*

In a letter to his father, Bobby described other charms of Harry Windsor, all leading to an odd conclusion. *He is like a grandfather to me. He spoils me and expects little more than my affection. He is certainly nothing like you, or how I have imagined your father, but he seems to have adopted me.*

In a conversation with his Accountant, Windsor instructed him to keep the *real* books away from the young man he had just hired to manage his bookstore. *But if the boy's as sharp as I think he is, there will come a time.*

Ellie Re-Writes Her Life

We just talked again and I mostly told you the truth. A year, twice a month, usually an hour, sometimes less. Twenty-four times, twenty-four hours, we have spent a full day of our lives together, and I finally made you laugh today. I was telling you a good story from my past but you stopped me.

—I already read that book.

And I said, you what? But then it hit me so hard that I must have blushed because I felt my face turn red. The other doctors never caught me, but you did. So I must have muttered something like oh fuck under my breath, and you laughed because you knew that I knew that I was busted. I had been telling you a story from one of the medical books I had read about people like me. I was using a real crazy person's story as mine. But you caught me. I said oh fuck, and you laughed, but not a mean laugh, it was a laugh with me, not at me.

—You have to remember. I am not trying to cure you. I am trying to understand you. Not those old case textbook studies you are hiding behind. You. Okay?

I hung up. I was ten years old again. I wanted to hide. I was so damn ashamed. So I sat here, assuming you would call me back, but you didn't. I waited but the phone did not ring. So I called you. It was the first time I had ever done that, call you. But I needed to hear your voice again.

—This is good, that you called back.

I was crying, something I almost never do anymore, and asked if I could call you back in a few minutes, but you told me to go ahead and cry, that you would stay on the line. That was an hour ago. Here I am now, my face looking like a melted kewpie doll. I used to be beautiful, Doctor PWR, I really did.

You asked if I had re-read all the earlier notes I had written. Re-read them? Hell, I had tried to re-write them. I would scratch out words, punctuate like I had learned, find subjects to go with verbs, un-fragmentize a lot, write in long hand and then type, as if I could remove (recover?) the very energy that went from my brain to my fingers on to the page. But here's the sad part. All the original notes? Perfect penmanship. I had beautiful handwriting. I remembered (how had I forgotten?) the time that Peyton brought a hundred envelopes to the bookstore along with an address list of all the people invited to one of his parents' parties and I had addressed all the envelopes. And he would take each one and slowly roll some sort of absorbent thing over them and then we would stuff the envelopes with the engraved cardboard invitations. I always looked forward to him seeing me the next week and describing the party to me, all the Charleston glory in formal gowns and stiff tuxedos, all the negro servants with white gloves and aprons, and I could imagine being a servant too. I hadn't seen the inside of his house back then yet, but he could describe every little detail. But he always told me how boring the parties were. There were no other people his age there. But he was lying to me, I think. I think that he secretly loved them. He loved his role as official greeter at the door, dressed up like his father, opening the front door and extending his hand, knowing each genteel couple by name. I would tease him, telling him that he was doing what the negro doorman was supposed to do. He would laugh and explain that the doorman was behind him, there to take coats and capes from the guests and hang them in a special room for such things. I was impressed. A room just for coats and capes. Peyton was the greeter, his father's son, his mother's son, the once and future Prince of Charleston. He made me laugh too, telling me how, as the party wore on, and he always over-drawled the words...wore on...he and his father would stand together away from the other guests, his father smoking a cigar, bourbon glass in one hand, and he would gossip about his guests, but always looking straight ahead and nodding or smiling as his guests looked toward him. According to Peyton, his father was a funny man. I had not met him yet, so how could I disagree?

Have you met Peyton's father? Surely, you must have.

You know the saddest thing about re-reading all those notes? Other than seeing how totally fucked up I was? I was reminded of all the other notes before then, all the notes I burned, as if that could really erase everything that had happened. I wish I had them back. Not the memories so much, all the warped fucking details of how P&P took me away. No, those, if I think too hard...or forget to think hard to not remember them...those come back like stump-legged pain. Residuals, does that make sense? Echoes of pain. Ghosts of pain. ED said it, elements of blank. Some...shit...like that. That shit never goes away.

No, I want to see those notes again for a different reason. I want to see my handwriting. I have this theory. My cursive was perfect from the very beginning. Just like me. I could see that handwriting and see the girl I was before P&P. Peyton thought my writing was perfect, but he never saw the earlier writing. Maybe the time that I knew him I was getting it back? Lord knows that when I wrote the notes I wrote after meeting him I was out of control, we all agree, but when I was literally with him every word I wrote was picture perfect. You do not have to understand this. I understand me. Before P&P, and while I was with Peyton, every single word I wrote, every dotted I or crossed T, was art. And now if there is anything like pornographic penmanship, every swirl and loop ugly and scratchy and vulgar, I'm the goddam poster child. Sometimes I cannot even read these notes to you after I write them, so I have to start typing again.

I think you are right, Doctor PWR. We finally need to meet face to face. I just wish I wasn't so ugly.

Sally Goes North

Sally had always known where she was going. She had told her girlfriends in Savannah, and they had always rolled their eyes and teased her. *You are going to be sooo sorry. You are much too nice to live there.*

Sally's parents had encouraged her, especially her father. *You are too smart to stay here. You need to go where you can really be a success.* Her mother had not disagreed, but she always offered a back-up plan. *You know, people actually do know how to read and write in Savannah. And you have kin there.*

No, Sally had her future planned, and New York City had ceased to be intimidating after the first few times she had visited. On a class trip in high school, her first time, she was appropriately awed. But then two trips with her parents, as they went to conferences there, a month-long trip by herself when she was nineteen to visit the only other girl she knew who had escaped Savannah. It was in that month that she felt like she actually lived in the city. She mastered the subways and busses, found the small shops and restaurants that would always be her favorites, discovered Soho and the Village, and even ventured through Harlem, albeit at noon, a feat that both appalled and thrilled her girlfriends back in Savannah. Then *the* trip, when she received the *New Star* prize from *Tinsel Magazine* for her witty reviews of bad movies. She had submitted a dozen reviews that had been published in an alternative newspaper in Savannah, with a readership of a few thousand. But, as her father proudly told her, "You're in print. That's what counts."

The *Tinsel* editors lauded her and eleven other young female writers as *Women to Watch*, and they were invited to New York to receive their awards. At their own expense, of course. With her parents' best wishes, a double-major in Journalism and English from Emory University, a folder with copies of everything she had ever had published in a newspaper or magazine, and money enough for three months rent on a three-hundred square foot studio apartment, Sally packed her bags and went North to stay. She was twenty. Jimmy Carter was headed to Washington, the Shah was still in Iran, and Sally had a half dozen job interviews lined up for the week following the *Tinsel* award ceremony. Flying into LaGuardia, she could look out the window and see the New York skyline as the 707 descended. She had seen it on earlier flights, but she still thought it was the most beautiful sight in the world, a world waiting for her.

Three months later, her original six and another six interviews later, Sally finally got her first New York City job, cashiering at the McKay Drug Store near her apartment. She had had two quick relationships, if *hello, how are you, would you like to come to my place and have sex* encounters qualified as relationships. She was twenty. It was the Seventies. She was broke but not about to tell her parents.

McKay paid the rent for a few months, and then Sally came

to an ironclad rule about her future. Any job that required a uniform was not for her. From McKay Drugs she went to a world of drugs at the Palladium on 14th. An old theatre, sex in the high rows, her introduction to unisex bathrooms, she loved the place. She was also offered a bar-tending job one night, only on the condition that she had to start immediately, that night, right then, that exact second, with the urgency of *we're in a goddam jam here, honey, and you look hot*. Personnel turnover seemed to be a problem. She already knew how to choose wine and make vodka tonics, but she learned a lot of the alcohol-catalog that first night by trial and error. She had arrived at the Palladium with a date. When she got off work at four in the morning, her date had already gone home with another woman. Sally had a hundred dollars in tips.

She would have worked at the club longer, but her parents' weekly question—*when will we see your first by-line?*—had to be answered eventually.

In the official biography she kept for herself, and to herself, Sally would credit the Palladium as an essential step in her dazzling career. She met Jimmy Tallman there, and Tallman said he was a fiction reader for *The New Yorker*, a first round reader for the hundreds of short stories that the magazine received each week. His own work, a *poignant roman clef bildungsroman mystery thriller*, he assured her, was soon to be published by Knopf. In the meantime—*hello, how are you, would you like to come to my place and have sex?* Sally was beginning to compile an unofficial and ever-evolving list: *Men I wish I had poisoned*. In the long run, Tallman eventually disappeared off that list, having been transferred over to the *Men who had potential, but never grew up* list.

Feeling both vulnerable and romantic about Tallman a month after she met him, Sally went to the *New Yorker* offices to surprise him and offer to buy his lunch. The receptionist was understanding and sympathetic. She had never heard of Jimmy Tallman, but that did not necessarily mean that he did not work there. A check of the directory, a call upstairs, and then *the look* that Sally understood. *I'm sorry*, the look said. Sally stood there, a box of chocolates in her hand, and wanted to get drunk. Other possibilities presented themselves as well: admitting defeat, going back to Savannah, a junior high teaching job, living with her parents again. A list of equally bleak possibilities. But then the sympathetic receptionist showed her a career door slightly ajar. *Are you perhaps looking for a job?* Sally blinked through tears and nodded. *Can you type?* Sally nodded faster. The receptionist was as old as Sally's mother. *We have an opening in the secretarial pool. It's not glamorous, but you'll make some contacts. Are you interested?* Sally was more than interested. *Does the Pope wear funny hats?* The receptionist did not laugh.

Sally took a substantial pay cut and typed for six months. Rejection letters mostly, short correspondence, computers and word processors were in the future. She met people, people whose names she had seen in print. She was invisible to them, but she still hovered in their world. From typist, she graduated to fact-checker, plus some copy-editing, and her world expanded. Fact-checking was essential work for the *New Yorker*, requiring persistence, discretion, and precision. Sally was perfect for the job. Even her friends knew that, and she actually liked the work. Within a year, she was a full-time fact checker and part-time fiction reader, the job that Tallman never had. Then, after Ronald Reagan had landslided Jimmy Carter back to Georgia, she came to an adult conclusion about her future at the *New Yorker.* She was never going to be a writer for them. There were too many other better writers whose work would always be ahead of her.

She went to work for an agent as a secretary/reader. "If Gabe Klein had been the only agent I ever worked for," Sally told anybody who would listen years later, "I would have thought they were all lying, thieving, womanizing assholes." Klein was a senior partner in an old agency, operating out of a brownstone in The Village. Sally was one of two women working directly under him. Her first hint of trouble was Klein insisting that she accompany him to a writer's conference in Mendicino. He was their well-advertised *New York Agent* who would be looking for new talent and sharing his insights about how to get published. On the Pacific coast, his basic insight was that any unpublished attractive female writer ought to sleep with him. The *not what you know but who you know* insight. As part of his fee from the Mendicino sponsors, he was housed in a model home overlooking a jagged inlet, the lighthouse a mile away providing a sweeping beam every few minutes. A spectacular view, and Sally was assigned one of the many bedrooms. Her role at the conference itself was to meet writers during the day and read the first thirty pages of their manuscript, because, as she had to admit, Klein *did* want new writers as well as new conquests. As he would boast, without seeing the irony, *I can smell talent a mile away.* In the evening, Sally was Klein's hostess, greeting a different fledgling female every night and then retiring discreetly to her bedroom at the other end of the house. Within a month of going to work for Klein, she had decided to learn as much as possible and then find another job. Sitting in her bedroom in Mendicino, watching that lighthouse beam sweep back and forth, she argued with herself. *Who's the whore here? Me, or her? Or Gabe?* And she would paraphrase the title of an odd new book just published. *Or are we all just a Confederacy of Whores?* She drank her wine, locked her bedroom door, and went to sleep.

For as long as her *Men I wish I had poisoned* list existed, Klein kept his top five standing, but she had to admit that he was a perceptive agent and that she learned a lot in the year she worked for him. He was vain and condescending, but he seemed to know everybody in publishing. And he loved to talk about how the key to being a successful agent was to know what every important editor was looking for, even before a manuscript crossed his own desk. *You got to drink with them, eat with them, party with them, and send their secretaries flowers. You've got to know people, Sally, you've got to know people.* In the months immediately after she left Klein for another agent in a larger agency, Sally actually got sentimental about him, realizing that she had been taking an adolescent view of an adult world.

Two agents past Klein, both of whom encouraged her to make a vertical move with their sincere best wishes, Sally went to work at Scribner's as an assistant editor. The first person to call her with a manuscript proposal was Gabe Klein. It was a good book, and she knew that Klein knew that she would like it. She fought for it in the editorial board meetings at Scribner's, making sure everyone saw what she saw in it, and it was her first done deal. She called Klein with an offer, which he rejected. She went back to the board for more money and then called Klein again. She could visualize him at his desk as he told her, "Damn, Sally, this book is worth more, and I've got other people interested, but for you I'll take the deal."

Her next day at work, there were flowers on her desk.

Ellie Tells a Story

The biggest surprise? Maybe the only surprise? You look just like your picture. Except that your hair is greyer and longer. I had expected somebody younger. The first time you called me, I went to the hospital to the old clinic and looked for your picture. I must have passed it a million times when I was there, that wall in the main office with all those pictures of the doctors posted side by side. I always thought it was like a post office wall of top ten most wanted criminals. Those glossy black and white mug shots of smart men with all sorts of credentials listed under them. You were there too, but I did not remember your face when you called. So I went back. I wanted to see your face when we talked on the phone. Did I ever tell you that I hate surprises? I like to surprise people, but I hate surprises.

But you are not your picture. Your hair says you are older. You say you are thirty-nine. You did not want to tell me, but I said I would leave if you did not tell me. Fair is fair, I said. But your face? Why is there not a line, not a wrinkle, no sign of wear and tear. No sign of smiling or frowning or anything. A mask? I must have looked like an old hag to you, but you looked like a boy to me. No big deal, but I was surprised. You are not a handsome man. But you are not ugly. You just are. And you are nice.

You had a plan, I could tell. You had said that you wanted me to write to you on my own, and then when we met I could sort of tell you in public what I had written in private. How did you say it?

—Upon further reflection.

That lasted about ten minutes. I told you I was bored with myself, with the old me, and anything I might have written after our phone conversations…that was already the old me.

—Fair is fair—we can talk about anything you like.

I told you that I wanted to talk about a new diagnosis, new drugs, no drugs.

—Horse before the proverbial cart? Talk first, then a new diagnosis, and then new everything else?

I said okay. I had all the time in the goddam world. I wasn't going anywhere. Yet? I almost said I wasn't going anywhere "yet," but I knew you were smarter than the other doctors. You would have wanted me to explain the yet.

I think you were mine when I did tell you one truth. I didn't realize it until I actually saw you face to face. All those early notes, the ones I wrote up until Peyton's father stole (cleaved?) him away from me, I was writing to you. About Peyton, but to you. Before you knew I existed, or me you, you were my audience. This between us now was not your idea. It was mine from the very beginning. I created you. And now you can play with me.

You? Diagnose me? Perhaps you can. More power to you. But tell me this. Why are you wearing a wedding ring? But there are no pictures of a woman anywhere in your office. Pictures of you and what I assume are your children, sure. Pictures of old versions of yourself, your parents. I know how that works. A big picture of you and some of the other doctors and their wives at some sort of party, but you are alone. But no wife anywhere in your little office world. I'll ask you later and you'll tell me. Plenty of time, remember? Evidently, neither one of us is going anywhere. Yet.

But I know I have to share with you. Quid pro fucking quo, Doctor PWR? I showed you mine first. You probably thought I would hesitate, right? Too painful to describe, right? You might have to settle for bits and pieces only, right? But it only took half an hour. The history of P&P from first touch until Paul cut (desecrated?) Peyton. My rule: one time only, the complete truth, and we would not go back there again. The P&P years, anything after that (even from my time in that hospital) would be a separate story.

I was ten, asleep, and I woke up, but it might have been a dream. Peter was touching me between my legs. I did not open my eyes. And then he was gone. It was only a dream. But he was back the next night. I dreamed again. One night he was under the covers with me and kept whispering to me as he pulled my pajamas off. He touched me and he took my hand and made me touch him. How very strange that was, as if that part of him was alive on its own.

Okay, you were right. I cannot do this again. I gave you all the details once. I cannot write them. I said them out loud and we could hear the words, but we did not have to see them, and they went away as soon as I said them. You were recording us, I knew that, knew that the words existed on some sort of tape, but I was never going to listen to them again. How many other words of other wackos are you holding captive on those tapes? How much of a sewer is your office? Am I just another case to you? More human waste? If I am, I will hate you. You know that, right? I will hate you.

The worst times were with Paul. He hurt me. He put himself in every goddam hole in my body. He hit me. He called me his dick sock. Every part of me fit him so well. Too much, Doctor? It's all there, still in your office, on tape to be played anytime you want a thrill, right? No, I am sorry. I am truly sorry. You are different. I know that. I wasn't sure until I met you. But you are not them, the others. You wear a wedding ring, but you are not married.

The absolute worst times were when Paul shared me. The first time he took me to the harbor and gave me to a man who took me to his boat. I was eleven. Paul made me wear lipstick. The other man reeked of...you ready?...reeked of Old Fucking Spice cologne. I knew that smell. I thought I could blot it all out of my memory, but those goddam commercials send me up the wall again. I have to get up and turn off the tv, but it is always too late. After that, Paul made his brother watch, he made him do me at the same time. But nothing was as bad as when he had his friends, his salt of the fucking earth friends, pay for me. Me on my knees, my mouth bought and paid for. One after the other. And poor Alice. One of Paul's friends brought her with him and we were partners. She was older than me. But she was on her knees beside me and we would take turns. Poor Alice. She always laughed. The man who brought her was her older sister's husband. Poor Alice. She acted as if it was fun, a game, but I knew better. She wanted them all to die. It took me a long time to figure out how to do that, kill them, but she did not know how it worked. I told the police about her, and they said they found her, but she said I was lying.

Rape tape? Tape rape? Those are two different things, if you really think about it. All the news that's fit to tape? Odd thing now? I do feel better telling you all those things. I never trusted the others. They were safe from me, too many other cases like me I assume, but you know different. You know I am different. You said you only wanted to understand me, not cure me. I know the reason you said that. There is nothing to cure.

Sex and the City

Sally had no illusions about what she saw in the mirror. An attractive woman, but not beautiful. Attractive in face and form, and when she was a teenager that form was especially attractive. Without her clothes, she was even beautiful, as more than one man had told her. The first man she went to bed with had her convinced that she was more than beautiful, she was perfect. That was the best part of the memory, the way he would make her walk around the room nude, bring him a glass of water, any excuse to see her body in motion, and just look at her. The sex itself was clumsy and painful at first, not much better later, but she never forgot the glazed look in his eyes before and even after the mechanics were done. *I wish I had a picture of you right now. Fact is, you ought to go into modeling, or at least have some professional take some pictures of you naked, keep them to yourself, for when you get old and wonder where it all went.* She had been offended when he said that. She was eighteen, he was twenty-four. She thought he was cynical, that he was implicitly suggesting that he take the pictures, and she never trusted him again. Twenty years of living in New York had softened her opinion of him and that first time, improving the memory of the sex itself. *And where is he now,* she wondered. *And what happened to the body he was in love with?*

Her twenties were the worst ten years of her life. Attractive *and* smart were not enough. She kept her hair long, knowing it was a compelling lure. She studied the make-up of other women. She seriously considered the opinion of the secretary who worked for Gabe Klein, "You ought to consider getting one of those makeovers, you know, to bring out your best features. Put some tint in that hair, some bounce, some more color around your pretty eyes, and then watch the dicks start wagging."

Sally knew it was silly, superficial, the *pretty woman army*, but she enlisted anyway. And she drank too much. Not a good decade.

How can a smart woman be so damn dumb? That was her retrospective question. *You'd think my parents were like some Wicked Step-Mother, instead of who they were, doting and proud of me. I was coddled and praised every day, even when they were yelling at each other. How did I turn out so spineless and insecure?*

Twenty years, how many men? She did not keep count, but, depending on her mood, or her audience, it was either *too many* or *not enough.* How many men that mattered? *That* was a consistent short list. And then, as she turned forty, Sally finally figured it out, the big picture, the sum of all mysteries, and she accepted her place in the universe. *I'm in love with a man who thinks I'm his best friend. Why did I ever think it was possible, his loving me, and why am I happy? How is that possible?* It was the happiness that took her the longest to understand.

She knew Bobby before she met him. Trade talk, party

gossip, a picture, acknowledgments by authors...*How to thank Bobby Beaumont at Windsor? I thought I had written a good book. He made it better, and all the glowing stories about him are true...* his voice the first time she called from Klein's office, that South Carolina voice that noticeably slowed down as soon as he heard her own Georgia voice. And then the surprise of seeing him in person for the first time, literally hidden by the taller people around him at a launch party. She had been looking at the back of Bruce Tucker, not knowing who he was but noticing how broad his shoulders were, and then Bruce had stepped away and there was Bobby, cigarette in one hand, wine glass in the other, black turtleneck sweater, wavy dark hair in need of a trim, with his shoes off. Remembering the moment later, she hoped that the look on her face had not revealed her first thought: *My god, you're so tiny. And how come none of the pictures ever do justice to those lips?* Tucker's place was taken by another man, and Bobby disappeared again.

Sally had wanted to work at Windsor long before she actually saw Bobby Beaumont. Most younger editors at other houses wanted the same thing. For them, it usually meant an immediate step up in status and then another step up in pay when they left for another house. Bobby's former assistants were sprinkled all over Broadway or the Avenue of the Americas or 55[th.] Agents wanted their first-time novelists to be published by Windsor, to be pampered by the treatment, to be adopted by Bobby or one of the other editors under Bobby. Most of all, they wanted the advance that Windsor was willing to pay.

Sally wanted to go to work at Windsor and stay. If Bobby and Windsor were synonymous, so be it. She understood, after too many years drifting, that she had a talent for reading, critical and commercial insight better than most. From her first job at *The New Yorker*, through Gabe Klein and the other agents, up to her early editor positions, she had been preparing for a career at Windsor, even before it was created.

Where's the line, she asked herself. *Would he be as attractive if he were somewhere else?* Where had the line blurred? *And that look of his, that mouth?* Sally knew all the rumors, the young women writers he had "discovered," the female agents by whom he had been wined and dined. The irony of all the gossip was that none of his escorts were the source. None of them ever spoke unkindly of him, except for his unwillingness to commit. His social life was an excess of beauty and talent. His private life remained private. Within months of hiring Sally, however, the romantic rumors went from current events to become history. For the first few years there might have been a notable public appearance by Bobby and a new woman, but more and more he went out less and less. Sally wished the new rumor were true: *Bobby Beaumont was settling down. Sally Graham was in the picture.*

Sally was flattered, but not deceived. Working at Windsor was enough by itself to garner attention and at least pseudo-affection by scores of agents. Working as Bobby's assistant elevated her status even more. But, to be Bobby's *special friend* was Sally's singular achievement. At first, she resented the idea that her own identity was merely a reflection of her relationship to Bobby. That, without her proximity to him, she would just be another bright woman in publishing. He had even asked her about it, whether she thought it would be better for her career to *not* be at Windsor. She had wondered if he were merely being polite, offering her a graceful way to make a decision that he himself wanted to make, to hire somebody new.

She had asked him a direct question, "Do *you* want me stay?"

He did not hesitate, except in the low tone of his voice and his eyes not meeting hers, "Very much so."

Sally was deeply moved. *Oh, Bobby, you're almost blushing,* she thought. Then, wanting to lighten the moment, "In sickness and in health, til death do us part?"

He smiled at her, "I do."

They had gone to bed with each other a few years later. The only time, and Sally had been drunk. That night was a fact, but many of the details were lost. Somewhere in her mind was a recurring image, however, that might have never happened, but around it she built an imaginary experience. She recalled sitting next to Bobby as he slept. She had gotten up and walked around his apartment after they had sex.

Wasn't that what I did, walk around that gorgeous place, without a stitch on? And there was a piano playing somewhere? But that might have been merely an echo of the hour earlier when I had played the piano for him. He had asked me to take off my clothes, and he had stood behind me, his hands on my bare shoulders, as I struggled to find the right keys, slow notes about summertime, a song he requested, and he leaned down to kiss the back of my neck. It was so warm in his apartment, and freezing outside. I went to the bathroom in the dark, and then I walked to the window and pushed aside the blue curtains that had been filtering the bright lights of the City. Then I went back to sit beside him, listening to him sleep, waiting for him to wake up and see me in the blue dark. Oh god, why can't I remember more?

Ellie Gets a Gift

You know, I think you like me more than your other patients. Like a parent with lots of children, and you say you love them all the same, but everybody knows that, down deep, parents have a favorite. The reason why does not matter. Am I prettier than the others? Hardly. Smarter? Who knows. More fucked up? I even doubt that. I yam what I yam. You know my dog I told you about? Remember her? Her only litter, four perfect pups, but the fifth was the runt. The others pushed her out of the way, but I loved her the most. I would bottle feed her myself, and I had a shoe box she slept in, right there on the bed next to me. I could lay in bed in the dark and listen to her breathe. Is that me to you? Am I your runt? I should not have named her. But I did, and she died. No such grief (luck?) for you, PWR, I will out-live you.

You told me that you wanted to understand one thing about me. If P&P had never happened to me, would I be me as I am now. Did they create me, or was I there all along? You think that if you know the cause of something, you can treat it, right? Or was it something about treating the consequence rather than the cause? You figure it out. You're the doctor.

All I know is that I am tired of being a fat cow who is tired all the time. Tired of being tired. I clean houses for the rich people in Peyton's old world. I am perfect for them...industrious, meticulous, dependable, and invisible. They go away and I do three hours worth of work in six hours, and I never tell them. They pay for three. But for those hours I can scrub and polish and wipe and then sit. I can read, or I can write in their grand homes, and then I clean some more. Heaven...right?

Do you have some sort of timeline for us? For me? How long until you fix me? My word, but your idea. Fix me. Different than cure? You told me about a soldier you were treating one time. He went to war sane but came back damaged. A perfect word for me, I knew you were thinking that. I was damaged goods. Caveat Emptor, right? Buyer beware. A handwritten sign pasted to my head...*Sold as is, no returns.* Peyton did it. He took it all. How about you?

You almost went too far today, finally asking the question that you thought would cause me to...reflect?...on myself.

—If Peyton loves you so much...

You would not look me in the eye when you asked.

—why has he not come back? Eight years is a long time, right?

You did not like my answer, I could tell by the look on your face. Oh, I suppose he might be a bit slow because I almost got him murdered, you think? Not thoughtful enough, doctor? How about, have you ever met his father? (Of course you have, surely?) Too glib? I don't care. You're so smart, you figure it out. But here's a written truth, not a spoken taped truth. Peyton is not ready, and he knows I am not ready. When those planets align, he will call me. And that's the only reason I am still talking to you and writing these notes. You are going to get me ready or else I will do it myself. Might take longer, but it will happen.

How very unprofessional of you, Doctor PWR. Should I report you? You were ever so casual at the end of our last meeting. You even leaned back in your chair and stretched your arms out as if every coil in your shoulders was unfossilizing. Would I perhaps be interested in meeting somewhere else next time? A change of environment. Perhaps coffee or lunch at a very public place of my choosing...my choice. Of course, if I was more comfortable here in the office, you would certainly understand. As if my choice, office or out, made no difference to you. But I knew the real reason. I am your favorite.

But you were right. Your office was a dead-end. Had I said something to you after about the tenth time I was there, a million years ago, about how nothing changes in your office. We sit in the same places. Everything else in always exactly where it was before...the pictures, the plaques on the wall, the books on the shelves (I think I could tell you know all the titles on the top shelf, in order. More time, I would have them all memorized.) Except for our lips and the spools of the tape recorder, nothing ever moved in your office. It was a fucking tomb. Collapsed lungs. You called today and reminded me about your suggestion. How very subtle.

—You pick the place—your choice.

I knew exactly where I wanted to go, and you never caught on, did you?

We went to where Peyton and I went to lunch the day after we first had sex. How many times had he taken me there? Back when I was beautiful. I tried to be beautiful for you too, Doctor PWR, but we both know that is a lost cause.

Did you really expect everything else to be the same, that we would be doctor and patient like we were in your office. Or is that the reason you really suggested it, so we would not be patient and doctor again. Cross that bridge, doc, you can't go back. How come I can see that and you can't?

Was it what you expected? Me, I had the best time I have had in years. I remembered some of the old negro waiters who were there when Peyton and I went, but nobody remembered (recognized?) me. I ordered what I ordered back then, my favorites of shrimp cheese grits and key lime pie for dessert. You were impressed that I seemed to enjoy eating so much. And I thanked Jesus God that you didn't order what Peyton would have ordered, the salmon and rice. You were boringly wonderful. A tuna salad sandwich, how utterly you I thought. And I saw you differently for the first time in years. How did I never notice how thin you are? Older and distinguished and still unlined and bony to boot. And how did I absolutely know that you and I were on our first date? You did not bring that damn tape recorder. But you did bring me a present.

I am sorry. I am being so unfair to you. You will never know why I chose that place. You probably think that it will be "our" place in the future, if we ever go back (and I think we will). You'll never know how cruel I was to you today. You thought I was there with you, but I was there with Peyton.

A long time ago you asked me how I knew that Peyton was in love with me. I just shook my head. I did not understand how I knew until I sat across from you today. You disappeared and I was back to that first time with Peyton. I was so out of place back then, in that world of white linens and sparkling water glasses, with a white man to seat us and a negro man to take our order and another negro man to bring us bread and a negro woman to refill our glasses. I was so scared and felt so small, like I was a peeping tom caught outside the window, and I had been looking inside at a world where I did not belong, and then I looked back at Peyton. He had been staring at me all that time, just like he had done for a long time everywhere we went. We would be at WPG or somewhere else and I would turn to see him staring at me, but it was that place today, that time ago, when I understood what he was looking at back then. I wonder if you ever saw the same thing in someone else's face, ever in your past. Did your wife look at you like that? Did you look at her? You'll tell me about her eventually, I am sure of that. But I still won't tell you why I chose that place for today. How do I know that Peyton loved me, loves me now? I looked around that room today, as Charleston dined and scurried itself into a blurry background, and I saw ghosts (apparitions?). Ghosts never die, do they, Doctor PWR. There's a poem somewhere I read and never understood. Until today. A boat crossing water between two worlds, the same boat that had crossed the same water for a hundred years. Only the passengers changed. The buildings and sky line, the pennants and flags, even the smell of the water, had all been there forever, to be re-seen and experienced by new people who were occupying the same material world that the dead used to inhabit. (I am working very hard here, PWR, to explain us to you. I owe you that, even if you never know.) Time means nothing. Space means nothing. (I will find that poem again and show you. You deserve to understand me, right?)

There on that boat the living were occupying the same space as the dead. Oh, fuck, I am losing it now, the thought that explains everything about today. All I know is that I was on that boat again, the boat that Peyton and I had ridden before, and we were still there. You were another passenger, but I was with Peyton.

And the saddest saddest part, PWR, about me and you. I think you love me. I am not even surprised by that. You were almost unable to speak as you handed me that little box, that red wrapped box with a bow on it.

You even mumbled something.

—-do not misinterpret this—I just saw it and thought you would like it.

Sure, cover your tracks. So, why the wrapping, why the ritual, sweet doctor. No, I did not misinterpret. You knew I would like it. Of course. You do know me well in some ways that nobody else does, probably even Peyton. Were you staring at me as I unwrapped it? You are so incredibly dear. That was my genuine true feeling at that moment. You are an incredibly dear man.

You gave me a tiny crystal piano. I held it in my hand, but I did not look up. You read all those early notes of mine. Did you not remember them as you bought that for me? Or were you only thinking about how often I had told you that I wanted to start playing again. How I missed the piano. Did you misinterpret? How incredibly dear you are, PWR. You thought it meant something between us, something we had shared. How we both loved the piano. Did you wonder why I stared at it so long? Did you think it was a mistake, or the perfect gift from you? For as long as I did not look up, did you consider the possibilities?

You are an incredibly dear man. But what did you see in my face as I looked up? You know what I saw in Peyton's face, his

146

eyes, whenever I looked at him? I looked up at you today, but I did not see what I saw whenever I looked at Peyton. I did not see myself.

A New Home

A few weeks after Bobby hired Sally, he gave her a tour of the Windsor Building, the same tour that Harry had given him years earlier, a tour that only a few others had received. Whereas Harry had started at the bottom and worked up, Bobby had led Sally from his office on the top floor down to ground level. She even got a tour of the floor that did not exist.

Bobby inherited the thirteenth floor from Windsor. *Inherited* was Windsor's word, conveying *de facto* ownership then and implying *de jure ownership* to come. When someone stepped into the ground floor elevator there was a button for the thirteenth floor. *Superstition be damned*, Windsor had always said, himself the most superstitious of men. The offices and apartments on that floor all began with the number 13. But it was actually the fourteenth floor. The real thirteenth floor was unmarked and accessible only by a private elevator that went to that floor and nowhere else. If you were on a floor above the real thirteenth, you had to go back down to the lobby to use the private elevator hidden behind a door in the lobby, and it required a key to open. Over time, of course, Windsor's secret could not be kept, and over time many people were in and out, but the necessary key was held closely by Windsor and his Accountant. Not even the Windsor sons were allowed there unless accompanied by their father. Those who did gain entrance were usually mystified as to why Harry Windsor was so secretive. From a hallway perspective, it was just like the other floors. Windsor himself had a mundane office and some storage rooms, but most of the other offices and rooms were empty. *Wasted space,* his sons told him, rent money forsaken. They never knew about their father's private synagogue behind one of the doors, nor his private apartment behind another. Nor did anyone, except Bobby, know about the labyrinth of internal hallways between rooms, the false walls, the hidden spaces. Harry Windsor had made sure that the official blueprints of the building were like his official tax returns to the government. True and false at the same time. *A man's entitled to some privacy,* he would tell Bobby, *and a fluid cash flow.* An office for him, an office for his Accountant, the only acknowledged uses on the invisible floor. His ground floor jewelry store had his public office, and he did most of his work there.

Truth is, he would repeat and magnify for Bobby, *I just wanted something for myself, some privacy, know what I mean? Nothing fancy. I'll fill it up one of these days. I made the ceilings a little higher, the walls a little thicker, but the important thing is that this is my space, and the lights never go out. These hall lights burn all the time, just like me. I go through this hallway, around the building, once a day for sure, forty wall lamps. And I carry a couple of spare bulbs with me. Small thing, I know, but I like to see them all lit all the time, and I can afford the bills, Con-Ed be damned.*

Bobby would remind his father, *It was all part of Harry's*

charm. Bobby was given his own key to the private thirteenth floor elevator, and he was allowed to live there as part of his eventual promotion up from the bookstore. Windsor more than allowed, he insisted that Bobby live in the Windsor Building. *You take any space you want there and make it your own. Send my Accountant the bills. I trust you to do it with class.*

Bobby told Sally this part of the story and she reminded him, "That's the first place I saw you, at one of your parties. I had wanted to see Bobby Beaumont's famous apartment ever since I got my first job. I went and you never noticed me. Of course, there were a hundred other people there, including John Updike and Joan Didion and Ed Koch, you know, the usual suspects, so I forgive you."

"I remember you," he protested. They were in the private elevator heading back to the ground floor.

"Yeh, right," Sally said, less and less self-conscious around her new boss.

"You wore a black sleeveless dress, very sharp, and, I think, you had a pearl bracelet? We talked for a moment."

Sally raced through her memory and then said, "I was wearing a black dress, but so were half the women there. You get no points for that, Bobby. And I sure as hell would remember talking to you."

"The bracelet?" he said, stepping back to let her out of the elevator ahead of him.

Sally stepped around him. She did not remember the pearl bracelet, but she did own one. She began to have a sinking feeling.

"I was drunk, wasn't I?"

"Quite, but a very mid-list sort of stupor," he said, steering her to the ground floor directory.

The ground floor tenants had changed over time. Gone was the bookstore where Bobby first worked, replaced by a clothing store. Gone was the small movie theatre, replaced by a restaurant. Gone was the Harry Windsor jewelry store, replaced by a music and video retailer. Standing in the ground floor lobby, Sally blinked at Bobby, and he knew what she was thinking, her confusion about the name of the jewelry store. It was his favorite Harry Windsor story, the feud with Harry Winston.

"I remember almost all the details of the time he told me all about it," he said. "It was the day he offered me my future life."

Harry Winston was the most famous jeweler in the country, his diamonds on display at every Oscar red carpet walk, his Hope Diamond donated to the Smithsonian, his services employed by Richard Burton and other Hollywood stars, so famous he was mentioned in movies without having to be explained, but Bobby's Harry Windsor was a New York jeweler before Winston, by two years. A jeweler of small aspirations, to be sure, but a precious gem retailer of significant legal income, or so his Accountant and ledgers asserted. As Harry Winston prospered in the headlines, however, Harry Windsor took notice. As he would eventually confess to Bobby, *I got too smart for my own good, and too greedy*. The Windsor letterhead and advertising crept closer and closer to looking like the uptown Winston designs. The final expropriation was Windsor's short-lived radio ad campaign: *Diamonds by Harry Windsor. Others may imitate, but none duplicate*. Two Winston attorneys paid a visit to Harry Windsor and suggested that he cease and desist from confusing the public.

Windsor had always loved telling this part of the story. "So I look at Abbott and Costello, there in their three hundred dollar suits, and I tell them to get out of my store, that I was selling rocks before their boss split his first carat. I told them that I would change the goddam spelling of my last name if I wanted to, *dsor* to *ston*, and claim I was a twin separated at birth, and they could kiss my ass and call it roses. I told them all that."

Bobby heard that story many times the first few years he worked for Windsor, but it was December 29th, 1978, when he heard the true story, the day after Harry Winston died.

Windsor had come into the bookstore trembling, an unlit cigar in his right hand, a copy of the *New York Times* in his left. When they had first met a few years earlier, Bobby had gently kidded Harry about his height. *You are the first man I have met here who is shorter than me.* Windsor had accepted the quip with good humor and turned it back on Bobby, *Short and sweet, both of us, right?* But on that Saturday morning, Windsor appeared to have shrunk to a child's stature. Bobby made him sit in the bookstore office and asked a clerk to get them some coffee. Harry protested, "Fuck coffee, get me some whiskey." Bobby sat and waved the clerk away, and then he listened to a rare Harry Windsor moment of truth.

"I loved that man, Bobby, I loved him like a brother. He had class, real class. Me, I was a knock-off guy from the very beginning. People loved Harry Winston because he was the real thing. Not a damn person in this town who loves me, Bobby, probably nobody that has any respect for me either. I know that. I know how it works. Some got it. Most don't. You…you got it, Bobby. And don't you fucking tell me you don't know what I'm talking about. That story I told you about his lawyers coming to lean on me, remember that? All true, I said all that to them. But I was a limp dick the next day when the man himself came to see me."

Bobby had leaned back, resisting an urge to reach over and hold the older man's hand as he talked, wanting to comfort him.

"Harry Winston himself, the real deal. He comes into my jewelry store, introduces himself, and asks if I have a few moments to talk. Moments...that was the word he used. Not minutes...moments. See, I'm ready for a piss fight, and then he asks if he can sit down. A moment of my time, a chair, all he says he wants, and I'm about to piss chicken soup in my pants. You know what he does then, after some small talk about how the weather is fine for that time of year and the city is so beautiful? You will not guess. He pulls the biggest goddam diamond out of his pocket that I have ever seen. A half-ton of stone, I swear. Got to be fifty carats, and he's handing it over to me for my opinion. Just like that. I had heard all sorts of stories about the man, how he carried diamonds with him sometimes, just to feel them in his hands, like they were magic lamps or something, rub 'em the right way and wishes come true sort of stories. And then he asks me the most profound question I've ever had somebody ask me. He says...*Harry, if this was yours, would you sell it?* Now you tell me, Bobby, what the fuck sort of question is that? I'm thinking then, is this a trick? Of course I'd sell it, in a New York minute. But as soon as I say that, I think it's the wrong answer. Harry Winston has got to be looking at THE mother of all New York Jews across from him. So I figure he's going to get uppity on me, but then the man says to me...*I would too.* And then he just looks at me, like he's waiting for me to see it. The big picture. The difference. Me, I'm as fucking clueless as a man in Gaza can be. So we sit there until he sighs. *But it would break my heart, Harry, to lose something this perfect. I would sell it. That is what I do. But not to the first offer, to just anyone. Not all my jewels are like this, of course, but when I find one this precious I hate to let it go. Sooner or later, I will sell it, but not yet.* Bobby, I sit there like a log. And then he tells me in his quiet voice...*You are not me, Mr. Windsor. You should not mislead the public. Your inventory and your clientele are different than mine. My customers would not be confused, but I fear that your customers would assume a value to their purchase that is not real. You are unfair to them. I ask you to stop what you are doing.* And there it was. Bobby, the request from the man himself, and I could have been myself and told him to go to hell, but it was also an offer. I could be his enemy or his friend, because I felt it, I felt him offering something, and I answered without too much thought. I said, *Yes, I'll do that.* He was the real deal, Bobby, and I was the phony, and he reached over and extended his hand for me to shake. And I was right about the offer. I stopped using him to sell my stuff, and he was my friend. Sure, we never went to the same parties. He never invited me to his place in the country. But he would come by to see me once in awhile, and we'd sit in my courtyard and have some tea, and I'd bitch about my sons not being interested in my businesses, just their shares, and he'd nod and tell me about his own sons. He was a great man, Bobby, the real deal, and he died yesterday."

Harry Windsor's Wish

"You want me to do what?" Bobby was suspicious.

"I want you to run a legitimate business for me," Harry Windsor said again.

The two men had moved from the bookstore office to the courtyard inside the Windsor Building. Harry Winston had been dead a day. In the center of that courtyard, two small children were sitting in a sand box, their Asian nanny hovering nearby, a tableau oblivious to the men sharing a bench and leaning toward each other.

"Harry, I can understand the *run a business* part of your proposal. It is the adjective that has me worried."

Windsor let out a deep breath. His face had a resigned *what you gonna do* look, but he flicked off an imaginary bit of lapel lint and continued, "Some things are better kept private, not that I have any secrets, of course."

"Of course," Bobby said, rolling his eyes. "As if I never wondered how you could keep the store open all these years when we were not selling enough books to pay the bills *and* my salary."

"Ah, Bobby, that store is a gold mine, a Red Sea of revenue. Just ask my Accountant, a man who makes my New York Jew credentials look almost papist."

"Harry, humor does not become you at this moment. I have worked for you for a long time, and I have never asked too many questions. You owe me nothing, but I am too old to keep doing this for the rest of my life. Yes, I want something else, but I also want you to trust me."

The older man shrugged. "I trust you, Bobby, more than I trust my own sons. Trust is not the issue. But you have to trust me too. Trust me to do the right thing. All I know for sure is that I want to own a business I can be proud of, something that gives me a good name like Harry Winston had a good name. Some respect, some admiration, something…*legitimate*. I know that's the word that you noticed. Some business with *class*, like diamonds, but I know that if my hands touch it then it will turn to shit, green dollar sign shit, but shit all the same. That's why I need you. You run the business. You create the business. I bankroll you for as much as you need to begin with. I step back. All I want is my name on it, and I want you to eventually make a profit, a legitimate profit. Not a fortune, not a thirty percent return on my investment, but more black than red on the books in time, a success. Can you do that for me?"

Over time, Bobby would look at Harry Windsor and see a man whose own life was a disappointment to himself, a man without a family and with only a few friends. He had met Windsor's sons, and their wives, but they were not *family*. Windsor wanted what Bobby's father had, a son who loved him, a son who respected him, a son happy to see his father anytime he could.

Forrest Beaumont had come to New York twice since Bobby had moved there, and each time he and Bobby were dinner guests of Windsor at the *Windows on the World* restaurant atop the Twin Towers. The three men were leisurely in the meal and their conversation. But each time, after the first half hour, Bobby noticed that Windsor grew quieter but also became more attentive. In the weeks after his father died, Bobby's grief was so profound that Windsor feared for the younger man's health. Windsor's unique contribution to Bobby's recovery was simply how he recollected those lunches at the top of the world. "Your old man was the luckiest guy in the world, Bobby. And a class act. I loved just sitting there listening to you and him talk to each other, like adults, like a father and son. I could see it, how much he respected you, and you him. He could kid you about not having a woman in your life, about him and your mother wanting grandchildren and you not cooperating, but it wasn't disappointment, just fun. And how he loved your mother...that was plain. I wish I had met her, but when the two of you started talking about her, well, I got to know her. And, hell, when you and your old man talked I thought it was the smoothest accent in the world. Music to listen to, and such proper English without sounding uppity. And I see you do that on your own too, how you talk with other people, but with him it was different. The man loved you...loved you...like a father... and I loved being there with you."

"And what kind of business do you want, Harry? The Windsor what?"

Harry smiled like a man given the perfect straight line. "I want the same thing you do, Bobby, the thing you told me about."

Bobby leaned away from Windsor, taking a circuitous route to an agreement. He looked at the children in the sandbox, studying their faces, brother and sister, possibly twins but not necessarily, blondish hair and pale skin. "Did you love your wife, Harry? Did she love you? Can you trust me with that truth."

Windsor flinched, but he had had enough conversations with Bobby over the years to sense that the younger man always had an eventual destination no matter what the beginning. "Why do you ask?"

"A friend of mine once told me that a child can look like its parents, as most do, but some children can actually look like their parents' love for each other, as if their appearance was produced by emotion rather than blood, and those are the most beautiful children in the world."

"Your friend needs therapy," Windsor snorted.

"And you did not answer my question."

"And you didn't answer mine…why do you ask?"

"I was just looking at those two children over there, and it reminded me of what she said, and I wondered about you and your wife. I will never meet her, rest her soul, but I have met your sons. You do not have many pictures of your wife in your office or your apartment, so it is hard for me to tell how much of her is in your sons. I can see you, and I can see signs of her, especially in their eyebrows and cheekbones, but I wonder what you see when you look at them. Do you see yourself, or her, or something like my friend described, how you felt about her. I am just wondering if my friend is right."

"Bobby, this is…"

"Yes, this has nothing to do with your offer, except I was

thinking about my future this week anyway. Those big picture questions. My father, I think, would agree with my friend about how children reflect their parents' love. And certainly my mother would agree. So, yes, I accept your offer. And, yes, I know what I want to do. How does *Windsor Books* sound to you? Or should it be *Windsor House?*"

"*Windsor House*. I like that. Sounds solid. The House of Windsor. *Windsor House*. But don't forget, you've got to make a real profit. Quality stuff, but a profit. Is that do-able?"

Bobby extended his hand to Harry Windsor, "Absolutely, with your money and my charm, absolutely."

Windsor was a happy man, "America…what a great fucking country, eh?" He was also happy that he did not have to answer Bobby's question about his dead wife.

Ellie Sees the Devil

Am I getting better? You said I seemed happier. Did you notice
that I was also thinner? I mean, I'm still a cow, but a thinner
cow. You told me to cut down on the medication. We'll go slow,
you said. A little at a time and watch for any changes. You know
what I think? I think you were looking at the pictures of me
from when I was first sent to the hospital. A decade ago? Sure,
I was a dazzler then. I was also sixteen. All girls are prettier
when they are sixteen. But you know how much I wanted to
look like that again. So, thank you. For letting me be beautiful
again, thank you. Not yet, but soon, and then what will you do?
You are too old for me, PWR, even if you are a good man. You
are too old.

    I am sorry I did not react like you thought I would (should?)
today when you gave me the news about Paul. You used a
wonderful and magic word, as if the word itself was self-fulfilling.
Is it a doctor word? Is it for all your patients? ...Closure... Paul
was dead. Perhaps closure was now possible? Close that door
and never look back? It's a stupid word. I told you it was stupid
and for a second I thought you were offended, as if I had just

told you that your entire profession was stupid. I'm sorry. But I'm not closed yet.

All you had were the basic details. Paul was murdered in prison, stabbed by other inmates, and none of them were known. Not enough, doctor. I wanted to know enough details to actually see him die. I wanted you to contact the prison and get more details, but you thought that was a bad idea. You want stupid closure for your patient? You get her the goddam details. But if you won't, I'll tell you how it happened. I'll tell you how it should have happened. Every day he was in prison Paul was raped by some bigger stronger meaner inmate. He was their butt-boy every day. Negro inmates fucked him every day. And they would ask him how he liked their nigger dicks up his asshole. You like that nigger dick—they would whisper in his ear every time they fucked him. And he would swallow their nigger cum. And that last time, the day they shoved a knife into his heart, a gang of black men holding him down as the biggest and blackest of them pulled the knife out so that in the last few seconds of his life he could see his own blood on that blade and know he was dying, right then the black man would tell him that I was watching him die, that he would be giving me the knife for myself to keep forever. Those are the details I need for closure, Doctor PWR, you good and decent man. Can you get me those details?

Thank you. How many times do I say that? I am always thanking you for something. You cut down on my medications a little. I didn't go all Lizzie Borden on you, so we went down some more. I owe you a lot. I am prettier. I am almost back to my old thin beautiful. And, praise the Lord, I don't have to pee as much. And even though I still feel like you are analyzing me when we go out together, I like you. You even laugh when I tell you that I will kill you if you ever write about me. I know that was your plan when we started. Know what I think now? I think you do not want to share me with anyone else.

And the new job for me? Thank you, thank you. Although I seldom say his name out loud to you anymore, I wonder if you made the connection. I used to clean houses in Peyton's world, but now I get paid more to take care of the children in Peyton's world. Are you tricking me? Was it supposed to be some sort of subtle therapy for me? Who cares. It worked. Thank you.

I take them to school. I help them with their homework. I give the little ones their baths. Some of the mothers let me pick out their clothes in the mornings. Best of all I take some of them to their music lessons and help them practice at home. (I especially think of Peyton when I do that.) And those homes, all the old and grand homes. I live in those homes now. They let me stay in my own bedroom. I can sneak into the kitchens late at night. And when they have parties I dress up and chaperone the children from guest to guest for introductions and greetings, and then we go upstairs to play. How is that not heaven? And one of the houses, the widow's house, she even lets me smoke as long as the children never see me. She's a smokestack herself and she gives me money to buy her cigarettes. I still pay rent on the sty I used to live in, but I have money left over. Thank you.

When did you think it was safe to have me around children again? How many times when we first started talking did I tell you about how seeing small children always made me think of P&P? And I would shut myself away and rock myself like a baby.

I think the worst is over. I think I can stop all the medicine. Can we talk about that soon?

There was only one time that I thought it was a mistake. I told you about Halloween a few months ago. Taking my children trick or treating. I even wore a costume myself. My two girls were Snow White and Cinderella. I was a Fairy Godmother. I know, silly. But the girls wanted me to be in costume too. I even had a magic wand. Kids in costume were everywhere. A lot of those stupid Rebel soldier costumes. But mostly Disney characters and witches and hobos and pirates. I used to love Halloween when my mother was alive. She always took me out, and we both gorged on candy afterwards, but P&P never let me do that after she died. So there I was last Halloween leading my girls door to door, making sure they did not grab too much at each door, making sure they always said thank you afterwards, and then at one house we turn around to walk down the porch steps and there is another group of kids coming up behind us. I saw it then. I saw my dead baby.

You read all my early notes, right? But I doubt that you remember what I wrote about me and Peyton having a baby, how we saw our baby as we looked at ourselves in the hotel mirror. Saw us as one thing. (I think I will tell you this when we talk again, and then you will know something about me that even Peyton does not know. Like some of the other things only you know.)

I was being followed by a little boy in a devil costume. A stupid Halloween devil costume. A red and black devil face with a twisted smile and warts and horns, an ugly grotesque more monster than devil face, a tiny child in a red costume with a red cape, a devil face that was melting on one side. I had seen it before, no big deal. But at the next house it was there again right behind me as I turned to go down the steps. It was in a group of kids who were always next in line. As we walked, it followed me. I told my girls to stop and let the kids behind us go ahead. That worked for a few houses, but then that child was behind me again. Laugh all you want, call it a delusion all you want, that child was behind me. But I know now, I learned with Peyton, a child is the union of its parents. That child reveals the "us" of the parents. I was pregnant when I was fourteen, a year after meeting Peyton, but before we did it for the first time. (And now only you know.) P&P were the fathers. I knew it. They never did. I was afraid they might even make me have the monster we had created. But you see, my good and gentle doctor, I could never visualize that child until I saw that devil's face. And it was following me. I thought I had killed it, but it was following me. What else could I do, my magic wand was useless. I was like some stupid Rosemary. I turned around and walked back to that child to tell him ...I will give you all the candy in my bag if you give me your mask. How could he resist?

Yes, yes, a good story for you the next time, PWR. If you want, I will bring the mask with me. Thank you.

Books in Print

Forrest Beaumont never pried too deeply into his son's life, but Bobby's *drift*, as his mother called it, was a recurring and much discussed worry for them. Both agreed that time was not important. Bobby could always come back to Charleston and become the Beaumont of the future. He need not seek his fame or fortune in New York. Fortune was in the Will, fame was merely another word for *position* in Charleston society. Bobby was guaranteed both. But New York held him. On his second and final visit to the city, Forrest had asked his son about the future, his plans. It had been almost ten years since Bobby left Charleston, and although he returned regularly for visits, called often, and wrote precious letters to his mother once a week, his absence began to wear on their hearts, and Forrest Beaumont grew tired of dealing with the predictable question from Charleston: *When is young Bobby coming home?*

Leaving New York for the last time, Forrest confronted his son, "Bobby, in a few years you will not be young. And certainly your mother and I are not getting any younger. I fear her decline more than my own, and some certainty about your future would be a balm to us both. Your mother says you drift. I defend you by saying that you are merely methodical and cautious. She is more right than I. You have much talent and great capacity for wisdom, but you seem still frozen in the moment you left home. Is there anything I can do for you?"

The two men were in Grand Central Station, each dressed in a dark suit. Bobby was much shorter than his father, so he had had grown accustomed to looking up at him when they spoke. "Daddy, I have some ideas, even a plan. I have come to love the book business, but merely selling is not my future."

"You will of course write, as I have always expected you to do," his father began.

"No, no…," and Bobby smiled. "I have had lots of free time here. The store is slow. I discipline myself to write for several hours a day, in the evening too, but…the honest truth is that I am not a writer. I have met many of them in my business and social life, and some have been kind enough to read my work. The false ones tell me that I have potential. The true ones tell me otherwise."

"You do not like selling, and you have no talent for writing. But you like the book business? Am I missing something? Writing and selling, is that not the book business?" A garbled voice was coming through the overhead loudspeaker, and train whistles were announcing arrivals and departures. Bobby and his father were surrounded by a thousand lives swirling around them like a river around a jutting rock.

"I like to read, daddy. I like to read books, and I like to read people. All I need is the right opportunity."

"You must tell me more when I see you again," his father almost had to shout amid the din around them. They shook hands, and then Forrest headed south to Charleston. He would never see his son again.

Ellie and Peyton: The Future

This must be a male thing. Peyton asked me the same thing. But you managed to turn it around. He asked me what I was going to be when I grew up. You asked what I would do with my life if I never saw Peyton again. You seemed so sure about that, me never seeing Peyton again. You might be right, right? God moves in mysterious fucking ways for sure.

But why do I need a plan? Why do men always have such big dramatic rule-the- world fantasies about their future? Good Doctor Freud, I never wanted to be anything. I told Peyton that I would probably end up being a teacher or a nurse or a virgin librarian (he laughed at that, we had already had sex in the public library). It wasn't like I wanted to be any of those things. I just assumed I would be something like every other girl. I couldn't tell Peyton that I only started even considering the future after I met him. Before him, if I happened to think about the future all I could see was P&P forever, so I stopped thinking. Before him, I did not want to think about the next day. I damn near failed school a hundred times. I would sit there and not care, so I am sure my teachers thought I was retarded. I talked smart, but I tested for shit on purpose in school. The hospital tests? I focused like I was going blind. (Did I ever tell you that I never cussed around Peyton, but I guess you bring out the best in me, right?) I told Peyton that I did not care what I was going to be in the future as long as I was with him. Sad thing is, as sappy as that sounds, I was never more truthful. That was my goal.

Peyton was different. I mean he was different from me, but I think he was like all boys. He had big plans. And I loved listening to him talk about them. One day one thing, another day something else. I told him about being born with silver spoon in his mouth. How could he not be successful? He could be a lawyer or a doctor I said, make a million dollars a year because he would already start with more than that just from his parents. He was born rich. If he had been born a girl he would be going to all the debutante balls and coming out wearing a tiara like Miss South Carolina and then sent to Miss Scarlett's School for Ladies and Turnip Greens. It was fun, telling him that because I could see that he actually had to stop and think if there really was such a place for about a half second, but then the turnip greens gave me away. It was fun, PWR, me and Peyton being in love. Didn't you have fun when you were in love? We were happy. Was that a crime?

You want to know his big plan? The only thing he was sure of was that he had to get out of Charleston. It was the only time he let me really deep deep into his other heart. He slipped up when he was talking about going away for his future. He did not know where.

—Some place where I won't disappoint my parents.

I understood immediately. As long as he was here he was always going to be their golden child, but never himself. I was fifteen, but I understood. He might write books, he might be a college teacher, he might be a scientist or a doctor (like you?). He might be anything he wanted, but it was not going to be here. But then he got quiet. I waited for him to say more, like I wanted to know where he wanted to go, but he never did, ever again. So I sat there in the gazebo at WPG and held his hand. Can I go with you?...I wanted to know, and he nodded yes. That was his plan. Eventually, we would be together in another world.

How about you, PWR? You grow up to be the person you wanted to be? Twenty years from now? Will you send me a postcard? Will you come see me and Peyton? That would be some sort of weird (fearful?) symmetry, wouldn't it? I won't tell him about how you love me. You do love me. That's okay. Makes perfect sense. But he wouldn't be jealous anyway. We can all be friends. We can talk about our children. Who knows, one of your pretty daughters might have made you a grandfather by then. You can look at how our children look, see if you can see me and Peyton like we will see ourselves. No, not really, I know. You will look at your children and see your wife and you, your long dead wife (thank you for telling me that she died before you met me, although it was always obvious). But not you, or anybody else, will ever see in my children what Peyton and I see. Never look at the sun, dear and kind doctor, or you will go blind.

Bobby Becomes a Legend

Bobby had never envisioned a career as an editor. The more he worked at the Windsor Bookstore, the more good and bad books that he read, the more he talked to readers, the more writers and agents he met, the more publishing parties he went to, the more book reviewers he met, the more of everything about books...the more he wondered at success and failure. He could envision himself a publisher, but not an editor. But, because he had always assumed that he would one day return to Charleston, he felt no pressure to decide his professional future. A personal issue lingered, love tangled up in blue, kept from his mother and friends, everybody except Harry Windsor and Mr. Taylor, and Charleston was not to be home again until he resolved that issue. Years passed. Although New York was to be a temporary home, he never left.

When asked to legitimize the Windsor name, Bobby knew the business he wanted to create. He had thought about it for years, but, in all those daydreams, profit never entered the equation.

When Windsor made his offer contingent on the business actually making a profit, Bobby was uncharacteristically naïve: *Of course it will make money.* Within weeks, he was disabused about the inevitability of a profit as he confronted all the things he did not know about publishing. Finding a good book to publish was the easiest part of the business. He would sit in the Accountant's office and lay out his plans, and Windsor's Accountant always had the same question: *How much will it cost?* Not, *How much will you make?* Windsor's Accountant had been Windsor's shadow for as long as Bobby had known the two men, and in all that time the Accountant always wore the same three-piece brown pinstriped suit, a suit which never seemed to fade. Windsor called him *My goddam Bartleby*, but the Accountant was not amused. Windsor also told Bobby, in the Accountant's presence, "When I die, talk to this guy. He knows where all the bodies are buried." The Accountant always smiled and nodded at *that* remark.

Bobby's best advice came from his father. After another frustrating meeting with the Accountant, Bobby called his father and told him about his plans, primarily to assure his parents that he did indeed finally have some specific plans. His father reminded him, "Make Mr. Windsor's money work for you. Use it to hire the right people. The best people you can get, those more experienced than you."

Bobby was initially irritated. "Daddy, I know that. I know how it works."

Forrest Beaumont was firm, "But have you done it? Knowing is irrelevant. Doing is the key."

After all those years in New York, having made hundreds of acquaintances in the book business, he started filling offices on the top floor of the Windsor Building. Mid-level people from other publishers, those he knew and respected, some skeptical, some eager for a change, but Bobby Beaumont was a persuasive young man, a young man already known in their circles as *special*. Bruce Tucker was hired early as head of Publicity/Promotion. Next came an assistant editor, and a secretary. Other jobs would be sub-contracted out in the beginning. Part of their salary, even for the secretary, was based on profit-sharing. A lot of book business eyes were rolling with *that* offer, but Bobby was totally confident, or so he seemed to them.

Windsor told him that he had five years to make a profit, much more time than Bobby had expected. "I thought you might need more, with all the start-up costs and everything, but the Accountant made me promise to cut you off at five. He's a cheap bastard, you know."

Bobby, Bruce, another editor, and a secretary...Windsor House did not step on to the publishing stage with a flourish, but it *was* noticed. Bobby was interviewed by the *New York Times*. That story never ran, but the Style editor did seek him out when Windsor's first noteworthy book crossed her desk.

Sally Graham certainly remembered that first book, even though she was only a teenager in Georgia. "Damn, Bobby," she told him soon after being hired, "I read about that book in the *Times* and tried to get our local library to order it, but they said there was no way in hell that pornography was getting on their shelves. I had to have my uncle in Savannah promise to get me a copy for my birthday, and my mother was double pissed at him for a long time after that."

Bobby's plan was simple. Start small and local. Get a reputation in your own neighborhood, and then expand to the rest of America. Of course, local was New York City, a country all to itself. For the first year, Windsor published books only about New York City, mostly non-fiction. Two were bestsellers in the City, and both lost money, as did all the Windsor books published that year. But that was part of Bobby's plan too. He wanted sales numbers first, then revenue. Windsor had given him a blank check, trusting his discretion.

For the first year, Windsor did not use a distributor. All sales had to be made directly through the publisher, but all the books were sold wholesale at seventy percent off the cover price. The only requirement for the discount was that the books get front window display space. Bobby had studied covers for ten years. As soon as he had decided on his first book to publish, he went looking for a graphic artist to add to his staff, somebody who could "see" the book Bobby gave him. Windsor wanted quality. Bobby knew that first impressions of quality began with the cover, but also included paper stock and fonts and glue and even the author photo.

He knew hundreds of booksellers in New York. He called each one of them personally, then he and his small staff, with a few couriers, hand delivered books to the stores. The invisible thirteenth floor of the Windsor Building was a warehouse.

Losing money profusely that first year, he still never lost sight of the Accountant's deadline. Losses still had to be made up by the fifth year. He tried calling the Accountant the *Grim Reaper*, as a joke, but the Accountant reminded Bobby about bodies being buried, *mostly in New Jersey*, the only attempt at humor the Accountant ever made.

Of the first two bestsellers, one was loved by young and old alike: *Ghosts in New York City*. A glossy coffee table book, pictures of locations, grisly tales of death and lost souls. Bobby had met a Columbia professor who had done all the research but who wrote like a professor. Bobby hired...*a ghost writer*... he loved using that line in interviews, and a photographer who turned black and white photos into art. And then he made sure that every radio station, newspaper, tv station, and magazine in the City got more review copies than they needed. He released the book on October first.

At the end of his career, when asked about his favorite books of all those that he had published, Bobby always put his other first year bestseller at the top of his list. He had many public reasons, but only Sally ever found out the private reason.

The Most Beautiful Women in New York.

His favorite book, and the only book in which he appeared. His concept was simple. He had walked the streets of the city for years and seen beauty everywhere. Even his father noticed when he walked with his son. The two men would sometimes sit at an outdoor restaurant and gaze, speaking to each other without looking at each other. Lust, for sure, but restrained by fidelity and manners, and never expressed crassly. A certain aesthetic appreciation of women in motion. How a skirt or summer dress revealed *and* covered, the curve of an ankle, jut of a hip and the bounce under soft fabric, wardrobes of color and style, hair that fell in straight lines or bobbed in curls or swirled as a shoulder turned, father and son as spectators to beauty. Forrest Beaumont once sighed and whispered to himself, "I will miss this when I die," and then, sensing that his son had overheard, he arched his eyebrow and leaned toward Bobby with a story.

"Your mother still does this to me, this longing, and I shall miss that more than anything else. Have I ever told you about the first time I ever saw her?"

Bobby nodded, lifting his hand to get a waiter's attention, and said, "More than once, but it is still a good story."

"It is *the* story, Bobby, *the* story of my life. And you shall, I pray, have your own version soon."

"Daddy...."

"Yes, enough of that subject, I know. Now, to my point. I was young, as was your mother, not yet teenagers. My mother had given another party, but I was uncooperative, almost sullen. I was about to go up the wide stairs to find a lavatory. Your mother was coming down those stairs, as if descending from heaven, her hand sliding down the banister, a scarlet gown contrasting her pale skin, her blond hair bouncing with each step, and utterly oblivious to my existence even though I was directly in her path. I froze, Bobby, pillared at the foot of those stairs, and then she saw me and each subsequent step was slower than the one preceding it. She entered my life in slow motion, her left hand extended toward me, and her first words were music. *You must be our host. It is my great pleasure to meet you.*

His father's story always ended with those words. Some minor details had changed over the years, but the last words were constant, confirmed by his mother's own version of the meeting. The last time that he told the story, autumn in New York, Forrest Beaumont added one more thought, "I wish I had a picture of how she looked then, so beautiful." Bobby agreed with his father's sentiment. There should have been a picture.

The Most Beautiful Women in New York sold thirty thousand copies in the city, was a topic of conversation by hundreds of thousands more, and it still lost money. Bobby's vision of beauty combined his father's appreciation of the sacred with the profane idolatry inherent in all men. Bobby wanted to stir body and soul, and he wanted women to buy the book for men. He released it two weeks before Valentine's Day.

Women was an over-sized coffee table book, and everything about it was Bobby's idea. He wanted Helmut Newton as a photographer, but Newton wanted to impose his own vision on the book. Bobby interviewed fashion photographers. They wanted professional models. Bobby wanted real women. Expressing his frustration to his newly hired secretary, he was handed her boyfriend's card. "Sully's place is full of women's pictures," she said. Bobby was intrigued by her blushing.

Sullivan Semken was the boyfriend, and he was hired as photographer, and he stayed with Bobby until the Germans invaded twenty years later, becoming the graphic artist that designed most of the Windsor award winning book covers.

Bobby told Sully that he wanted freshness and spontaneity, no studio pictures, not too much make-up, but motion if possible. The two men hit the streets, Sully with a camera, Bobby with a folder of contracts. Sully loved to re-tell the stories of their meeting women and surprising them with an offer to be in the book. But Sully did not know that Bobby had also pre-arranged many of the models. Not those on the streets, who were always surprised. But Bobby made a point of seeking out beautiful women he had already met, the wives and daughters of men he knew, men who were book critics or reporters or radio executives or disc jockeys or television producers and morning show hosts. He went to their homes or offices, and those were the only studiously posed shots, and more profane than sacred.

Bobby had told Sully the basic goal, "I want you to capture that first moment of attraction, when face and body provoke desire, but not lust." Sully had no idea what Bobby meant by that distinction, but he did his best.

A hundred women were chosen, all stunning, even with flaws. The first and last were especially guaranteed to get attention in 1979. The one in the middle almost got Bobby arrested. The first was his secretary, Sully's girlfriend, a Marilyn Monroe look-alike without even trying, resting her bottom on the edge of her desk, her arms reaching behind her for support, her feet planted far apart on the carpet, her sweater one size too small, her nipples almost apparent, her skirt hugging her thighs, her face looking like she had just had the best sex of her life a minute earlier. The last picture was the wife of an NBC vice-president, walking toward the camera, nude under a full-length sheer negligee, her breasts and pubic hair clearly visible, but it was her face that was the essence of the picture. Bobby had told her to walk toward the photographer, and he had already told Sully the signal when to snap the picture. The woman was too self-conscious, but Bobby, off to the side, sighed...*I wish I were your husband...*and the woman turned and tilted her head toward him, smiling at the compliment, and Sully captured that face at that moment.

Ninety-seven of the other pictures were unique in their own way...a woman alone, a woman in a crowd, a woman talking to a lover, a woman looking back over her shoulder at the camera. Beautiful women who had never been in a book before. The problem was the middle picture. It was not a woman. It was a child. A ten year old blond girl walking down a staircase, wearing a red dress, one of the thin bodice straps hanging loosely off her shoulder, her hand on the railing, a blazing chandelier on the ceiling beyond the top of the stairs. Was she wearing too much make-up? How to explain the full lips, and the dark adult look of her eyes? Bobby had told Sully what he wanted, and Sully thought he had captured the image of an angel. Bobby almost did not use the picture. It was not what he had seen in his own mind. But Sully was right...it *was* a dazzling image.

A Methodist minister disagreed. In his world, the angel on the staircase was child pornography. Bobby would tell Sally about that minister years later, and all she could say was, "Thank god that guy didn't live long enough to see an *Abercrombie and Fitch* catalog."

The minister wrote a letter to Bobby, got no satisfaction, and then wrote a letter to the *New York Times*, which refused to print it. The *New York Post* was more accommodating, and also seemingly outraged. By the time the story was absorbed into the gossipy air of the city, a lot of people, who had never seen the book, thought the last photo in the book, of the nude wife, was actually the underage girl's image that everyone else was talking about. *Nude* and *child* was a combustible combination, even if not real. And then the *New York Times* wrote about the controversy, complete with a picture of the book cover. It was reviewed in the Style section, and Bobby was a celebrity. Harry Windsor was impressed. The Accountant was not. *The Most Beautiful Women in New York* cost nine dollars a copy to produce. Bookstores paid ten dollars wholesale and sold it for $19.95 retail, but Bobby had given away a thousand copies. Not to mention, as the Accountant made a point of mentioning... *We've got overhead to cover. Either of you geniuses remember that?*

Ellie Goes to a Funeral

YOU BASTARD. YOU FUCKING BASTARD.

You bastard. You think I'm illiterate? You think I never look at a newspaper? You think that if I do not know, then you do not have to tell me? You bastard. You think that I would miss the goddam front page of the Post today? Front page news above the fold, right? I know all that stuff. I know more than you think I do. Front page, and his picture too. You would have thought that John Calhoun had been resurrected and wrapped in cotton balls to march down Church Street again. A great loss to Charleston, all those people who knew him said. Another link to our past snapped and down we tumble, right? I looked at that face for hours this morning. I know his other face, the face he showed me as I was bleeding out my nose, and my eyes were looking for God and there he was in white.

Peyton's father is dead. Weep sweet Jesus. The King is dead. Long live the King.

And you weren't going to tell me. Because I know why.

Peyton is coming home. He is the new man of the house. And you know that I don't need you anymore. So take your credit, dear doctor. You cured me. I am beautiful again. Just in time. Perfect timing. You fixed me for Peyton. And I don't care if you think it is a bad idea. Seeing him again. Going to the funeral. You are too predictable. And you never believed me when I said he was coming back for me. Mysteries abound, but everything has a reason. Science and God agree. Everything happens for a reason. His father had to die before Peyton could come back. Check. He did not contact me as long as his father was alive. Check. He is coming back now. Checkmate, Doctor PWR.

Three days from now and I will see him at St. Phillips. Three days to wash and re-wash myself. How do I know all this? Why anything? You said he had forgotten about me. Silence spoke volumes, right? But how did he know where to find me. I wasn't gone at all. His eye was on the sparrow, right? I am living in the Pinkney house, no home for me anymore anywhere else, but the note was hand delivered today. He knew exactly where I was. He had just been waiting. An invitation written by him.

—I have thought about you every day.

So few words, and I still I cried like a baby.

Isn't that a breakthrough, PWR, me finally being able to cry in spite of all that damn medication? I cried and Mrs. Pinkney held me tight as her children stared like I was being born, bawling like a baby. She was so gracious.

—We must get you a proper dress.

She was shocked that I had never been to a funeral before. In my brain, in my brain, I wanted to tell her, marchers to and fro, but only Peyton would understand. Or you. You want me to talk to you before I do anything rash, right? That is a good idea in your world, probably you are sure, but I am not in your world anymore.

Peyton took me to St. Phillips a few times in the past, like I took him to SJB, but never on a Sunday or for any services. We were our own congregation.

—Our own congregation.

You probably think that is something I would say, but it was Peyton. He and I saw the world the same. After he went away I went by myself as soon as I got free of your doctor friends. Time and Space avail not, remember? So all this makes sense, this reunion. I should have known it was close months ago. I went by myself, sitting there in the same spot that Peyton and his parents sat years before, where he always sat me down. But I was alone and then the earth and sky split open and I heard his father's voice. But it was just the new organ they had installed, some tuner going through scales I suppose, getting ready for the first public performance the upcoming Sunday. Just a giant organ going through scales, and then I could hear two men talking in the balcony, one laughing, and then it boomed again, this time a real song, a hymn announcing...something. But it was an announcement for sure.

Mrs. Pinkney wanted me to sit with her. She did not know about me and Peyton, but I told her that I wanted to sit near the back in case I had to leave early. She said she understood. But she didn't. But I like her anyway.

I was a death virgin. Not the event, the ritual. I had seen pictures of funerals in magazines, famous funerals for famous people like Bobby Kennedy and Martin Luther King, but I was not there at those. Today I was in St. Phillips with a thousand other sad people. I was a traitor, or a spy. I was not sad. I was happy. That is what I did not want Mrs. Pinkney to see.

With a rolling organ thunder, the world went silent and Peyton's father entered. I saw the casket first, and then I took the deepest breath in the universe. I saw Peyton, his right profile. I closed my eyes. He did not see me. I opened my eyes and watched him lead the procession following the casket, his arm supporting his mother, and I saw her black-veiled profile as she passed by, her husband ahead and her son beside her. Behind Peyton and his mother were an old black man and woman, the only negroes in the church.

Peyton was that close to me and he never looked toward me, but I knew he knew I was there. He was ten years older, ten more years perfect, and I was beautiful. I had forgotten how beautiful I was until he walked past me.

And you thought it was a bad idea? Oh, PWR, I wish you had been there. I'm sorry that I did not wish that as it happened, for you to be there, but I do now. Of all the people in the world at that moment, you would have come closest to seeing how beautiful I looked.

Do you remember me telling you about how many times I had thought about killing myself? I really did. And when I killed my baby that was the closest I ever came to actually doing it. On purpose. The very next day, as I was still bleeding down my legs. And for that hour, as I walked around Charleston looking for a damn bus to step in front of or a bridge to jump off, I started to imagine my own funeral. I could even see P&P acting sad. Some people from school. For a second I even imagined my mother looking at me in a casket. They would all be sorry, even P&P. But my funeral was not like today. It was not grand.

It was petty and small. There was no music, no singing. Even my mother was not singing. And nobody wore black. If I had known you then, I suppose I would have imagined you there too. You could tell everyone how I would be missed. How you loved me, even if they did not. But there was no preacher there at my funeral. I had been talking to Peter and Paul at SJB but they were not at my funeral either. I think they would have been ashamed for me, taking my own life, playing God, such a sin, and they would have been right. I wasn't going to be mourned by the cream of Charleston, as Peyton's father was today. Life would go on without me. That was what I was thinking as I walked around town, even past that church today. I forget, did I already tell you about me killing my baby, or did I just write it to myself? I never wrote about it when it happened, did I? You read those notes...did I? About killing that baby and then wanting to kill myself? So here's the last thing I want to say about it, and I only remember because I saw a real funeral today. I once wanted to kill myself. I was serious, I imagined all the people at my funeral, and then I imagined Peyton. I had gone through the sum total of my life and left him out. And then I thought of him and I ran to the bookstore, ran like I was chasing myself, but he was not there. That was okay, because I knew he was still alive. I was never going to kill myself as long as he was alive. That would be like killing him too. So I sat on a bench near the store and smoked a cigarette. Then I went home and took a shower.

Is this typical, Doctor PWR, all this obsessing about death when you go to a funeral? I know they say that funerals are for the living, not the dead. To make sense of this stupid thing we do, being alive. Lord knows, the preacher sure tried to do that today, and maybe he did for most of the people there, but I wasn't listening to him. All I thought about was Peyton talking about his father. There was no divine plan in his voice, no eternal mystery about the mind of god. He was describing the man who had unioned with his mother to give him life, the man who saved that life at my mother's house, but he did not tell that story. He made the people laugh and he made many of them weep, summing up the life of a man who had not even turned sixty yet. In my father's house are many mansions. He even told the story of how his mother and father had met, on that stairway in the Peyton House. Just for that eulogy, PW, I wish you had been there. My tiny Peyton was the biggest soul in the room.

An hour later, we were finally alone.

Peyton had taken me to the St. Phillips cemetery a long time ago, to show me the family plot. Do you hate new cemeteries? All the open space and manicured grass and trees. That's why I liked St. Phillips even back then. It was so old and cramped with stones everywhere. Stones worn by time, names and dates smoothed out until they were disappearing, no more permanent than smudges. Peyton had obviously been to that cemetery a hundred times. He knew the histories of his kin and almost everyone buried around them. Me, I was looking for ghosts in grey uniforms. The thing that confused me? His family plot had space for two more graves, but even they had to be wedged in tight. You, Peyton...I wanted to know...where are you going to be buried? Your mother and father have a future here, but you? He thought I was being too morbid.

—Figure that out later, perhaps we dig up the kin from a

hundred years ago and take their spot?

He did not seem to worry about dying. I was petrified like a forest.

—Neither one of us is going to die. Science will save us all, right? No more death.

I will die if you die, I told him. He laughed, he really laughed. And then he stepped over his grandfather's slab and hugged me.

—Neither one of us is going to die.

I waited in the back of the crowd that squeezed around his father's open grave. More words, flowers on the casket, more words, and then the other people started to wander away. For the first time, I was able to see Peyton's face clearly and closely. He did not see me. His perfect face with that dark line from brow to cheek on the left side. The scar I had given him. My scar. But then he turned his back to the crowd and stood by his mother, holding on to her as she reached out and touched her husband one last time, as if caressing the mahogany casket. She had never been real to me in the past, unlike Peyton's father who had been as real as thunder to me. I wanted to introduce myself, to tell her that I was sorry for her loss. Common words, but I, more than anyone else there, could imagine her pain. I was her.

PWR, you ever go to a burial and the only sound is the wind? Barely moving, but enough to stir the leaves overhead, enough to feel it move around your body. Maybe a bird too? But no human sound. No words, no breathing, no rustle of clothing. You ever wondered what would be the last sound you hear as you die? I love that poem. I said it in my head all to myself when I sat by my mother as she died. (Why can't I remember her funeral? She must have had one, but I do not remember it at all. Did P&P rob me of that too?) The stillness in the room, that poem, the blue uncertain stumbling buzz poem. I think that is what I will recite to myself as I am about to die. Peyton was wrong back then. We all die. You too, PWR, you will die too. You are an old man, remember, and you will die. I will go to your funeral, I promise. You have always been good to me.

Can you imagine a tomb with no walls? That was what I felt like as I waited for Peyton. A hundred mourners dissolved into twenty, and then just me. Me and Peyton and his mother and the old black man and woman, all with their backs to me. There were other things there too, but they were not people, not real people. They were merely hands. A hand to turn a crank, hands to shovel dirt, hands without bodies. The work of hands done, Peyton's mother turned and was escorted past me by the old black people. I could see her face through the veil. She did not see me.

Peyton and I were alone in our own tomb, but his back was still toward me. I was in no hurry. Seriously, PWR, I had waited this long, why worry about a few more minutes. Peyton was still talking to his father. Me and Peyton were never going to die, I wanted to remind him of that, but I could wait. I wanted to walk up and touch him, but I waited. When he finally turned around I looked straight into his eyes, and I died.

I did not see myself. I was not there. Peyton was looking at a stranger. For that fractured and then suspended moment I thought of you, thought of how you had been right, why should I assume he would remember me, wait for me, want me again. How utterly delusional was that, right? See, for that second, all I had left in my life was you. But here's the worst thing I will ever say to you, PWR, and if I go to hell it will be for this reason only. Ten feet away from me at his father's grave, but also ten years? Peyton tilted his perfect and scarred face, stared at the thing in front of him, and finally smiled as he slowly spoke for the first time to me.

—Ellie?

I saw myself again, saw how beautiful I was, and I abandoned you, PWR. I was your Judas.

Peyton held out his hand, and do you know the profound and romantic first words out of my mouth? As if the prior ten years had never happened? Time and Space merely choices that could be erased and re-done. An etch-a-sketch life of infinite possibilities. All that kind of flowery talk, right? All I could say as he walked toward me?

Can we go somewhere for a smoke?

He looked off toward the past, Time and Space when bookstores and music stores and parks were our world, then back at me, seeing himself for the first time in forever, smiled again, and reached inside his coat to retrieve a pack of those damn Marlboros.

I am so truly sorry, doctor friend and lover. Instead of groom at the altar, you became the father of Peyton's bride. I am about to leave you forever. I am truly sorry. If I had met you first, you could have adopted me and made me whole again. I am sorry, sorry, so truly sorry. I will miss you.

The Bobby Stories Begin

Bobby could not remember the first book he had ever read. He was asked that question by an *Esquire* reporter who was doing the first profile on him. The reporter had followed him around for three days, and was even allowed to visit Bobby's Windsor apartment, a privilege that subsequent reporters were not granted. Beaumont was still relatively unknown to anyone outside of publishing, but *Esquire* had heard cocktail party stories about the editor who had fired his most profitable writer a week before another of his writers won a Pulitzer. So, who was this Bobby Beaumont?

The truth was less colorful than the rumor. Beaumont did not "fire" a writer. He simply refused to edit his latest book. He was willing to publish it, but he did not want to work with the writer on the editing. The writer went to another publisher. It was rumored to be a battle of egos, but Bobby insisted to the *Esquire* reporter that ego had nothing to do with it...at least, not his. The writer was Stephen Malloy, a man who had taken seven years to write his first novel, a carefully researched study of the world of mediums and séances, fictionalized into a thoughtful story about love surviving death, under two hundred pages, and as Beaumont wrote to the Arts editor of *The New York Times*, "every sentence was worth re-reading." It was a crystalline book, but even those books get published and still perish. For his first book, however, Malloy's stars aligned themselves in the right order. A glowing NYT review, which alerted other media, a producer on the *Today Show* whose sister adored the book and insisted that he read it too, an interview with Jane Pauley, more positive reviews, fanatic word of mouth, short-listed for major awards...the book sold a hundred and five thousand copies in hard cover. Windsor House had paid Malloy, who had no agent, a twenty-five thousand dollar advance. His next book was a guaranteed bestseller. Malloy hired an agent, and the agent suggested a quarter-million dollar advance. Beaumont paid it. The second novel was not as good as the first, but good enough. Malloy's fan base was established, and the quarter-million dollar advance was easily recouped. Malloy then discovered a formula for expanding his reader base. A veneer of his former prose quality, but more and more emphasis on horror rather than the spiritual, more sex and less love, and each new book was longer than the last, despite Bobby's efforts to trim them. He would explain to the *Esquire* reporter his view of his role.

"The bottom line is that it is not my book. I can cajole and threaten, but I will not make a writer do something that, down deep, he thinks is not what he wants to say."

The *Esquire* reporter knew too much about publishing to accept that answer. He pushed Bobby toward the truth, "And you were making money regardless, right?"

Bobby was not offended. He merely shrugged, "A lot of money for both of us, but it was still sad. His first book was wonderful. For his second, I just told myself that Windsor could take the money we made off him and find some more good writers. Eventually, Steve decided he wanted to sell books more than he wanted to write them. But, please do not quote me on that."

Malloy had assumed that Bobby would be his editor again, but Bobby merely told him that his assistant editor would work with the latest book. Malloy insisted, "You're my editor. I don't want to deal with the second string. And, hell, Bobby, my son is named after you. We're friends." Bobby declined, and Malloy tried to joke, but Bobby heard a threat, "My agent wanted me to auction this one out, but I told him that I wanted the Windsor imprint. But, Bobby, there's no point in being published here unless you're the editor. I can sell books with anybody."

Bobby made the *Esquire* reporter put down his pen and turn off his tape recorder. "You can paraphrase this any way you want, but the truth was that I had lost interest in Steve. His previous book should not have been published at all. I was disappointed in myself for not telling him that, lord knows his agent should have, but you were right...I knew it would make money, and I knew that Jan, my assistant at that time, would benefit from the experience, but Steve took his manuscript and went down the street. Jan was not disappointed. But I was. I was too rigid. I could have been more persuasive about the changes that needed to be made, instead of just turning him over to someone else. He was a good man. Perhaps it was my fault. I had let a friendship turn into a professional relationship."

Bobby did not tell the reporter all the truth; that, as he looked back at that time, he could see the first signs of his gradual disenchantment. Just as he was becoming a celebrity himself, Bobby wanted to go away and be left alone. As the news of Malloy's exit from Windsor was becoming mythologized, a first time Windsor novelist won the Pulitzer. The first thing that writer said when a *Times* reporter called him was, "This belongs to Bobby as much as me. He made me find the book I thought I had lost." That had been Bobby's favorite editing story for a long time. How the writer had been rejected a dozen times by other houses, each with a glowing "wonderful, but not quite right for us" letter and a few specific criticisms for the agent to pass along to his writer, and those criticisms leading to another re-write, re-write compounding re-write, until agent and writer lost all hope, and then agent and writer parted company, with writer mulling a career in sales, making one last contact for a new agent but not telling him about the prior rejections. That agent took thirty pages one week and the entire manuscript the next week, and then called Bobby the week after that, and then called the writer and told him to "sit down because your life is about to change."

Six months later, as the writer sat in Bobby's apartment, *nervous as hell* he would say later to anyone who would listen, the two men went through the manuscript from the first word to the last. Three days. At the end, the writer asked him, "With all these changes, why did you even buy the book in the first place?" Bobby asked him if he was satisfied with the new version, and the writer confessed about the book's rejection history. He had finally told his agent the week before, and the agent had exploded, calling the writer dishonest, and that if he had known that he was not the first agent to see it, and that it had already been rejected a dozen times, then he would not have touched it, and under no circumstances was the writer to tell Beaumont the truth. But the writer was compulsively contrite. Surely, he told himself, Bobby would find out anyway. Some other editor would tell him, surely. But that was not the most important reason the writer had for telling Bobby the truth. It was much more important than the truth.

"This is my original story," the writer told him, in response to the question about whether he was satisfied with the editing job. "This is almost the version that went to the first editor two years ago. It's tighter, a few pages shorter, and the chronology is clearer, but it is almost what I had in the beginning."

Bobby told the *Esquire* reporter the Malloy story, and his face did not conceal his disappointment, but the other story, about the first time writer, that story melted lines in his forehead and led to a long pause of obvious pleasure. "I told him I was not worried about how many other people had seen the story and rejected it. And I told him that I bought it in spite of the sloppy writing. I knew there was a wonderful story in there. All I had to do was retrieve it. But I did not tell him, after he told me about the past, I did not tell him that it was more important that he believe in his story more than I did. He was an insecure young man, I could tell. I wish I could have given him courage, but he was too nervous."

Esquire wanted to know what happened to that writer, but Bobby did not know. "He fired his agent, and I understood that, but he never wrote again as far as I know. One brilliant book, a long time ago, but no more." Bobby then almost snorted, "Of course, Steve is still selling parodies of his original talent, by the boat load. It does not have to make sense, it just is."

Ellie Redux

This is more difficult than I had imagined. Without PWR, to whom am I writing? In the past, I used him as an audience, even before I met him. But that was a trick I played on myself. I never wrote to Peyton. Looking through a thousand pages now, it seems like he was all I wrote about, but never to. The words before Peyton (B.P. ?) were all burned, and thus, I suppose, their reader(s) as well. I wrote about versions of myself, but I can see those now as fiction. Those thousands of pages are now down to a few hundred. Sometime in the future, I will give them, and all that is to be written, to Peyton and he will make them a story. That is what he does now...makes stories.

I am not who I was. I read those notes and see someone I do not recognize. (That is a lie, of course. I know her too well.) PWR must be given credit, my first and former doctor, who deserved a better patient than me. He never wrote that book he thought I would become, his most famous case. He stopped when he fell in love with me. But he turned me over to Peyton with a special "how to" kit. How to treat me, medicate me, manage me. Peyton never knew his name, but he read the reports and hovered over me, a surrogate angel for PWR. He made me go to doctors in his world, and all they did was agree with PWR. I eventually cheated, as I think PWR anticipated, so when I reduced my medication I was still okay. I stayed beautiful, but I was not dead, like I had been at the beginning. None of the doctors, not even PWR, understood the most profound truth of my life. Peyton fell in love with a girl unhinged. But I read all those notes from back then and did not see who I was when I was with Peyton. I was unhinged, so what? But unhinged in a world from which Peyton was excluded. In our world, I was Ellie. I was sane, as hinged and solid as a new car. (No, I was never insane, PWR understood that much, at least. I am sure of that.) Thus, the great fear of my life. To be cured of being the person Peyton caught stealing books. I cannot let that happen, ever.

Back to my first question. If not to Peyton, nor to PWR or any imaginary version of myself, to whom am I writing? When people think to themselves, who is listening? The most intriguing question of my life? Is it possible that there might actually only be one me? One real me. If that is so, then everything about me and Peyton makes sense. Peyton found me and made me real. And only he sees the real me.

If I were honest, I suppose, I could say that he is the only person who sees any version of me. How many times have he and I been in the same room and nobody else has seen me? All those parties in his apartment, dozens of people from his world, even his staff, his writers, the other women who want him and cling to him. I was always there. I talked to them. I drank with them. I was invisible.

Me, not quite right in the head? Tell me, Ellie, is it possible that Peyton is as daft as you? We buried his father, we went to a hotel and had sex, and then we went to his house for a reception two hours later. As if we had seen each other every day for the previous ten years, as if neither of us had been exiled from the other. But our new life began that day. We did not arrive together. He did not introduce me to anyone. It was our first party together. I was invisible. It was our mutual creation. In a room with other people, but only we could see the lines between us, arcing electric lines that flowed through or around other bodies and back to us. (Peyton understood that when I told him, about the arcing lines. He nodded, and he smiled.)

You are too much of a gentleman...I would tease Peyton later when we were alone, even after his parties in New York,...too inhibited to admit it, I would say, but I knew what you were feeling. You wanted to touch me as much as I wanted to touch you. You wanted all of them to disappear. But you are so much the master of your emotions, so in control of your life, that you posed as if the public you were real. I am your first love, Peyton, your only love, your worst purest passion. The parties, just like the reception to honor your father, were a dance. I was your first partner, and we both knew I was going to be the last. An hour before, you had been inside me; an hour after, you would return. Did anyone ever imagine how base you could become with me? Do you remember the playground? Stupid question. I should ask, will you ever forget the playground, that time in the dark with a thousand people tucked behind the windows all around us at midnight? (Note to self: you are not really writing this to yourself, are you?) That secret chapel, me on your lap in the front pew, Christ on a cross behind us. I was rocking slowly, but I could see a woman come into the chapel from a door in the back. She saw us, Peyton, but you never knew. She did not leave. She and I made eye contact, and I moved faster on you as she and I shared you. I knew the sound you would make when the time came, and I wanted her to hear it. She waited for us, and then she was gone. At least, I think I saw her. The couch in your office? Seriously, you kept that bloody relic? And we traveled back in time how often? Re-covered or not, it was the same couch. You know, if we're lucky, a hundred years from now, because we will never die, you promised, if we are lucky we will go to sleep on that couch together and never wake up. We deserve that. Your apartment in that weird building, my apartment on the floor that doesn't exist, how do we...the us of us...manage to stay invisible.

Am I the only person who knows the real Peyton? And he knows I know. Perhaps I have been wrong all along. Perhaps it is me who is supposed to write his story. But only about the world unique to us. Your world is one circle, mine is another, but then those two circles cross each other, like a partial eclipse, and the dark spot created...that is us.

Sun or moon, Peyton, which one do you want to be? And have you ever considered how perfect a total eclipse would be?

How well can I act? Appearing older and smarter is easy. I do that all the time at the parties, topped off with an impersonation of a person who barely knows Peyton. He and I agreed on who I was from the very beginning, and Harry W helped us. New girl in town, bright future ahead, perhaps a secretary on Wall Street in my cards, but just somebody who worked in one of Harry's other businesses for now? We would both laugh at how many other people lost interest in me when they found out I was not really in the book business. Harry made me keep track of those people, tell him who was too obvious. Most of the time, if they themselves were actors without lines in the play, I never saw them again. If anybody had ever asked me to describe Peyton in three words, and I could not talk about him and me, I would have said he was a judgmental person. Judgmental. He judged people, and he could then either reward or dismiss them. For how strangers treated me, even if I was invisible, he judged them. Down deep, only I knew, he judged himself the harshest of all. The other two words? Still to be determined.

Truth is, coming here terrified me. I could act old and smart, but I was a child who was scared of the dark when Peyton asked me to come here. Charleston had been my world, and I had always been a tiny fish in that ocean, but I knew where to hide. Here is not an ocean. It is a universe, I told Peyton, full of alien life forms and malevolent forces beyond my control. He told me to stop acting. He was going with me. I would not be alone.

—Stop being a drama queen—Stop over-talking life.

But I knew he did not mean that. I knew that how I talked was part of why he loved me. He had told me that in the bookstore.

—Ellie, you cannot write a script for the future. How could I have imagined you if I were scripting my own future?

He was wrong. I had scripted him before I met him. (No, the real surprise was PWR, who was not in my script at all.)

We rode the train, just like he had done a decade earlier. He was my guide. This is a magic place, I told him as I looked at the buildings, holding his hand as we walked to where he worked. It was magic and loud and crowded and smelly and foreign and beautiful. I acted brave, but I was scared to death. I wanted him to take me back to Charleston and come with me. But I acted brave. And then I came to his world, that weird building, and I listened as he described its history. And as we walked, he told me about a man named Harry.

—Do not let first impressions fool you—Harry is a true friend.

Fair enough, I discovered eventually, but Harry was not my first introduction. It was the old black man at the door. He saw us coming as he stood behind the glass door and opened it as we got closer, standing aside as we passed him. But Peyton made a point of stopping and introducing him to me, me to him, and the old man welcomed me in a voice that was not from here, a variation on a voice I knew, a voice from some version of my true home, and I felt safer. He would guard that door for me, protect me, just as I imagined him doing for Peyton. He was older than God's dirt, but I think he will outlive me and Peyton and all the others.

Bobby Interviews Sally

Sally wore black. She knew all the stories about Bobby Beaumont. Black was his favorite color. So, of course, he wore blue denims and a red sweater for the interview. He walked shoeless out of his office, extended his hand, the smell of sweet tobacco trailing him, and Sally's first two thoughts were, *he's even shorter than I thought,* and then, noting his wardrobe, *I am so fucked. I must look like a goddam undertaker.*

And then he spoke, and she fell in love again. With his voice, that was her first love. He spoke softly, and South Carolina wrapped itself around her, and the years of her own self-conscious efforts to sound like she was not from the South, all those years seemed wasted.

"You are from Savannah, is that right?" was his first question, and she thought it was more an accusation than inquiry, so she hesitated, and then she lost her professional balance without even trying to respond. Without a word from her, he said, "You do not sound like you are from Atlanta. Georgia for sure, mostly

Savannah, but not Atlanta."

"My parents were from Savannah, and certainly sounded like it, and I grew up there, then went to Atlanta for college," she said. "How did you…" He motioned her to sit on the old couch in front of his desk, and then he sat on the edge of the desk in front of her, finally looking down at her.

"You introduced somebody, or was it that you were interviewed afterwards, at the NBA dinner, and it was obvious that you were the right editor for that author…"

"Bill Summers, who won that year, as I recall," Sally interrupted, trying to sound assertive, feeling less overwhelmed.

"Yes, not the best book that year, but good enough. And I heard about your struggle with his ego, that story made the circuit, and we all thought you should have been named co-winner."

"Mr. Beaumont…"

"Bobby, just call me Bobby."

And that was her signal that she had passed the first test. Nobody called him Bobby without his explicit permission.

"Anyway, it was a good speech you made, or interview, or whatever, but I thought to myself at the time that you were trying too hard to sound like you were an editor, too precise in your words, and your accent suffered. And when I looked at your resume, I was a bit confused. You listed Atlanta as home, but you are not really from there, are you?"

"Like I said, I went to college there," she almost drawled. This was not the interview she had expected.

"Would you like a drink?"

Sally could not stop herself. She laughed too loud, and she could see the receptionist in the outer office turn toward her and Bobby, pausing to smile at the two of them.

"Is it five o'clock, Bobby?" she tried to joke.

The smiling receptionist appeared with a bottle of merlot and two glasses. Not a word, just a smile.

"It is always five o'clock somewhere in the world," he said as he poured. "So tell me one thing," sitting on the other end of the couch, "tell me how you know you like a book, how you know you want to publish it."

Sally looked at the glass of wine and wondered if it was a trick question. Anticipating this moment, she had read every book that Beaumont had personally edited and published the previous year, a half dozen, and two so far this year. There were no clues, and she had not liked all of them, but there was one in particular that made her hold her breath as the end approached, and then weep at the last word.

"Do you only publish the books you like, regardless of the market," she asked him, stalling for time, editing her response.

"I only publish the books I love, regardless of the market," he almost whispered, pouring a second glass of wine for himself, tilting the bottle toward her, ignoring her full glass. Fall in New York, late afternoon, the office was dimming. "Me, I understand myself. I want you to tell me about yourself."

Sally looked at the glass of wine and thought, *You will stop at two glasses. You will not drink too much. You will not start slurring.* And then she talked for an hour. She talked about the first book she actually loved, *To Kill a Mockingbird*, and the last book she edited, the one about corrupt Texas politics, soon to be short-listed for non-fiction awards. She talked about the difference between fiction and non-fiction, truth versus fact. She talked, not caring if Beaumont watched her rub her finger across her wine-soaked lips and then seemingly caress the rim of her glass with the tip of that finger, unconsciously circling and circling and then touching herself again, as her mother had always done, appalling her father. Sally talked about what she had learned from her boss at Viking, and she held up her empty glass and wordlessly asked for more, talking about a book she loved but which Viking turned down, only to see it go to Windsor and win a Pen/Faulkner, and Bobby listened to her and waited for her to catch up to him as the smiling receptionist appeared with another bottle of wine and disappeared. Sally noticed other Windsor people walking past Bobby's office door, peering in, studying the tableau of Bobby and his new aspirant, and then waving as they began their descent and exit from the Windsor Building, manuscript boxes or briefcases in hand. The lamps in the office seemed to glow warmer as the sun outside drooped behind the most beautiful skyline in Sally's imagination, leaving her and a silent Bobby Beaumont with empty glasses, the smiling receptionist nowhere to be seen.

Sally stopped talking, but Bobby did not speak. *God, how I want this job*, she thought. *And I wish the hell he would say something.*

"Okay, Bobby, here's the truth. You wanted to know how I knew I like...love...a book, right? The litmus test? It's real simple. I can't wait to get to the next sentence, but I don't want to leave the one I'm in. I slow down. And I stop. I re-read, and I can't wait to read more but I don't want it to end, so the closer it gets to the last page, the less I want it to end. And there's no single best example of that. It just is. And it only applies to fiction. The best non-fiction people can do the same, but it's still different. You did that book about the race horse a few years ago, wonderful prose, insightful and a pleasure to read, but I wouldn't read it twice, so there it is, I guess, the difference. I've read some novels over and over, years apart, and they're new again. And then...."

Beaumont stopped her with a wave of his hand, saying, "We all do that, Sally," and she knew he was disappointed in her answer. *God, I want this job. God, I want this job.* Sally looked for help, a cold glass of water, fresh air, anything to clear her head, and seeing Beaumont about to light another cigarette, which she hated, she blurted out what she knew would sound like a teenage girl's starry-eyed wisdom.

"I hear music, Bobby, I hear background music, soundtrack music, I hear strings and horns and pianos and especially saxophones when I really love a book. I see the characters and settings in perfect clarity, but most of all I hear music. Sure, not on every page, but a lot. It's not written there, the author doesn't supply it in words, doesn't even tell me there's goddam music in the air, but it's there, and I can hear it."

Beaumont took a slow drag on his cigarette, careful to exhale away from her, and Sally stopped talking. *God, I want this job, and, God, I am such an idiot.*

Beaumont took another drag, but then he stubbed out the freshly lit cigarette and rose gracefully from the couch, surprising Sally by how unfazed he seemed by the wine. "You are going to like it here, but I am going to make a special rule just for you," he said, extending his hand to help her up.

"I'm hired?"

He let go of her hand as she steadied herself, then he walked around turning off the lamps. His corner office had no curtains, and the electric illumination of the city was barely enough to let her see him, but he moved in the dark like a blind man.

"You were hired before you got here. The interview was just to see if I would change my mind."

"I'm hired?"

"You are hired, but on one condition. When the rest of us open a bottle of wine, you are not allowed to drink unless it is after six o'clock. And I am serious when I say this. You are not allowed to drink before six o'clock. Understood?" Sally nodded, thinking, *You sound like my father but I don't give a shit. I will stop drinking entirely if that's what you want.*

"Now, please come over here by the window and tell me a secret about yourself, something nobody else knows." Bobby stood peering out, as if looking for something lost, and Sally tread a careful path around the furniture toward him, afraid of stumbling. A few months into the future, she would have the office map etched in her mind, the exact number of paces from this to that. Beaumont never moved his furniture. If new chairs replaced old chairs, their legs were positioned into the rug indentations. That first night, however, her hands led her feet. Finally next to him, wondering if he would reach for her again, disappointed when he did not, she finally said, "I guess you figured out that I don't handle alcohol very well, so that's not much of a secret, is it."

Bobby laughed softly. "No, I have heard those stories before."

Thank God it's dark. A red face isn't my best feature, Sally thought, her shoulders tightening.

"Well, I get tired of all the jokes about my last name, all the comments about Graham Crackers and milk. You know, big problems like that," she said, suddenly feeling dizzy.

"You know, it could be worse. You could be named Bobby Lee

Beaumont, like a Yankee's version of some spitting whittling good old boy with straw in his teeth and tobacco in his back pocket."

"Bobby, have you got name issues?" she snickered, blinking in the dark, feeling her stomach start to turn.

"No, not really. Just Yankee issues. And, for the record, I love Graham crackers. My mama always held them out as a treat for me when I was young."

Oh God, Bobby, you say mama like you were back in Charleston, lost and looking for home, Sally wanted to say, but stopped herself.

"Something else, Bobby, and I'll only admit this in front of you. As much as I might bitch about the South and being glad I escaped it, the truth is that I actually miss it. I miss my home in Savannah. I miss my parents, the parents I had before they got divorced and started the piss fight that eventually killed their souls."

As a child, Sally thought her Savannah house looked just like the gingerbread one from *Hansel and Gretel*. Ornate white latticework framed the double-decker porches, and the shingles were painted baby blue. Situated in the heart of the Victorian historical district, the wooden house was a favorite with tourists who snapped photos of Sally waving proudly in front as they passed by in their trolleys. Once inside, Sally always took off her shoes so she could feel the smooth pine floors while she pranced up the wooden staircase to the second floor. Occupying the smallest bedroom upstairs meant that she had private access to her home's best feature, the covered porch. After her parents went to sleep, she would often tiptoe outside to sit beneath the grand oak whose branches she could almost touch from her rocking chair. If she fell asleep, in spring she'd wake up to a dawn chorus of songbirds; in late summer, she'd hear the roar of cicadas. She spent most Saturday mornings in the fall playing in Forsyth Park, only two blocks away. And when it got too chilly for the park or the porch, on winter evenings she would curl up in a chair in front of the living room's bay windows and count the stars. The details of her childhood came back easily when she was with Bobby. Nobody else was allowed to see her past.

Sally felt herself swaying, so she wasn't sure she actually heard the voice, but just as she was about to lean toward Beaumont she heard it again as the light in the hallway came on.

"Bobby, the car you ordered is at the front. Sally, I've got your stuff, so whenever you're ready I can take you downstairs. We should hurry. I told Mr. Taylor that he could lock up after we leave."

It was the smiling receptionist, silhouetted in the doorframe. Or, so Sally thought. The woman walked into the office and turned on one lamp. Sally's eyes adjusted. The receptionist was Whitney Randall, Beaumont's assistant editor, the woman Sally was replacing. She was leaving to become a senior editor at Harper-Collins. She was younger than Sally.

Five minutes later, standing beside a Lincoln Town-car, driver holding the door open for Sally, Whitney shook her hand again and smiled, "You'll love this place, and I know you'll do great. Bobby wouldn't have picked you otherwise. He was afraid you might turn him down, so I know he's a happy man tonight. And you'll love the rest of the staff."

Sally was too self-conscious to talk much, still swaying, her stomach still churning, but she did have one question, "Are all the stories true?"

Whitney took her elbow and nudged her into the car, leaning

down, "None of them. But you should still be careful. Bobby will break your heart. But don't take it personally. And, if you ever get him to explain the scar on his face, call me. It's one of his famous secrets. Who knows, you might be the one who gets the truth. Whatever happens, this will be the best job you ever have."

Ellie and Harry

And then there was Harry. If Disney made Jew cartoons, Harry would star in all of them. I had known Jews in Charleston, but a Southern Jew and a New York Jew are not the same. Every Southern Jew I had ever known was immaculate and polite and reserved and gracious. The first thing I notice about Harry? His fingernails were almost black. His breath reeked of tobacco and fish. For a rich man, he dressed like a poor uncle. A few seconds after introducing the black doorman, Peyton saw Harry rushing toward us in the lobby. Before I knew what was happening, Peyton had stepped away and Harry had my right hand wrapped in both of his. He was laughing about finally meeting me after all the stories he had heard. I looked at Peyton and he just shrugged. I was on my own. My first thought...Peyton had told this man about me, when he would tell no one else? Out of nowhere, Harry asked me if Peyton and I were going to get married. Out of goddam nowhere.

—The two of you will convert and I will pay for everything.

I looked at Peyton. Just that damn shrug. I had known Harry two minutes and he was planning my marriage.

—You will be my children, the parents of my grandchildren.

Behind Peyton, the old black man was stone-faced, but then he winked at me, or so it seemed. I saw him lean forward and whisper something to Peyton, and Peyton broke into more than a smile, almost an un-Peyton grin. Harry was still holding on to my hand.

How to script the future? It was only a few more years until I figured it out, but I could not have predicted that first day that the only world in New York in which I was actually visibly real was populated by just a few people: Peyton, Harry, the old black man (whose name I can never remember), the ghoul of an accountant, and a very select group of writer friends who Peyton allowed into his inner circle. I think I loved Harry as much as Peyton did, just for that opening question. He was the first outsider who understood and assumed the inevitable conclusion of my life.

Perhaps Harry was right, perhaps he should have been Peyton's real father. I ran a gauntlet that first few minutes, from him announcing my inevitable marriage, to him asking if I had any Jewish relatives, anybody who survived the Holocaust, to him asking if I knew any Fascists in Charleston. Would I like a new watch? I was actually having fun, and I think that Peyton knew I would like Harry once I ignored his opening inquisition.

—Will you read some poems to me? You must let me tell you about my good friend Harry Winston, rest his soul. Will you live with us here in my home?

His home, that strange building? I liked him quickly, but I was not sure he liked me. How could he? He never shut up. I should have realized that he already liked me because he knew that Peyton loved me, and he loved Peyton as a son. But

I thought I might have lost him when he asked me about Anne Frank.

—You read her book, I am sure. You are pretty like her. Sure you are not Jewish? You remind me of her. Sad child, but you are safe here. I have secret rooms here. Peyton will show you how safe we are. The world is not a safe place for Jews, not even here in Jew-cropolis, my word. Jew-cropolis, more Jews here than in Israel, but even here we are never safe. Between me and you, I hate kosher food.

Harry, shut up, I told him. I am not Anne Frank.

—No, no, I know you are not, but she is important. She suffered much, but she was love herself.

Harry, she let herself die.

Harry was quiet, looking down, not at me.

—She was love herself.

Harry, I said, I am not her. They will never kill me. I will fucking kill them, as many of them as I could, I promise you that. Trust me, Harry, I am not love myself.

Out of nowhere, in the middle of a fun conversation, I am telling Harry that his goddess Anne Frank was a victim, and I was never going to be a victim again. I had escaped Charleston and my past. All I had in front of me was Peyton and a future. What cage in my brain had he rattled? If PWR were around, he and I could process this to peace. Peyton and the old black man stood a few feet away, mute but not deaf.

Harry, I'm sorry, but I hated that book. I wanted her to kill somebody. I wanted her to find a goddam gun and kill somebody before they took her away. I'm sorry.

I could see him tremble a little, almost a shudder, and a low mumble.

—Yes, yes, Miss Ellie, I understand. I wish my rage would make me courageous, like you. No, you are not the lost Anne.

Harry, I'm sorry.

Sally Goes To Work

Sally had wanted to work at Windsor ever since she got her job with Gabe Klein. Part of her education was to learn who to trust, who to respect, and Bobby Beaumont was the most frequent citation. The more she worked for Klein, and then the other agents that followed, the more she understood how different Bobby was from most editors. He had complete autonomy. No committee buying decisions, a process that she would endure with the other publishing houses for whom she worked. The trick as an agent had been to study Bobby's prior decisions and try to anticipate what he would like in the future. He could not be pigeonholed by genre, fiction or non-fiction. But everyone agreed that Bobby's books, with the exception of a few notable bestsellers, were quality pieces of writing.

Unlike many other editors, Bobby did not do a lot of social networking. Not a lot of lunches and drinks after work, with their small talk and gossip. Bobby's great domain was *The Party*. Small talk and gossip, even at those for sure, but on a massive scale of impersonal contacts. He seemed to love parties, and few people understood that parties were where he did his rare interviewing and recruitment of new employees, as well as launching new writers. Everyone who worked at Windsor, except for Sully Semken and Bruce Tucker, first met Bobby at a party, not knowing that he was already interested in them, that he had studied their work and absorbed others' opinions about their professional skills. Days later, he would call that person and ask him to come see him. Sally met him at a party, but she was fuzzy about the details. He would tell her, after she was hired, that she did not make a good first impression, but he knew he would see her again at some other party. She would get a second chance.

Bobby was on everyone's A-list of party invitees, and his attendance was always a coup, but more important was to be on *his* party list. In the beginning, his parties were huge, a hundred people filling a giant lounge on the infamous thirteenth floor of the Windsor Building, and you had to get there early because the single elevator to that floor could hold only five people, and the black doorman Mr. Taylor was a rigid gate-keeper. No crowding, and only he was allowed to push the single button. Sally had been there when Mr. Taylor restricted one particular ascension to three people because one of them was Teddy Donahue, a three hundred pound editor whose self-esteem was commensurate with his girth. Donahue complained to Bobby about *the damn embarrassment of it all, as if your man was my keeper*, and Bobby assured him that it would never happen again. Bobby kept his word. Donahue was never invited to another party.

As Windsor became more successful, and Bobby more well known, the Windsor parties became smaller, moving from the lounge to his apartment itself. The guest lists shrunk, their value rose. Sally's second chance was at a party in Bobby's apartment. She was stone cold sober. Her invitation had allowed for her *and a guest,* but she went through her mental list and realized that there was nobody in her life with whom she wanted to share this particular experience. She decided to go alone, making a note to herself as she came to that conclusion: *What the hell is wrong with this picture?*

She had stepped into Bobby's infamous apartment and started seeing her future. At least, her future as she wanted it to be. *I want this,* she thought. And *this* was an apartment of wall to wall, floor to ceiling books, antique furniture, wood floors covered with rugs from India and Persia, an eclectic assortment of styles that should have clashed but instead seemed to have melted into some soft version of wood and cloth beauty. Sally's first vision, however, was not the room itself, but Bobby, who opened the door to greet his guests, offering one hand to lead them in, the other hand to take their coat. She would come to understand that the look that he gave her at that moment, which she took as some sort of personal recognition and intimacy between them, some singular pleasure for him at seeing her, was the same look he gave all his guests. "Sally, thank you for coming." And she glided in.

Unknown to her, the other Windsor people at that party already knew that Bobby was interested in hiring her. They had seen it before, the subtle final test. That night, the test was a simple question about *Stones,* a memoir she had rejected the previous year, a memoir grabbed by the next editor who read it, a memoir about *hard luck and perseverance and redemption through faith and love* that had gone on to be a phenomenal bestseller. Sally had heard the whispers about how she had *let the big one get away.*

She was soon talking to Bruce Tucker, a tall man almost too handsome for the business. Tucker had seen combat in Vietnam, a former life he never discussed. He had swatted down his personal demons just in time to accept Bobby's offer to handle publicity and promotion for Windsor. Introduced to Tucker that night, Sally discreetly looked for a wedding band. Seeing the gold ring, she fell back on her standard defense, *Either gay or married, always the case.* As she stood there with him, they were joined by Sully Semken, the Windsor graphic artist, and Ashley Bancroft, a new Windsor author. The party was in honor of Ashley just being announced as a finalist for the National Book Award.

Sally never realized that it was a set-up, nor did she realize that Bobby was watching his trio surround her. Steps one and two, small talk and gossip, out of the way, Sally was asked if she had any second thoughts about rejecting *Stones.*

"Oh, I wish the house had the money it's made, but, you know as well as I do, these things happen all the time, a book rejected one place becomes a best-seller somewhere else. No big deal, right?"

Ashley had been designated to ask the key question, "But we heard there was something else going on with that book. Any truth to that?"

Sally had looked around at the rest of the party, scanning the room for anybody that looked like a media person, anybody from her own publishing house, pausing to sniff out a hidden agenda in Ashley's question. If she had been in almost any other business, she would have had no qualms about undercutting her competition, but publishing people were too aware of their collective marginal status in American culture. The answer to another's success was to find your own successful book. Sally was a true believer: *You might envy another publishing success, but you did not resent it.*

She thought that her real reasons had been well kept, but Ashley's question itself implied knowledge of the answer. Still, a discreet evasion would be understood, and even respected in some quarters. Sally was leaning toward discretion, but then she saw Bobby cross the room, a tall woman at his side and obviously his escort for the evening. Bobby put his hand on the young woman's waist as he introduced her to a producer for *The Today Show*. Sally wanted him to glance back at her, but his back remained toward her as she finally spoke.

"The book's a lie. At least fifty-percent bullshit. I made some calls. Too many *facts* were fiction. It was still powerful stuff, and I even wondered if it should have been published as a novel instead of a memoir, but a novel would have required better prose than he could write. That was the real problem. It was dishonest non-fiction and crappily written fiction. And I thought the guy was, you get down to it, a con-artist. He wanted everybody to believe something that wasn't true. I don't think the editor who bought it did any checking, or else she chose to ignore the signs. And then, wham, the damn book and phony writer become a cover for *People* magazine, and sales shoot to the top of the World Trade Center. Sooner or later, it will happen again, but the rules will have changed. The next phony will get caught, and the publisher will be seen as a total whore." Her audience leaned back when Sally said *whore*. "Yes, yes, we all publish crap for money. Not ya'll as much as most of us, but you're not immune. Anybody remember *American Killer*, from two years ago? Well-written for sure, but a book so vile that the first publisher, when it finally woke up out of its coma, swallowed the advance money and released the writer to re-sell. I mean, come on…"

"I'll take responsibility for that," Semken interrupted her. "I convinced Bobby that the book would be a hit. And I had a great cover in mind even before we bought it."

Well, who said I would ever work here, Sally told herself, but she did not back down. "Sully, since when did you people ever need a hit. And, please…skull-fucking? A full page describing a man poking out a woman's eyes and fucking her in the empty sockets?…and the chainsaw scenes…" but then she stopped herself. *I sound like an obscene Baptist preacher. And how the hell did I get from that wretched* Stones *book to criticizing these people?*

Ashley nudged Bruce Tucker with her elbow as Sully Semken winked at her. Bruce was blushing, but he was also smiling as Ashley finally said, "Sally's right. The book was shit. I was embarrassed to have it in my apartment. Fact is, I never finished it."

Tucker was more chastised than Semken, but not repentant, "Well, pornographic violence or not, profits from that book paid *your* advance, plus a few other first-timers."

Sally was still not forgiving, "Would you do it again, Sully?"

"Not likely, but, then again, I'm not the guy to ask. I supported its publication, but Bobby made the offer."

"I guess that he saw something that the rest of us missed, eh?" Ashley added. "I mean, after all, even Norman Mailer thought it was good, pornographic or not. Isn't that what he said in *Vanity Fair?*"

Sally remembered that piece, and she was about to disagree with Ashley, but then she realized that the young woman in front of her was not... and she would not be so unkind as to say it out loud... but Ashley was not relevant to her own future. Bruce and Sully were Windsor. Ashley was not. She had one book, but not a career. She was not an Updike or a Doctorow or a Roth or Anne Tyler, writers who had become integral flesh and blood to their publishers. She was not yet a *Windsor writer*. She had potential, but Sally had seen other writers with potential never get past their one good book. But, Sally sighed, *Ashley Bancroft is certainly a trend.* A talented young woman whose persona as well as prose could be marketed. Bobby Beaumont had published more than his share in the past few years.

Sally was hired a month after the party. A year after that, Ashley Bancroft jumped to another publisher for a bigger advance. Windsor had been generous with its second book option offer, but Ashley's agent had found a better deal. Sally understood, but she also understood something about herself: *I do not fucking forgive.*

Sally went to work at Windsor in 1990, the start of a good decade in publishing, especially for Windsor. Every month brought another reason for another party. Windsor books were number one in fiction and non-fiction, hardcover and paperback, the four top spots owned by Bobby Beaumont, all in the same week. It was time for a party. New star writer signed after an auction...time for a party. Windsor titles dominate the lists of award finalists...time for a party. Those parties were also industry galas. Sally swirled with all the other publishing people, contacts initiated or re-confirmed. She had always loved the drama and, in its own way, the glamour. For her, writers and editors, and even agents, were all part of a caste system as glittering as Hollywood, with A-lists and B-lists and even a C-list of stars. The A-list had parallel tracks: writers of commercial bestsellers and writers of *serious* literary merit. A serious literary writer who was also a bestseller...that person was on the A+ list. The publishing parties were unlike the few Hollywood parties that Sally had ever attended. The people at the book party were recognizable only to themselves, and then often not at first glance. On the street, they were all invisible. At the Hollywood parties, *the deal* was paramount, with name-dropping as an art-form in second place. At the publishing parties, *the book* reigned, with rumors about unpublished or soon to be published books a satellite conversation. The best thing about Hollywood parties, in Sally's mind, was that *those people could all be characters in a book.*

Her first day at Windsor, Sally attended her first in-house party, complete with champagne. Bobby had discovered another first-time author whose book he had fallen in love with.

The author was not young, a man in his forties, but obviously overwhelmed by his good fortune. A first novel, a two hundred thousand dollar advance, and to be edited by Bobby Beaumont. All the major Windsor people, Sully Semken and Bruce Tucker and a half dozen other players, along with the *new girl* Sally, were in Bobby's corner office when the author arrived and was ushered in with applause and smiles. It was ten in the morning, and the champagne was chilled. Everyone in the room had read the manuscript before ever meeting the author. Bobby had made the decision halfway through his first reading, and the manuscript had been passed around after that. Everyone at Windsor was excited, and proud. Sally knew the feeling, a brilliant book discovered and shared, prepped, and then presented to the world, a treasure for which they could all taken partial credit, the author's excitement their own, the author's talent validated by their judgment, and they wanted to *love* the author as much as they loved the book. Any book could be publicized, and Bruce Tucker was a master of that, but not every author could be promoted.

Sally had seen versions of the ritual in other houses, but the difference that first morning at Windsor was Beaumont's self-assigned role. His shoes off, Bobby padded softly around his office, introducing the author to each person in the room, and then he faded into the background. He had already had dinner with the author, had the author back to his apartment for drinks, and had formed his own opinion of the author. In his office, he wanted to see how his people reacted. Sally did not stare, but she slanted her attention toward Bobby as discreetly as possible, studying his face as he studied the others. Small talk, sincere praise lavished on the author, some jokes from Sully, witty responses, the author was a funny man, and Sally could sense that Bruce was visualizing this author across from particular media people, on *that* particular show, interviewed by *that* special critic, and Sally herself started to like the author as he described his life before he ever wrote the book, a life that did not imagine a book, but a life of children adored and wife loved, a good man who had gotten lucky and knew it. Sally could sense what Bobby felt. *This author, as well as his book, deserved all our support.*

The book would be a commercial failure; its advance was never earned back. The early reviews glowed, but an insidious review in the *Times*, a review so poisonously personal, written by an established author, claiming that the book was an insult to the reading public, a review so damning that Sally had called the new author and asked, "Did you ever meet this woman before? Sleep with her and dump her? Piss her off?" The author was dazed, and the inexplicable review would stall an invitation to the *Charlie Rose* show, and then NPR moved it back in line, then off. A reverse collapse of dominoes. Bobby had loved the book, but it was a commercial failure. All that was in the future. That morning in Bobby's office, however, everything good was possible.

Sally did not know about the last part of the ritual because it was not included for every first-time author, only those whose books had turned Bobby back into a reader as well as an editor, those who wrote stories that Bobby had never heard before. The first person to read the manuscript after Bobby had been Sully Semken, who was given an image that Bobby wanted on the cover of the future published version of the book. Sully would read the manuscript, understand the image that Bobby wanted, an image that captured the essence of the book, and then he went to work in his own studio, drawing the cover. He had to have it done in time for the in-office party. Only Sully and Bobby knew, so, when the moment happened, the rest of the Windsor people were often as dumbstruck as the author.

On Sally's first day, she watched the author glance around the room and then freeze in mid-stare. She had been lucky. The others had been distracted by something Sully was joking about, but Sally saw the author's face and then followed his eyes toward the shelf behind Bobby's desk.

Bobby's idea, Sully's creation...the cover was wrapped around another Windsor book and turned full face out, the title in bold letters, the author's name below, and clearly visible from the first moment the author had entered the office. Visible but not seen, and then, casually but inevitably, as soon as the author had finally seen the cover, Bobby reached up and took it off the shelf and handed *the book* to him. A woman's slender raised hand, a thin bracelet, holding a blazing sparkler exploding with a thousand shards of light on a gauzy orange and yellow background. Sally almost wept when she saw the author's face as he accepted the emblematic book. The room was silent as everybody else, Sully Semken most intently of all, looked at the author hold the book in his hands, staring at the cover, and they all had the vicarious thrill that he must have had at the first sight of the cover on the shelf, that his book was real. It would be another nine months before the actual book hit the stores, but this was the moment that mattered. It was Bobby's gift to the author for his work. Sally looked at her boss, seeing his pleasure, as he was oblivious to her, a moment between him and the author only, she and the others now only spectators, and she wondered if Bobby ever looked at a woman the same way, because surely this was how someone looked who was in love.

She could have used *that* look as an illustration for that emotion. Others might even agree with her, but then she found a better example. Next to the empty space on the shelf from which the author's book had been removed was a framed black and white photograph. A picture that Sally had seen years before in another book: *The Most Beautiful Women in New York*. She had to step closer to the shelf to study it as closely as she had done when she first saw the book in the past. That first time, she did not know about Bobby Beaumont, but she had been struck by the man's face in that picture at that time. *A face*, her adolescent mind had spontaneously exclaimed, *as beautiful as some of the women in this book. How can a man be that beautiful?* He was in the background, off to the side, most readers' attention directed toward the woman in the center of the frame, and he was merely one of many smaller supporting images. Sally had noticed him in the picture years earlier, a cigarette in his left hand, leaning back in his chair, sitting in the smoky bar, his face focused on the woman sitting across from him, a woman whose back was to the camera, her right hand resting on the table, holding a cigarette whose smoke was drifting toward Bobby. She was the only woman in the book whose face was not seen.

Sally stepped closer to the shelf, peering closer at the photograph, seeing the look that had always been there but which she had to grow up before she could really see, and she realized that no man had ever looked at her the way that Bobby was looking at the woman in that picture, a woman whose own face was hidden.

Everyone else in Bobby's office at that moment was still absorbed in the story of the new author. Sally was in her own story.

Ellie Goes Home

How have I lived here this long? Peyton does not let me into his office until late at night. The spooky accountant still has not spoken to me. I only see Peyton's select writer friends when he is with us. The old black man never seems to be more than twenty feet away from that front door. How can I live here like this forever? Especially now, with Harry dead.

For the first few years he was all I had. He was the only one who had time for me. He was a dirty old man. We both laughed about that, and Peyton had warned me, but he was not worried. Harry had a look when he wanted to tell me a dirty joke, like he had to look all around and over his shoulder to make sure we were alone. And the jokes were always so lame. I knew better, dirtier, and I could make him blush. He would show me his private albums of pictures, old tired plump women with mounds of pubic hair.

—The hair, the hair—he would whisper—you don't get to see that very often, eh?

No, Harry, only when I look in the mirror. And he would blush again. He would tell me about the women in the old vaudeville shows he went to, the bubble dancers at the burlesque, all the women he supposedly went to bed with. I made him a bet that I had had more sex than him.

How many, Harry? How many did you do the deed with? He would snort, look around and whisper.

—More than twenty.

Okay, Harry you win. I'm still in the single digits.

He was lying I was sure, puffing up his numbers. I was lying too. But I soon realized that as much as Peyton had told Harry about me, he had not told him about P&P. I wasn't quite a virgin to Harry, but I was still chaste. Harry was border-line great-grandparent material, and to him I was just one of those modern fast girls coming out of the flower generation. I was Peyton's...girl.

I miss Harry a lot. When Peyton was busy being publisher Peyton, Harry took me to all the nooks and crannies of this city. Peyton warned me about Harry's tendency to exaggerate, and any history of any place as described by Harry was not to be trusted. I told him that made me and Harry a perfect couple. Plus, all three of us were chain smokers.

Harry loved Broadway, and he especially loved musicals. Over and over, how many times we went to see dancing cats and opera phantoms. He could take me backstage and introduce me as his distant niece. He took me to Carnegie Hall and he introduced me to Leonard Bernstein. A swishy Jew—-Harry would whisper to me, as if only he knew about Bernstein's private life. (I always knew a "secret" was coming as soon as he lowered his voice.) I would roll my eyes.

I'm shocked, Harry, so totally shocked. He seems so rugged. Harry missed the joke.

Is that what happens to all of us eventually, we get stuck in some sort of personal time warp, the world changes but we still think we're in the world from thirty...forty years ago? We're all trapped in the fears of our youth? The present and future always judged by our past? (Those are the sorts of questions that PWR liked to talk about.) But, for all his drama, Harry made me wish I had known him in the Thirties and Forties. How glamorous and glittering he made me imagine this city used to be, when he was a young man.

I owe Harry one thing for sure. He taught me to not be afraid of this place. Within a few months I could go anywhere here I wanted, knew all the subway routes, where it was easiest to get a taxi, which movie theatres had clean seats, where to shop for groceries. (God forgive me, I had learned to cook in my ten-year exile, and Peyton says he loves everything I fix. He is a better actor than me sometimes. I had tried cooking for PWR, but he soon disabused me of the notion that I was Julia Child.) Best of all, Harry showed me the art museums and the big public library. I never ran out of things to see when I was alone. I would tell Harry or Peyton about where I had gone during the day and they would just watch as I re-created the people and voices. I learned to ignore Harry's over-reaction to me telling him about some of the places I had gone to, but I knew that when Peyton did one of his eyebrow-arching head tilted down looks...I should not go back there.

As much as Harry made me brave about this city, I could never tell him that I still did not like it. Most of all, the more I am here, the more I know that Peyton is not totally mine. This city takes him away from me. I could hate this place if it were not so wonderful.

I owe Harry one more thing. He saved me and Peyton. Saved...us. He had the answer to my only question. Why wouldn't Peyton marry me? I had gotten used to being invisible, but sometimes I wanted to scream at Peyton. In the middle of being happy, perfectly happy, I wanted more. He had taken me to the Guggenheim on one of those perfect Spring Sunday afternoons. I did not tell him that I had already been by myself months earlier. He liked being my guide, introducing me to newness in the world, and I wanted him to think I was entering a strange world with him holding on to my arm. So we walked the spiral to the top. He knew a lot, but I had already made up my mind about the art. Truth is, modern art bores me. The art on display bored me. I tried to fake interest, but he caught me. But it was okay. He did too. He preferred the Renaissance and up to the twentieth century. Me too. But we have to give it a chance, he told me, not have closed minds. Absolutely, I told him, and I love this building. The art? I stuck out my tongue. In that giant round Wright house he reached over and pulled me to him and kissed me. How could I not love him even more at that moment. Both of us, not just me, became invisible. But then the thing happened, the thing that PWR always told me about, the thing that destroys me, the thing...the moment... when I want more. And we almost ran down the spiral, knowing where we were headed, back to his apartment, back to a bed that we would destroy...again. I wanted to scream because I was so happy. I wanted to scream because I was miserable.

Harry explained it. We were sitting on a bench in his own private playground inside his building. The next day. He had never seen one of my patented meltdowns, and I was giving him everything I had repressed since I had moved to his city. I told him about the Guggenheim from the day before, told him how I had almost asked Peyton the *When are we going to...?* question. But I had stopped myself because I was afraid of the answer. And for one moment I had leaned against the wall of the spiral walkway and wondered if it would hurt if I jumped from that spot and fell through circles of art that I hated. I yelled at Harry that I was going to be my own fucking Jackson Pollock creation, splattering myself on the floor and then they could hang me on a wall and people could pay money to see what I really was down deep, a collision between flesh and blood and concrete, scraped up and spread on canvas with a spackle. I would create the real me. Harry was weeping as I paced around him, my arms flailing like a jerky string puppet. I could not stop to help him. I was spewing my life out, including my life with Peter and Paul, how Peyton got his scar, all the past that Peyton had denied to Harry. I felt like I had been bitten by a snake and my life inside me was venom that had to be sucked and spit out. (I had done that to PWR a lot, but I had only done it once with Peyton.) Poor Harry. I kneeled down in front of him and began slapping his knees, demanding that he listen to me. I wanted him to share my nightmare. I don't understand, Harry, how this can be. I thought that when his father died then Peyton and I would finally be together again forever. The man is dead, Harry. I saw him put in the ground. I believe in ghosts, but sooner or later, his father's ghost has to go away, doesn't he? Harry, how do you kill a ghost?

And then I was empty. No secrets left, my abominations shared with an old Jewish man who was crying in front of me. Children were playing on the swings a hundred feet away from us. Peyton was in his office twenty-two stories above us. I got off my knees and sat beside Harry, feeling his shoulders tremble next to me as I pressed against him, holding his hand. All I could think of was how I wished I had never said those bad things about Anne Frank. How long? Minutes or an hour, neither of us spoke again, and then Harry put my life back together. He told me a story

—-His father was a good man, Ellie. I met him a few weeks before he died. Right before our Peyton created the books named after me. Me and his father were proud of him, like we were both his father. I had already heard some stories about you from Peyton, and his father did not add or subtract, but I could tell that he knew you too. He said that he had been taking care of you for a long time. That was news to Peyton for sure. But the thing is, Ellie, Peyton's father and him both agreed. Nothing could be done for you and Peyton until his mother passed. She was sick. The father was well. Neither man would hurt her, son or husband. See, Ellie, it was never the father. It was always the mother. She had never known about you. Soon enough she would be gone, they agreed, but it was Mr. Beaumont who went first.

Harry is gone. My world here is smaller. But I understand it better. I told PWR that I was willing to wait for Peyton to come back for me. And he did. We are here now together. Anything, all things, are possible. Perhaps I will be redeemed in the end. Like a piano in storage, dusted off, tuned up, strings replaced... someday. But I know the sins for which I will never be forgiven. Right at the top of the list will be me not paying attention to Harry as he finished telling me about Peyton's mother. I was forgiving Peyton when Harry said something about being sad he would never see me and Peyton get married. I was accepting another postponement. All things were still possible.

Harry was dying. He was trying to tell me, but I was not listening. In Ellie world, my story was more important than his. I never got a chance to apologize. All I know for now is what Peyton and I will name our first son.

I'm sorry, Harry, truly sorry.

The Death of History

Sally knew that Bobby was dying, but neither would say it. In her own office, she would sometimes sit and stare at the wall, berating herself for not confronting him and making him share it with her. But she had known him long enough, as had Sully and Bruce, and the others who had been at Windsor longer than her, to understand that Bobby made the rules. Even after many years with him, she was always intrigued when Sully or Bruce told her how Bobby had changed a few weeks after she was hired, that the Bobby they knew for the previous ten years was not the Bobby she had a chance to know.

When she asked about the difference, Sully had said, "He was happier, seemed to me, laughed more."

Bruce explained it more precisely, "He seemed to lose interest in a lot of things around when you were hired. He used to have opinions about everything, thoughtful ideas about more than books, but he got more cynical and indifferent. And the odd thing is that the last ten years have been our best. And you deserve a lot of the credit for that too. More titles in print, more sales, more awards, and the backlist is starting to pay off too.

But he seems to have enjoyed this decade less than when we were still getting kicked around by Random and Scribner's and the others. He still works as hard as ever, and his social life is a lot more public than before, but you can see it sometimes, that blank look." Bruce had told her all this, knowing how she felt about Bobby. "You should have known him in the old days. You just showed up too late."

Showed up too late? Sally wondered if Bruce meant that she would have had a better chance with Bobby if she had gone to work for him sooner. Worse, she wondered if she was any part of the reason he changed. But she quickly bounced back. *This is very odd, how Bruce sees him. His description of Bobby in the past is how he always was around me since I have known him. Until the Germans came, Bobby seemed to enjoy having me around. Now he walks around muttering about conversations with Harry Windsor.*

"Bruce, have you ever wondered why Bobby has never gotten married, or at least kept the same woman in his life for longer than a few months?"

"All I know is what he told me a long time ago…that he wanted what…"

Sally stopped him, knowing how the line would end because she had also heard it from Bobby, heard it even if the question was only hinted at, heard it sober and drunk, heard it in his office late in the afternoon as they watched the sun disappear, heard it at a party when he had a drink in each hand, one for him and one for his date flavor of the month, as Sally stood alone and too obviously smitten by her boss, "He wants what his parents had," she told Bruce.

Tucker nodded, but then reminded her, "You know, you're the only one of us who ever met his mother. That should tell you something about how Bobby feels about you."

"Do you know *why* he took me to Charleston, Bruce? How pathetic I am?"

"Sally, why is it that your self-esteem goes *down* when you're sober, unlike most people, who begin to wallow when they drink too much?"

Sally ignored him. "He wanted his mother to meet the woman he was going to marry." Bruce's expression was worth the humiliation she knew she was about to inflict on herself. "She was dying, and Bobby asked me to go with him and be his *fiancé*, the future mother of his children, her grandchildren, so that his mother could rest in peace. He literally asked me, *Do you think you can act like you are in love with me?* You can imagine what I *wanted* to say to him, about why the hell he thought I would have to act, but I went along with him and we spent an hour in love in front of his mother in this Tara place back in Charleston. *That's* how pathetic I am."

She did not tell Bruce everything about that hour. *Christ, I had the easy part. I was in love with him. But for that hour I actually thought he was in love with me, that's how good of an actor he was. His mother must have thought we were some confederate Romeo and Juliet, and I knew that Bobby asked me there because I didn't have to fake southern, and southern was important to his mother. God, I would look him in the face as he spoke to me, and I would have sworn that he was in love with me.*

Bobby's mother outlived his father by a decade, surprising every Beaumont relative in Charleston, but she died a few weeks after meeting Sally. Leaving after the first visit, Bobby had told her to expect another trip soon. It was in the time between when Sally met his mother and the time she went to his mother's funeral that Sally went to bed with Bobby for the only time in her life.

The Beaumont plot in St. Phillips Cemetery was close enough to the bones of John C. Calhoun to satisfy all the friends and relatives whose sense of history demanded eternal proximity to the Great Man himself. Even Sally, whose cynicism about all things southern was usually a solid defense against historical seduction, even she was impressed. Of course, as she explained later, *cool dry weather helped.*

The day was atypical for early September in Charleston. Sunny, but mild, and just enough breeze to make the air almost cool. The service at St. Phillips had been high Episcopalian, with a choir of pure voices, and the procession to the cemetery had almost a hundred cars. Sally sat with Bobby in the front limousine, commenting on the large outpouring of grief and condolences, but he had shrugged and said, "You should have seen my father's funeral."

At the graveside services, Bobby told the black-clad mourners, *In my Father's house are many mansions,* and Sally wondered if he believed it. Shaded by an expansive green tent, the mourners focused on the last Beaumont while Sally discreetly looked at them. *Is she here,* she wondered, *the woman that Bobby loved and left behind as he went north twenty years ago?* That was the sum of her knowledge about Bobby's past love. He said he had been in love once, but he left her in Charleston. He had had one drink too many, Sally had asked a direct question, but all she got was one sentence. The door shut.

She studied faces, looked for a woman by herself who would reveal herself by how she looked at her former lover. But everyone looked too old. Most were of the mother's generation, and it occurred to Sally that in the two visits she had made to Charleston with Bobby, he had never introduced her to any friends of his.

The first time, to convince his mother that he was indeed soon to marry a proper southern girl, it was just a one-day trip and there was no time for social reunions. Sally smiled at that memory...his mother remarking *you seem so young for Bobby, dear*...and Sally had thanked her, while thinking, *I haven't felt young since I turned thirty.*

The second visit lasted three days, and Sally thought she was introduced to every gentrified heir in Charleston, but not one of them was introduced as Bobby's "friend." The last opportunity had been at the reception back at the Beaumont mansion after the funeral. Bobby had stood just inside the front door and welcomed each of the consolers, and she, fortified by a single glass of wine, had stood beside him for the first hour, forgetting names as soon as she was herself introduced over and over again as *my friend from Savannah*. No mention was made of living in New York City. Charleston would nod at Savannah, but the response to New York would have been an arched and quizzical eyebrow.

Tired of role-playing, Sally had excused herself from the line and wandered through the house, marveling at how long and wide the hallways were, how red the carpet, pausing in front of the infamous Lankford Beaumont portrait. She found her way to Forrest Beaumont's study, where father and son had sorted out various rites of passage, and she would have stayed there longer, it being the quietest room in the house, but an elderly black maid had appeared, as if out of the curtains themselves, and informed her that *Mr. Beaumont requests that you witness his presentation.*

Bobby's *presentation* was a gift to Charleston. The Beaumont mansion was to be given to the Charleston Historical Society as a living museum, the repository of his father's papers, and such gift was to be maintained by a properly funded foundation in the Beaumont name. Charleston was properly impressed, acknowledged by sincere applause and vigorous head-shaking, but Sally wondered if anybody else had known, as she immediately did when Bobby finished his presentation, the true meaning of his gesture.

Bobby Beaumont was never coming home.

Ellie Solves a Puzzle

Did you expect this? Sweet doctor, you and me in session again. But here you are, my old audience, my new audience. Even though I should have killed you when I figured it out. (Yes, I am joking.) Were you surprised to hear my voice? With Harry turned to burnt toast, who else could be my friend? But you and I both know that we are not friends. Why is it that I forgive you? Down deep, I don't even think I forgive Peyton for making me wait so long. And I sure as hell cannot forgive myself for the pain I have inflicted on others (Yes, you are on that list too.) But I forgive you for a simple reason. I called you and demanded that you tell me if you knew Peyton's father. It had been two years, and the first thing you hear from me is a banshee voice demanding the truth. You answered immediately, in that calm Carolina voice. You were honest. You told me the truth. How could I not forgive you?

You had been hired by Peyton's father to...treat?...me. ("Treat me"...why is that funny to me?) All expenses paid. The book idea was serious, but abandoned. Peyton's father had gotten me all those jobs in the big houses in his world. For me? Like fuck, it was for me. You didn't deny the obvious...him paying you, keeping me employed...I was never out of the old man's sight, was I? The man in the white suit had his eye on me all that time, and you were his paid rat. I should hate you, and I sure as hell should not forgive you. But I do. You said that you had stopped being paid by him as soon as we went to lunch that first time. But you still talked to him, didn't you? And you knew that he had told Peyton about caring for me, but he did not tell him about you, did he? How does it feel to be invisible, PWR? Welcome to my world. Thing is, Peyton told me the truth too. Why is it that the people I care about will actually be honest with me when I press them, but I never can be honest with them. Peyton knew his father was watching out for me, but you never existed.

Why is it so hard for me to cry? I can scream when the sun goes behind a cloud, but I cannot cry. I wanted to cry as Peyton told me about the agreement between him and his father, all about dumb Dora me. I wanted to cry because Peyton was crying, apologizing for staying away from me, but admitting that he was never sure if I was the real single ONE for him, crying as he talked about how he never found anyone else ever like me, but he stayed away anyway. Poor Peyton, I wanted to tell him, I could have told you that. There will never be anyone to replace me. Poor Peyton. It was so obvious listening to him try to explain why we were separated for ten years. So obvious why. So obvious he adored me. And I was willing to wait forever, even if it meant until the last day of time, and we only had that one day to be truly one. We were sitting on the same bench where Harry and I had sat weeks earlier, and the same children (surely?) were playing on the same swings. A boy and a girl, and

I told Peyton to watch them. They were us.

Deja vu all over again, PWR, me talking to you about me and Peyton? Sorry, I guess you got on the train and can't get off either. Here's a secret I won't tell you. As soon as I heard your voice I felt safe again. I was back in Charleston. I heard your voice, and I wanted to cry. But I couldn't cry, not even as I listened to you cry. And, yes, I will come see you again. And, yes, thank you for asking if I still played the piano. Almost everyday, but I did not tell you where. I did not tell you about the piano in Peyton's apartment. Please do not cry in front of me. My enormous talent, right? I make men cry.

Stephen Malloy

Bobby had not seen Stephen Malloy in a decade, but he always saw his name on a bestseller list. When Sally had told him that Malloy wanted to see him, Bobby was perplexed, but on his scale of questions to be answered before he died, the re-emergence of Malloy was not anywhere near the top. Still, as he waited for Malloy to arrive, he gradually elevated his first bestselling novelist into the *Was all this inevitable?* category.

"Mr. Malloy's here," Sally announced, and then she left the two men alone in Bobby's office. Before she left, however, she tried to read body language. As Bobby walked across his office and extended his hand, and Malloy took his first tentative step back into the scene of his first success, Sally knew that Bobby was utterly relaxed, while Malloy, even in his thousand dollar suit and with his hundred dollar haircut, was a collapsing house.

Small talk, always the small talk first, and Malloy slowly thawed in the presence of Bobby's genuine affection. He knew all about the Germans capturing Windsor, the move to Park Avenue, the demolition of the Windsor Building, but he had not known about Bobby's own decline, a decline no longer hidden.

Bobby's first sight of Malloy had erased all the past disappointments, all the gossip about how Malloy had supposedly spoken harshly of his first editor. They were the same age, and each was responsible for the early success of the other, and each was dealing with the loss of the most important thing in his life. Bobby noticed the thin manuscript right away, but he let Malloy initiate the request.

"You look good, Steve," he said after awhile, a courtesy.

Malloy, who already knew about Bobby's heart problems from a few years earlier, hesitated before answering, "Are you okay, I mean, other than all the German intrigue? The move, all that?"

Bobby was looking at a desperate man, he knew that, a man who used to be a very good friend, a desperate man who wanted a favor from a dying man. Why not tell the truth?

"Well, other than the fact that I find myself talking to Harry Windsor too often lately, and I have lung cancer that seems to be spreading, I am fine. My doctor is convinced that I have got less than a year. Well, he actually told me that a year ago. He thought I could extend it with some treatment, but the news came at an odd time in my life. The Germans, of course, and a personal loss a few years ago that somehow affects me more now than then, someone close to me, so I decided to let go."

"Just like that? Let go?" Malloy said, slumping deeper into the couch in front of Bobby's desk, previously aware of bad news about his former friend, but not *this* bad. And *a personal loss?* Then, the flashback. He remembered a dinner at the Kiosk restaurant, an evening to celebrate his first book's contract signing, almost twenty years ago, Bobby eating his hamburger almost raw, expensive vodka re-filled over and over, two friends who had the world of print by the tail...the moment when he knew Bobby Beaumont was in love. That phrase...*personal loss*... Stephen Malloy was beginning to understand.

They had been in the corner booth, discussing the progress of Malloy's first novel, still being revised. He had his back toward the door, and he had seen Bobby's attention shift from him to somebody who was approaching behind him. Bobby's face had softened and his eyes had opened wider, a look that Malloy had never seen, and, without taking his eyes off the person approaching, Bobby leaned forward and whispered to Malloy, "I want you to meet someone nobody else knows about, my secret." Malloy had turned slowly, but once his own eyes saw her he did not move. She was wearing white, a form-fitting dress and seemingly sheer, but perhaps it was his imagination, or the vodka, at that moment. A small red purse in one of her hands, a cigarette in the other, and, as she looked toward the darkened booth, Malloy had realized that she did not see him, only the person behind him. A week later he and Bobby were together again, with Sully Semken with them at the Kiosk. The woman came back. Sully had his camera and sat out of sight. Bobby had told him that they needed one last picture for *The Most Beautiful Women in New York.*

"Just let go?" Malloy repeated.

Bobby shrugged.

"The loss? Was it someone I know?"

Bobby stared at him, took a cigarette out of a silver case, but then put it back. "The great irony, and, believe me, irony seems to be wearing out its welcome in my life, the great irony, Steve, is that you are one of the few people who does…*did*…know her. And if I had been sober that night, she and I would have kept our secret, even from you."

"That woman you introduced me to, back in…hell, a long time ago. I wish I could remember her name."

"Would not matter if you did," Bobby said, "We never used her real name when we were around other people in the city."

"She's dead?"

"Yes, she is dead."

Malloy hesitated again, not knowing what to say, but he sensed that his mission to Beaumont was shifting from him being a supplicant to him being a friend again. The two men lapsed into small talk, again circling around Malloy's original purpose. Bobby talked about his plans for a post-Windsor life, his temporary home at the Plaza, his new apartment that nobody had seen yet, his plan to go to Europe on the Queen Mary II, a leisurely ocean voyage to embark the morning of the German demolition, salt air rest, *looking for icebergs* he joked. Malloy finally realized that Bobby was merely waiting for him to speak about his original purpose in coming.

"I have a memoir I want you to consider publishing," Malloy said, exhaling, nervous again, knowing that if Bobby was not interested…*and who could blame him?*… well, if Bobby was not interested, some sort of symmetry that he had imagined for the past month would have been proven an illusion. "About my son and me, our last year together. It's my secret, this story."

Bobby spoke too quickly, a reflex that he instantly regretted because, absorbed in his own drama, the meaning of Malloy's request had not yet registered with him, "You have a publisher, Steve, a good one, and they have been very fair to you. Do you not think…" and then the enormity of Malloy's request dawned on him. "Your baby, I mean, the child you and your wife had when I first met you, right before your book came out? Oh, god, Steve, I am so sorry. I have been so self-absorbed this past year that I did not know…" He stopped because he realized that he really did not know anything, he just assumed the worst.

"I want you as the editor for this one book," Malloy said, lifting the manila envelope off the couch next to him and handing it across to Bobby. "It would mean a lot to me. Fact is, I'm just afraid you won't like it."

"Steve, I am not doing anything for Windsor anymore. No more books, but I am sure the new people would love to have this. Or, I can give it to Sally. Her new house would be perfect for it."

"You haven't read it, Bobby. You don't know anything about it. It might be worthless." Malloy was getting agitated. "Goddam it, Bobby, I know that you don't owe me anything, not after what I did, but please don't make me beg. Please, this means a lot to me. Just read it, please, and tell me if it's any good. I want him to be remembered, that's all, but only if it's worth reading."

Bobby left his chair behind the desk and came around to sit on the old couch with Malloy. It was six o'clock, and the rest of the Windsor people were leaving the building, all except Sally. Malloy was almost trembling, his composure gone, his grief exposed.

"Will you wait with me," Bobby said, taking the manuscript out of its envelope. "We can talk as soon as I finish it."

Malloy nodded, sniffling, and mumbled, "Of course." Smiling, "Just like the first time you read my stuff, remember? We sat in this office and you read all 200 pages while I waited."

Bobby smiled. "It was a wonderful story. I felt lucky to have it."

Malloy stood and walked over to the windows, not wanting to be sitting close enough to actually see Bobby's expression as he read. Traffic below was thinning out, and the taxis were yellow blurs whenever a green light flashed.

I was a good writer once, in the beginning, but the more books I sold the less I cared about words. Books were easy, plots were everywhere, prose came out of a faucet, and I was a success. Not the most successful writer, but enough to be envied. Airport bookstores loved me. I told myself that I would eventually write a really great book. I wasn't sure if it would be fiction or fact, but the book would become the one book that was essential reading for that one year, and I would be respected as well as envied. That book would be my last book. I often told my son about that magical final book, as part of a bedtime story I made up for him. I know, you do not believe me, about the bedtime story, but I can show you a crayon note from him, written when he was five, waxy mis-spelled words, telling me to hurry and write that "finl" book so I could read it to him. I think he believed me when I told him it was a magic book, all about words that had the power to cure the sick and raise the dead, words that would wrap around small children and protect them from wolves at the door. I was glib, for sure, stealing the language of fairy tales, but perhaps, I thought as time passed, my final book was itself a fairy tale. Once upon a time, I would begin, there was a boy named Bobby…

I was a good writer once, never at a loss for words, always finding the right ones, too often more than I needed. Yes, I was good in the beginning, but not good enough at the end to protect Bobby from the wolves.

Sitting in her office, Sally waited for the meeting between Bobby and Malloy to end, but an hour passed, then two, and she wondered if they might have left without her knowing. She went to Bobby's office and knocked lightly. With no response, she opened the door slowly, smelling cigarette smoke even before she saw it. The two men were drinking, and smoking thin Cuban cigars, a contraband gift from Malloy to Bobby.

"I'm about to leave for the night," she said. "Would you guys like me to order some dinner delivered up here?"

Both men looked at her like she was the funniest woman in America.

"Or perhaps a haz-mat team to fumigate this place?"

That convinced them that she was, indeed, the funniest woman in America.

"Sally, Sally...come in," Bobby said. "It is after six o'clock. Join us. Steve and I are the two most wonderful and brilliant men you will ever meet."

"Princes..." Malloy slurred, pointing at himself and Bobby, "...goddam princes."

Sally felt an emotion she had not felt in a long time. She wanted to cry, not from sadness or depression, but cry because she had not seen Bobby this happy in years. Unabashedly, peacefully, all was right with the world happy. And if Stephen Malloy was responsible for that happiness, then he was, in her view, indeed, a prince.

"Order dinner for three, Sally. Stay with us. Pretend it is midnight, and you have to be our designated driver," Bobby said. "I want you to get to know Steve. I am going to edit his book, and you are going to publish it. We will all be famous."

Sally looked over at Malloy. If *happy melancholy* could exist, he was its personification. "Okay, it's a deal," she said. "But no more drinking, and nobody leaves this building until I understand what the hell you're talking about."

Bobby spoke to Malloy, "I told you. This is the woman who will make it all happen. If the Germans had been smart, they would have figured out a way to keep her, make her the new Windsor chief, but…their loss." Turning back to her, "Right? Their loss?"

When she went home that night, Sally was still sober. She had made sure that Bobby was in his apartment and also arranged for a town-car to take Malloy back to his hotel. She stayed up for another two hours reading Malloy's manuscript. Bobby had been right. It was a precise and spare memoir about a young man dying of leukemia, his father's grief and reconciliation, but it did not really need an editor. The prose was exquisite. It would have been published by any other house that read it, but Malloy had gotten what he wanted, Bobby Beaumont's collaboration, Bobby's name on the acknowledgement page, Bobby's blessing and validation. Sally imagined what would be on the dedication page as well: *For Bobby*

Ellie Tries to Explain

Put this on that list of questions I want you to answer. Why do I feel safe with you, but I only feel...calm...with Peyton? You have never seen me at peace, have you? And so it always comes back to the first question. You use the name I want, the same name that Peyton gave me, but I do not think you know that me. So the new question is...does Peyton know the Ellie that you know? Make sense? I know I am the same person, but I feel different around you, different than I do with Peyton. Trust me, sweet pea (yes, good mood, insert laugh here) you are the only other person I have ever known that I cared enough about to actually want to understand. (So, does this mean that I am not really a narcissist, like the other doctors said I was? I thought that was a bit harsh of them, treating poor abused me like I was a villain. The fuck-holes. Especially the one who fucked me.)

From the first day, Peyton made me calm. You making me feel safe took years. Gold star to you for your patience. Peyton got his reward the first day...me. My adolescent and ravaged heart, served up in that silly kiss on paper. Your reward? Oh, hell, PWR, you tell me. My brain? You want that time bomb? I give it to you on a platter. Write your damn book. I'll write mine. Peyton can write his. We'll all be rich and famous authors. You want my soul? Deal done. I think I read about that in a book somewhere, selling your soul. But I would give you mine free, no strings. Wait, wait, I hear violins. (Gag)

I wish you could see me and Peyton in the calmest center of the universe. How many nights have we spent there? His apartment in Harry's building, or in my secret apartment down the hall from him. His office is my second favorite place, but even when we are alone there I can feel the vibes left over from all the people who came and went during the day. (Especially the always goddam attractive woman editor who works in the other office.) His office is messy and the space is shared with others. His apartment is our world. It's like living in the oldest library in the world, thousands of books stacked floor to ceiling on shelves that were probably built by the same guys who built Noah's boat, that's how old they look, some of them with leaded glass doors, but all the books arranged personally by Peyton, his own secret system that he learned back in Charleston. Two giant rooms of books, thousands of books, and a long table against one wall, topped by neatly arranged stacks of manuscripts. No street noise, no music...hell, no neighbors...absolutely quiet. And we read. Poor Peyton usually has a manuscript a night to at least start. In the beginning, I would browse his shelves and choose anything I wanted. And those were the calmest moments of my life, PWR, when neither of us spoke, but we sat close enough to be able to reach out and touch the other, without taking our eyes off the pages in front of us. That was some sort of perfect equilibrium, us in separate stories but still attached. The only time we ever went wrong was when he asked me to read some of the same manuscript he was reading. Everyone in publishing knows that Peyton does NOT ask for a second opinion, does not need anyone to validate his own judgment. (Sort of like you, PWR, in how you diagnose?) But he asked me. And he would listen to me. And then he would do whatever he was going to do anyway. And he was almost always right. He would listen to me respond to a chapter and then ask me questions. But the best part was when he talked to me about his own responses. As much as I could joke about being jealous of his assistant editors, the revolving door brainy beauties who fluttered around his office, it was when he told me that he "loved" a book...the excitement in his voice, the energy in his hands, and always the final proof...when he would read passages aloud to me...I could be jealous of that love. Sometimes he would invite a writer to his apartment to go through the editing together, side by side at that long table which had been cleared of all other manuscripts, leaving the two stack of pages in the honored center position, two copies of the same manuscript, and they would turn the same page of the same story at the same time. I only saw it once, that process, with the writer who would become our singular personal and mutual friend. They would bicker about words, and I would serve them pineapple juice (one of the myths of the Peyton experience with writers, but true.) I was always puzzled by the fact that Peyton had people who idolized him, but he had almost no friends. That writer, that first-time writer was a true friend, but then he went away and Peyton seemed lost for months. No other writer filled that void.

And there it is, PWR, the calm I feel with Peyton. The eye of the hurricane? You figure it out. Last clue? For as long as Peyton and I slept together, I never had a nightmare.

You want me to come see you? And you seemed surprised when I said I would? You are so so professional, Doctor PWR. You insisted that I tell Peyton, so there would be no misunderstanding. Of course, of course, I said, we would not want him to misunderstand anything. I thought you knew me, your version of me, better. Of course I am not going to tell him. You and he are different planets. But if it makes you feel better, dear PWR, you can assume that he knows all about us. Fair is fair, you know all about Peyton and me. He should know about me and PWR, right? You are a very sweet man. But I thought you understood me better than the others. Me and you have nothing to do with Peyton and me. Nobody exists in the same world with me and Peyton. (PWR, I'm sorry.) I'll come see you. I actually look forward to it. Correction: you are not a planet. Peyton and I are a single planet. You are a moon but only I know you are there. You revolve around us. Wait, better. You are a planet, but Peyton and I are the sun. But you are my favorite planet, my earth.

I still do not like this city although I love it more and more. I know a thousand places here, but there are always more. My days are almost always free. I am my own escort. I have gotten used to the crowds on the sidewalks and the subways. Sometimes I can melt into some sort of rhythm here, moving at the pace and in the mood of everyone around me. But some images still overwhelm me. Without knowing it, I can be walking on a crowded sidewalk but going up at the same time, so that when I reach a certain point I am higher than the people walking up toward me. From seeing only the backs of the people in front of me, I am lifted up, like being in an ocean wave, and suddenly there are waves of people packed together and moving as one body up toward me. A wave of people? A something else? But it takes my breath away. Dorothy in Oz, not in Kansas anymore, that's me.

I've learned an important skill, PWR. I know how to judge the speed of a taxi. And I have learned to shut out the noise. Have you ever been here? You must have been, right? I will ask you when I see you. But this noise barrier skill of mine... that's a lifesaver. Another skill? As you know, I am shit for remembering names, but I think I cannot forget a face. I see somebody on the street, somebody who makes eye contact with me for a second and then keeps going. But for that second, I know, I was not invisible to that person. And then a month later I will see that same person and even though he might not make eye contact with me this time I do remember his face. And I can remember what he was wearing a month ago. Thing is, I probably recognize hundreds of people I do not know but cannot forget. (Put that on one of your magic tapes and explain to me later...Laugh track inserted.)

My favorite place here, other than Peyton's apartment? The park. Peyton and I go there at least once a week, and it is the closest I can get to forgetting where I am. His apartment is a new place, a unique place, but the park reminds me of WPG back in Charleston. The same feeling. Instead of hundreds, like in WPG, there are thousands in the park here on any day. A zoo with sad animals, carriages circling around outside and sometimes through the park (Yes, I have ridden them, sometimes by myself.) Peyton and I both salute that statue of that damn Yankee general right there at the entrance. We are traitors for sure. Have you ever heard of the Plaza Hotel? It's right there next to the park and sometimes Peyton will surprise me and have a room reserved so that if the proverbial urge ever strikes us all we have to do is walk a block. There is a giant pond in the park, and when I go there by myself that is where I sit. I watch children play with their toy boats in the water. (But I think I am beginning to hate pigeons.) Statues in the park. Alice in the park. Mad Hatters in the park. Mad me too. I never read that book. I should, I know, but I know the song. One pill makes me large. One pill makes me small. (Agenda for me and you…my pills. I have been cutting down. I think I can cut them out soon.) Some days, when my blood is flowing good, I can walk and walk through the park and then do it over. You will be surprised by how much weight I have lost since I moved here. But I am still beautiful.

Sometimes I think about you as I wander around this city by myself. Some things I think to myself…PWR should be here now to see this too. The first time I ever really thought about you was in the first year. I was by myself and I discovered a stage near the docks. Well, hardly discovered since I just followed the crowd that was going there. This was before I had gotten comfortable in crowds here, so I was trying to not let anybody actually touch me, bump into me, so I had to go where the wave was taking me. Was it June? I think it was a warm June night. A band was playing, some folky band I thought, but it was a story band. The songs were stories. To this day I cannot remember the name of the lead singer, but I remember his voice even though it was not like really a good voice, but I remember it anyway. You? Where do you fit in, PWR? One song about a father being tangled up like a puppet in strings held by his daughter. I thought of you. Right out of nowhere I wished you were there to hear that song. I thought of you as a father to your daughters (all grown up now). How you talked about your daughters was the first chink in my armor, Doctor PWR. You talking about them made me like you for the first time. You slipped through the shell I lived in. I need to remember the lines. I'll find a copy of that song and bring with me back to Charleston. I want you to hear about how the little girl grows up into a fine work of art.

I remember now. I remember the singer's name. How could I forget! It was Harry...Harry something. A Harry, like Harry Windsor. But he died. I remember reading about it in the newspaper. He was a young man and he died while driving somewhere. Just dropped dead. But he was young, I know that. That night near the water, that was his last concert in the city, and I was there. So were you.

Did you ever notice something about me that Peyton saw right away, because he does the same thing. He takes a single word or concept and then he starts to wonder about all the possible meanings and uses of that word. It only takes a few words to create a universe...he said that to me. He said it to me the very first day we met. I was scared to death of him. He caught me stealing. Like a smart criminal, I refused to talk in the beginning. He waited, explained how the universe of words worked, and waited again. How could I not talk to him after that?

And I do the same now. See more meaning to life than what most people see. I listened to that song that night in the city and I thought of you and your daughters, and then I saw the other meanings too. I thought of you and me, how I was the daughter of the song and you were waiting for me to take shape from a jumble of parts. To find the grace and form of a fine work of art? Something like that? Words like that? PWR, I'm sorry. I'm sorry you got tangled up in me. And I'm sorry that singer died. I would like to see him again. Harry...Harry something.

Sally's Critique

"The author is dead!! The goddam author is dead? Did you perhaps stop to think that *that* bit of information might just be a little important to me?"

Sally was not having a good morning. She had finished her second reading of the pages and had asked Bobby when she could meet the author so they could go over her notes. She did not tell him that what she really wanted was to meet the woman and ask her about Bobby. The tall German had just left Bobby's office, so he was not in a good mood either.

"Sally, the author is not the book. You know that. You do not need the author for this book."

"Then why the hell did you tell me...something I recall as... *the writer will be glad to work with you*...or some shit like that?"

"She is gone, Sally. Perhaps I was a bit distracted when I gave you those pages. Dead a long time. I received the material from a lawyer representing her husband, a man named Peter Stone. She had told him to wait a year, and then send it to me. I had known her, but lost contact. The lawyer sent the material and an affidavit, assigning ownership over to me. Excuse me, I was distracted. I had not seen her in a long time."

Sally inhaled a barrel of air and was about to use it to vent her displeasure. She knew that Bobby was lying, but she then realized that he was having trouble breathing. It was happening more often in the past few months.

"Okay, forget this for now. You need to go rest. You need to go to your apartment and lay down, right now. And you better not be having a heart attack, or I will kill you. Are you? Are you feeling any pain? Any tightness?"

Beaumont had dark bags under his eyes, but he smiled, "Sorry, I am just tired. Only that. Nothing dramatic. But you are right. I should rest for awhile. The only problem with going downstairs…"pausing noticeably, "…is that I find myself talking to Harry Windsor more and more when I get there."

Sally ignored his comment about talking to a dead man and walked around his desk to kneel next to him so she could take his wrist and check his pulse. Then she stood up and stared down at him.

"You're forgiven," she said, and he puffed out a weak laugh. "We'll talk about the manuscript tomorrow. In fact, I think we need to agree to stop calling it a manuscript. That's too generous for whatever this is, these scenes, whatever. You think about that for awhile. As for me, I can take my first question off my list."

Bobby did not respond.

"The first thing I thought when I started it was that the writer wasn't sane. I was right about that, eh? So all I'm dealing with now is a dead insane woman, thank you very much."

"So you liked the story?' Bobby said as he stood to leave his office, accepting her offer of a hand up.

"It's a mess, like you said, and damn sad, with a bad ending, if that is indeed the ending, but I think it has…potential." *And now I am lying to him?*

"Did you hear music?" he asked.

Sally paused, remembering her interview years earlier, "Oh, Bobby, of course I did." *Why am I lying to him? Why can't I tell him how angry I am with him right now? I had everything prepared to unload on him, but it seems so pointless now.*

"I thought you would. I counted on it. Later, please tell me more about your reaction to the ending. It was my great disappointment as well."

Sally went back to her own office and revised her notes. She had other manuscripts to start, phone calls to return, lunch with a new young agent who wanted to introduce himself, a long and typical list of things to do, but she sat for a few minutes, wondering how Bobby was feeling at that moment downstairs, her anger subsiding. *Bobby Beaumont, you little bastard. Did you really think I would not see the truth within a few pages?*

As part of her appraisal of any manuscript, Sally would make notes in the margin of the manuscript as well as keeping a separate list of questions about larger issues, but that separate list was only made on her second reading, after she had determined that the story was absolutely good enough to deserve publication. Some manuscripts did not get read past thirty pages, but most that got to her desk, having survived the winnowing process of early readers, especially agents she trusted, were given a full reading. The marginal notes were usually about some mechanical problem, a verb tense shift or spelling or an awkward transition or any imprecise diction, a residual habit of hers left over from her days as a copy editor at *The New Yorker*. It was Pavlovian. This particular story was an encyclopedia of errors.

She never thought that verb tenses ought to be consistent? And how the hell was I supposed to figure out where her voice was and where she was telling what somebody else was saying? And some of the scenes simply jumped out of nowhere?

But as long as she kept reading, she would reflexively mark an error and keep going. Even manuscripts rejected and then returned by her became notorious among some agents, ridiculed by others. A two-week affair with one agent ended when he joked about how he had always wondered if she would be as critical in bed as she was on a manuscript. In hindsight, she regretted her decision to dump that agent. He actually *had* been good in bed.

Sally knew that Bobby would not even look at the marginal notes, but they were all things that the author had to correct, and the official Windsor copy editor was even more surgical than Sally. This manuscript, however, had a more obvious problem. The author was dead. It was a mess. Huge gaps in chronology. Any editor could correct the marginal problems, but Bobby would be more interested in her insight about the structural problems, the problems that an author would have to negotiate with the editor. With a dead author, who makes the decision? Was it worth the effort to read the mind of a dead writer? As much as Bobby had insisted to her that it was *her* decision, the subliminal message was clear: Bobby *wanted* this story to be polished and then published by *somebody*. But Sally knew that what she had read was...un-publishable. Still, she started a list of her concerns, knowing that he would want her to be honest. But she also knew that she had a unique problem with this manuscript. With others, she had trained herself to keep her distance. It was not her book, not her story, and all she was supposed to do was help the writer write his own story. True, like all editors, she had to also imagine who else would want to read any particular story. The non-fiction market was a lot less mysterious. Good writing, fresh insight, relevancy to current events or trends...there was an audience somewhere for almost every non-fiction book. Not always a big audience, but still identifiable. Fiction was much more problematic. And the trouble with this particular manuscript was that she was suspicious about her own objectivity. Suspicious, she admitted, was an understatement. Bobby had admitted his lack of objectivity about this story. Sally was not objective about Bobby, she knew that about herself.

Still, why do I feel like I connected dots of a picture I am not sure I want to see? And all the implicit and explicit rules of editing were useless. Hell, I feel more like an archaeologist than editor. I tried to be an editor. I let Bobby think I was trying. But he doesn't really want an editor. He wants an audience. Me. I can act...act...like an editor for him, but why play that game now?

She also asked herself why she had been so tentative: Did she really say that it had ...*potential?* The truth was that she had re-read certain passages just for pleasure. She thought it was more than wonderful. With that response to any other book, she would not have hesitated to tell Bobby, *We must publish this, buy it now and smooth out the rough spots later*, and in the past he had simply accepted her judgment without reading the manuscript himself. But she was absolutely sure about one thing...she hated the ending. Peyton and Ellie, and even the saintly doctor, deserved better.

Sally sent the hundred or so coherent pages and her comments back to Bobby. As soon as he read her notes, they would talk.

But he would know that he was uncovered, so why not forget the editing charade and start telling her the truth? She wanted to know more about the woman who wrote the book, and she wanted Bobby to explain that woman's role in his life. Coyness was not an option anymore.

Ellie Plans Her Future

How's this for a profound revelation? Went to a matinee today, another poor me left alone day while Peyton juggles the strings of American culture day. (He laughs when I tease him like that, but sometimes I am serious.) Did you know that I don't think I ever went to a movie when I lived in Charleston? Surely my father or mother took me when I was very young, but I do not remember. (Fucking meds) I watched a lot of movies on tv, but we both know that is not the same thing. No, movies in a movie theatre, those are movies. And this city has a lot of old movie theatres that show old movies. Movies from places that are not America. Peyton and I go together when we have time. (Balcony sex, PWR, you should try it.) But I go by myself during the day. My favorites? I wish I could figure it out. No particular type. They just have to be good at what they are trying to do. But I usually hate westerns. And that is why I am so proud of my new wonderful insight that I realized today while watching an old black and white western. Out of nowhere, I realized that I was on top of a mesa. Me and Peyton.

I used to think all this between me and Peyton was like

climbing a mountain, that once we got to the top the only way to go from there was back down, so sometimes I wanted to slow down, to not really be too happy, because I know that is what reaching the top would be like...being too happy, and then splat, the fall. But there it was on the big screen today, in black and white. A panoramic shot a thousand miles wide. Cowboys like little dots on the landscape, and there in the distance was a range of mesas. All those flat tops, and it hit me. Going up a mesa was harder than going up a mountain, the sides were steeper. But but but...when you get to the top you can walk for miles at that same height. There was no drop. You can be really happy for a long long time. Make sense? Surely you, of all people, understand this. I so want to tell Peyton tonight... We have reached the top of the world and we have Time and Space enough to be happy Forever. Unless I kill you first. (I am kidding. You know that. He would know that.)

Did you ever feel this way, back when your wife was alive? It would last forever. Did she? (You know what I still have? That little crystal glass piano you gave me. I see it and I think of you. Don't let that go to your therapist head, that your favorite former patient still thinks of you years since she has seen you. You know what I mean, about thinking about you.) You finally told me how she died, but I think I knew all along. You know what, dear Doctor PWR, what I am thinking about doing? I am thinking about going to school again. And you get all the credit even though you never suggested it. There are lots of wonderful colleges in this city, and Peyton said he would pay for everything. (Did he think I would assume that he wouldn't?) Of course, my high school career was less than stellar. No, it was more like shit-hole awful. But I am smart. You know that.

Peyton knows that. My future teachers will know that. I'm not a spring chicken anymore, sweet Peter and Paul (the SJB P&P) know that. But why would I or anybody else want to waste our youth on going to school, right? But here's the wonderful thing, PWR...I want to do what you do. I want to be Ellie Freud. (Joke alert) I always thought of my future in terms of simply being with Peyton, but even he is impressed that I want to become something on my own. In other words, Doctor PWR, I want to be you. I want to help people like me. And here is the revelation that I had about myself...I understand people like me. Better than you, I see myself. Better than you, I can interpret my life. I hear things I do not say out loud. And I can do that with people like me because I realized that I had been doing it with you. I knew your wife had killed herself even before you admitted it to me. You will eventually give me all the details and you will talk and talk about it and I will help you. And the thing is...I could do the same for Peyton, but he tells me less about his family now than he did when we were kids. I know everything about him except for why he is afraid of his mother. He and I talk all the time about the now of our lives, but we seldom touch the past. I'm okay with that, trust me. The past is that damn ball and chain I would like to dynamite. But I think that Peyton's mother is going to have to die (her body...her heart died a long time ago) before he will talk to me about her. You, on the other hand, I am guessing, will gush like a ruptured dam once I get you to talking. And you already know more about my past than Peyton ever will. I showed you mine...time for you to show me yours.

So I will start looking at colleges here. You can help me. And we can talk about the books I will read, probably a lot of the same ones you read. And when I am done I will stop being invisible in Peyton's world. Here's the serendipity. I will get my license at about the same time that Peyton's mother lays down beside his father. I will have my own coming out party then. I'll tell you all about this next month when I come see you...finally, right? You are in for a shock. I am cured. (Ha!) Well, I am down to taking my meds only every other day. I am happy. I live in the best of all possible times and worlds. I see the future too. ED was right. I dwell in possibility. Go ahead, laugh. Did I ever tell you about the time I dressed up like ED and went to some sort of open-mike poetry session in some club (an old stage theatre?) here and I was spectacular. And here's a secret that Peyton will kill me for if he ever found out I had told anybody...he went with me...dressed like Poe. Edgar Fucking Poe! How wonderful is that! He recited those awful Poe poems about dead Lenores and ravens and Anna-fucking-Belle Lees. See, nobody in that club knew who he was, or me, and we were totally perfect as dead people. I should stop telling secrets about him. He is so proper, just like you. (And your secrets?) Even Peyton admits that he wishes we both lived a hundred years ago.

This is not where I thought I was going. Me and Peyton and our literary slumming. I do this with him, jump around as I speak, but nowhere near as bad as I used to do with you. If he ever heard some of those early tapes you did with me, I am sure he would think I was a retarded idiot, or at least I was somebody with a goddam learning disability. I will give you credit, PWR, you always seemed to understand me. I wanted to tell you about my epiphany, about being on top of that flat mesa, and then tell you about my plans to be like you. We'll go through those more coherently soon. The fun will never stop. But here's a confession.

I really am nervous about seeing you again. I want you to be proud of me. But not like a father proud of daughter thing, like that song I told you about. See, I figured out something else about you and me. You don't want me to be a daughter you can protect. You want me to be your wife, the wife that does not kill herself.

Ding Dong, I'm back in Gotham. I wish I could bring that Charleston smell back with me to this city. Even you thought it was better than usual this Spring. All of Charleston smelled like a garden compared to here. Especially WPG. Thanks for taking me there. Was it supposed to be some sort of secret therapy? Mission accomplished. I think that even I smelled better back there.

So where do I begin? Seeing you again after all this time? I am sure my face gave me away. How is it possible that your looks never change? You had grey hair when I met you, but no more now than then. No more lines. You must weigh exactly the same, to the ounce. I even recognized the same clothes. I have this weird feeling that if we still know each other in fifty years you won't have changed and I will look like your mother. (You must show me a picture of your mother and father on my next visit. I want to see if you are there, if they are young looking too.)

Your face gave you away too. Admit it, Doctor PWR, you weren't looking at a patient. You were looking at me. You tried to make me think that you were still my doctor, but seriously...a walk in the park?

The answer to your last question, as I was leaving...yes.

Of course, if you were trying to be my doctor you ought to

be disbarred. Going to the park was fine. But taking me to my mother's house? Did you think that seeing that it had been demolished and wiped off the face of the earth...would make me feel better? I can see the textbook logic. Scene of trauma no longer exists, ergo trauma recedes? P&P dead, scene of crime gone, new life in big city...life goes on? Oh, please. Did I ever tell you that I actually wanted to come back here and live in that house again? Makes no sense, you think? Makes perfect sense to me. It was my mother's house first. The only good memories of my childhood came from that house. Fuck P&P. On a really really clear day, I can smell her and my father. So we drive by there and I think I missed it because...you jerk...you did not warn me. So all I see is that godawful brick blocky shithouse where my house used to be. Does that make it safe from the big bad wolf? My mistake was living in a wooden stick house? Huffed and puffed down? And you were surprised that I almost cried? Almost, always almost. You did not anticipate that? Sometimes I think I am smarter than you. The music store is gone. Peyton's bookstore is gone. My house is gone. Thank god that SJB and WPG are still there.

I am still glad I went. I am still glad I saw you again. You were right. And thank you for listening to all my Peyton stories, as you always have. If I were you, I might hate Peyton, listening to me swoon like a thirteen-year old girl who gets invited to the prom...something like that. But you are the King of Patience for sure. (patients?)

And thank you for finally letting me see your house, inside and out. Back then, did you think I would bite you if we ever got alone in your house? I would pounce on you like a maniac and then scream rape? You were always safe with me, Doctor

PWR, just like I am with you. In one of Peyton's new books last year, some history about the 1950s, I read this wonderful term...MAD...Mutually Assured Destruction...MAD, and I thought how perfect that was for something else, some other relationship, and I asked Peyton if he had ever heard that expression used in any other context. I told him that I thought it was a good title for a book.

Does where we live, how we live, reveal us? Not an original question, I know I know, but your house says a lot about you, just like Peyton's apartment does about him. (Although I have a hard time separating his apartment from that weird building he lives in. A calm space within a copycat space, and then all those secret spaces, where I live?) But your house is an open book. No secrets there. Old and quiet, just like you. Lots of windows, lots of sun, lots of empty rooms full of furniture. Your daughter's bedrooms full of teenage daughter stuff, time warps from the 70s? Rooms warm and rooms where perfectly beautiful daughters would grow up happy and safe and mature and well-adjusted. See, when you talk about them, that is what I hear between the words, how perfect they have become. Their pictures are everywhere too. Cradle to graduation. Will I ever meet them? And your bedroom, your old man bedroom...has any woman ever seen it? Trust me, you will never get laid in that bedroom. A monk dormitory is probably sexier. I know, I know...it is not the same bedroom you shared with your wife. That room is closed up, you told me. (And so you do have a secret?) And the rest of your house? You and Peyton share one thing (other than me), you want everything around you to be in perfect order, a place for everything and everything in its fucking place. But there is a difference, an absolutely charming difference between you two.

Peyton can afford servants. His place is spotless, as clean and neat as a showroom. (His office needs some sort of office maid service. Is there such a thing?) But you, sweet PWR, your world is covered in dust. Has nobody ever done what I did...rub their finger across a table or bookshelf? Drawn a heart and put an arrow through it? Haven't your daughters offered to help? You got a goddam rag? I told you that I felt like I was in the ashes of Pompeii, and you laughed, as if you had heard it all before. You need help cleaning, PWR...dusty house equals dusty mind, right? You need a good woman. (Which, surprise surprise, rules me out, as much as you might wish otherwise.)

But you knew I would forgive you as soon as I saw the piano room. Not just a piano, a goddam room for a piano. Books along the walls, but only two chairs, two Queen Anne chairs stuffed like fat Christians. And there was not a speck of dust on that piano. Not a speck of dust on that polished hardwood floor. With the sun coming in late that afternoon, that piano, from ivory keys to brass pedals, glowed and sparkled and breathed. You said it had always been that way, that room, but I do not believe you. It was not there when I first knew you. That room is mine, isn't it. How do I know that? You think I would not notice the tiny crystal piano sitting on the shelf, the same tiny piano you gave me years ago? There it was, but I did not say a word. But I knew why it was there.

How is this possible? I get back here and realize that I had actually missed it while I was gone. This gigantic dump of a city, I missed it. That was a surprise, a good surprise, unlike some of the other surprises, like finding out that Peyton had hired a new assistant that he was very impressed with. I've seen her. She is not as pretty as the others, but he says he thinks she will be the best. Actually, she is not pretty at all. All the others were head turners, but this one is...not. I mean, she's okay. After I found out, I waited outside the building and watched her leave. Then I realized this was a good thing. Peyton must have sensed that I was not happy with his other assistants. This new one is proof that he cares about my feelings. Then again, I am not worried. Never have been. Is that true love, PWR, never being jealous? If I were going to be jealous it would not be about the women who work for him. I just might, just might, however, give a shit about some of those damn women writers who always seem to float around him. Even the ones from other publishers, the ones who always come to the parties. It's them who are jealous of me. Even if I am not there, they want to be me. I have Peyton, they want Peyton, they want to be me. Very simple, but they cannot have him. The bitches cannot have him.

The other news? You'll love this, especially considering what I said to you a few months ago. Peyton's mother is sick. Praise Jesus, said I, the Wicked Witch of the West. I know I will feel different tomorrow. I will be a better kinder more generous more mature person tomorrow. In fact I am a better person as I write this. But first emotions must be honored, right? Are they truer? Go with your gut, so to speak? But I was different when I first heard. I was myself for sure.

Peyton had that look on his face...his Charleston look...his Charleston has its hooks in me look. He was working late in his office but he let me come and wait for him. All the others were gone. It's our favorite place to smoke. Not sure why. But a lot of times he can get on a toot over some new manuscript or some hot deal that is falling fucking apart or maybe he is pissed at some agent, and then he goes through a pack or two a day. I love those times. So we were in his office and I was laying on our virgin couch, listening to him ream some writer for not doing the revisions he had wanted. Poor writer, not to realize that Peyton's suggestions were commands. This time it wasn't that Peyton was mad because the writer had not done as he suggested, but that he had not even tried. It's your book...he would say calmly...but it could be better. So sayeth Peyton. Me, I'm laying there on that couch with a cigarette in my hand, an ash tray propped on my stomach, happy as a clam. Eyes closed, I'm blowing, I am sure, perfect smoke rings over my head. How long did I lay there not noticing that he had stopped talking? Had I gone to sleep? Smokey the Bear would not be happy, me going to sleep with a cigarette in my hand. Houses burn for such small mistakes, right? How about weird buildings in a big city? My eyes were still closed, but I felt my hand reach up and put a cigarette in my mouth. (By the way, I really like this new medicine you gave me. I think. Some days are weird. But if I start gaining weight again I will kill you.) I felt it on my lips as I took a drag. The breath, the smoke going in, the smoke going out. The only sound was my breathing. And then his voice, so calm and quiet.

—My mother is sick.

And then nothing. I had heard it before, too many times. The woman was Biblical. I knew she would never die. But this was different. The other times, he always made me sit down because he had something to tell me. And then the details. Symptoms, diagnosis, treatments, prognosis. Doesn't look good lament. This was different.

—My mother is sick.

And then silence there with me in his office as the sun faded outside. A dimming office, and neither of us spoke.

And then it hit me, how and why it was true this time. Peyton was not talking to me. I wasn't there with him. He was all alone and his mother was dying. He was talking to himself. I did not exist. But, dear PWR, I understood. I really really understood that at that moment Peyton and his mother were one person. His father's death had been sudden, with no time for dying. Just alive, then dead. I know that was awful for Peyton, but this was different. Like Peyton and I are one thing, so are he and his mother. That thing is dying. A long time ago, before his face was cut, we played a game of memory. How far back could we remember? I was lousy at that game, no surprise, except for certain smells and faces. Peyton was like a camera. He was a baby, he was sure, probably not a year old. (I would not believe that from anybody else, but I believed Peyton.) He was in some sort of crib, but all he could remember seeing was a gauzy netty thing over him, and then the netting was pulled back and his mother was looking down at him. That was the first face he ever saw. When he told me that story years ago, I told him it was how the blind man must have felt, when his new first sight was the face of Jesus. Sight was Jesus. Life was Jesus. In the beginning, I surprised Peyton a lot. That was one of those times. I was fifteen, but I knew my Bible.

So there we were tonight, PWR, and I was witness to Peyton's first sight disappearing. I heard it in his voice.

—My mother is sick.

I eventually saw it in his Charleston face.

—My mother is sick.

I wish old Harry were still alive. The three of us could smoke and get drunk again, but I know what Harry would be thinking. The Queen is dead, long live the Queen. Harry had always been on my side, so I could forgive his loyalty to me rather than Peyton's mother. But I am loyal to Peyton. PWR, I am not sure how long this will take, but I know it is a one-direction decline. She will die eventually. I never really felt that before. She will not recover this time. Like always seemed to happen before. I had even thought it would not happen until I became a doctor like you, years from now, but it will happen sooner. Not soon enough for poor old Harry, who is not going to be at the wedding.

I wish I had known her, instead of known about her. She would have liked me. We could talk about Peyton, and she could tell me all about Peyton's father, the things that only a wife knows. I would have been a good daughter for her. And if I can never go back to my mother's house, there is always Peyton's house. I know he will not stay here forever. I know that he will not want to raise our children here. He will want to go home again, where he was created. PWR, don't die on me, okay? I will need one friend all my own when we come back to Charleston.

Sally Prepares A Speech. It Is Not Delivered.

I wasn't sure when it became obvious to me. Probably the first time I read it, not even the entire thing, but the bells and whistles were screaming about something within thirty pages. The second time for sure, even though I wouldn't admit it to you. I felt like a voyeur, but I wasn't sure I wanted to stare. And I was pissed. As if a joke was being played on me, a cruel joke. How could you not know I'd figure it out? So, why the game? You're not a cruel man, I thought, and I knew how you felt about me, I thought. You'd always respected my feelings, hadn't you? Respected for sure, but not reciprocated. But the most damnable thing you could have done was force me to read the story, this whatever it is, as if we had no history of our own. You knew that all these pages did not make a book. Over 700 pages, and only about a hundred were coherent and original. The rest was mostly repetitious. She wrote and re-wrote. Words and sentences crossed out. A child's language becomes a woman's. The horrible things that happened to her were obviously re-written. Some typed pages were simply second drafts of the handwritten pages. Publish it? Fuck you, Bobby. You bastard, you could have saved me a lot of trouble, you know. You could have told me all this from the very beginning, or at least sooner. So maybe I wouldn't have wasted my life loving somebody who was in love with somebody else. How about that, Bobby? Or should I call you Peyton? How about before we screwed each other? Or maybe that's why we only did it once? A guilty conscience get you? And you sat there while I played the piano for you...were you thinking of her? And the goddam couch? Seriously? Is it really the same? Bobby, this was all so unnecessary. Everybody else around here thinks that I know all your secrets. Hell, I thought I knew most of them, and those I didn't weren't important, right? But, this? Oh, Bobby, you could have told me a long time ago. I knew my place. There was you, and then everybody else. I had a life, I wasn't lonely. I went out, had a few boyfriends, even a few good ones. But the more I thought about it, the more I could accept things. I'm successful. Hell, even the girls I know back in Atlanta are jealous. I've never thought I needed a husband or, god forbid, children. My biological clock stopped when I had an abortion. And I never regretted it. See, I could tell you things like that, tell you all my secrets, the worst about me, because I thought we had something special. Am I a complete fool? All these years. And then you go and hand me this story and then give me some hocus pocus about the author being dead, about a lawyer sending you the manuscript. Was it to be our little secret? What were you afraid of? Was it just simply that you just wanted some sort of artificial, even if it wouldn't last, some sort of editorial objectivity? Why not give it to somebody else? Why not tell the truth? And why, if it's all true, why did you break her heart? She might have been crazy, but you hurt her. You must have. And why, which I know you can't answer, why do I wish I had been her, not those horrendous parts for sure, but the parts about you and her. Why am I jealous of a dead woman?

The Truth

September was Sally's favorite month in New York. Summer vacation was over for the rest of the country. The City was no longer *the* destination for tourists. It had become just a snapshot or video memory. Were the sidewalks less crowded, the lines shorter, the traffic less congested? No, but Sally knew there was a difference. Perhaps it was something as simple as the weather, bluer skies and cooler temperatures, but still warm enough for a slow motion afternoon in Central Park. She and Bobby had done it a lot in the past ten years, usually by themselves but sometimes with a few other Windsor people, simply closed the office and gone to the Park. Lunch at the Plaza, an ironic wave from Bobby to the statue of General Sherman, and a walk through the Park.

As soon as she knew the questions she wanted answered, Sally had planned on asking Bobby to go to the Park with her. Give themselves lots of time for a casual conversation, ease into the truth, come to an agreement about how to handle the story, but Bobby had another park in mind. More private, but much less sunny. Sally would have been more adamant about Central

Park, especially since it was such a gorgeous day, but as soon as Bobby suggested his alternative she realized the truth…he was too weak for long walks.

They sat in the Windsor Building courtyard. The noon sun gone, the courtyard was shaded and childless. The surrounding apartments had been vacated months ago in preparation for the demolition, so Sally had Bobby all to herself as they sat on his favorite bench.

"Do I have to pry all this out of you bit by bit, or do you already know what I am going to ask?"

"I suppose we could do that scene in *The Godfather*, where Al Pacino tells Diane Keaton that she can ask one question and he will tell the truth," Bobby said, "so why not ask your most important question first."

"As I recall, he still lied to her."

Beaumont sighed, "I keep forgetting. You were a fact checker in another life, right?"

"Bobby, I'm past forty. I've cared about you even before I met you. I thought I knew you better than anybody else did…"

"And you do."

"But not everything, right?"

He nodded, shrugged, and slipped further into an accent that Sally heard only when they were alone, "I have always been a private person, you know that. And *nobody*, not even old married couples, know everything about another person."

"You are beginning to piss me off, Bobby," she said, shifting her body to face him more directly while at the same time sliding further away from him on the bench. "You are going to fucking tell me the truth, Robert Lee Beaumont." Instantly, she regretted what she said, but she also told herself, *Dammit,*

Bobby, you owe me. You really do. After all these years, you owe me. And of all the people in the world, you know that I would never hurt you.

He did not look at her, and they sat in silence for a minute while he gazed around the courtyard, pausing to stare at the remnants of a children's slide, and then he looked back at her.

"She always told me that we were a story and that she was going to write it one day. I never believed her, but I did ask her one favor if she did write it." He was back in Charleston. Sally was relieved, but she did not speak as he continued, "I simply asked her to make me taller."

Why do I want to laugh and cry at the same time, Sally thought to herself. *And I suppose I should be grateful that he can at least try to tell a joke...even a lame joke.*

"Bobby, it has so much potential to be a wonderful novel, or a wonderful something, a memoir, something. But we both know that is not why you wanted me to read it."

His smile was surrounded by a blush. "Yes, it is very good, not what I expected, but a true love story in its own way."

"Bobby, this is what I want. I want you to talk to me about her. Tell me the truth. Don't make me interrogate you like a divorce lawyer."

"Sally, you read the story. You already know the truth."

"Even the ending? Is that true? Did you stop loving her? Did Peyton? Do you see why I'm confused? *You* wouldn't have broken her heart, would you? How could *he*? And if that part is not true, then how much else is not the truth either?"

Bobby took a deep breath, and Sally wondered if he was merely stalling for time, or was it like he did more and more lately, deep breathing like a drowning man coming up out of the water. Almost a gasp. In a minute, his breathing became more relaxed and he said, "Oh, Sally, I am not a monster, am I?"

She wanted to reach over and touch him, to put her fingers on his lips and tell him to be quiet, that he was not a monster, but all she could do was finally whisper to him as softly as a mother putting her child to bed, wanting the child to go to sleep with one last thought, "You are a prince, remember? Isn't that what you and Steve Malloy finally decided? Both of you, princes among men. You're not a monster, Bobby. You are a prince."

A confused look first, then blank, but then an embarrassed smile as he recollected, "Of course, I forgot. A prince." He took another deep breath. "Still, it was the most difficult part for me to read, her conclusion, how she ended the story, so bitter and so angry, and so wrong. And your critique was right about that ending. It was inconsistent with the rest of the story. But I think I understand now."

Sally saw her opening. "I'm back where I began. If this story is about you and her...," She stopped, clearly exasperated because she realized she had avoided the one thing she really wanted to understand. "Oh, goddam it, Bobby, will you at least answer one question for me? Forget her manuscript. Just tell me one thing."

"The *one* question that gets a truthful answer?" He asked, but his irony was no defense.

"Yes."

He nodded.

"Why didn't you tell me? Not at the very beginning, I understand that. But soon enough. Years ago. When it was obvious how I felt about you. Why didn't you tell me that you were in love with her, in love with somebody invisible or mysterious, or whatever, but in love with a real other person, out of town or not. Why did you let me act like a fool for all these years, being in love with you, like a puppy! Why did you give me hope all those years? You gave me hope, Bobby. Surely you can see that."

She stopped talking and stood up quickly, wanting to walk away from him, but unable. Instead, she looked away, toward the ghost of a playground, finally speaking to herself as much as to him. "You gave me hope, Bobby. Why did you do that?"

From behind her, Bobby spoke quietly, "I never gave you hope, Sally. That was you, giving yourself hope. Not me. I am sorry."

She walked away, not looking back, to the other side of the courtyard, and then she turned back to him, still sitting on the bench, small in the distance. Something her mother told her a long time ago came back to her. *Sometimes, honesty and the truth are two different things. Big picture, little picture, that's the best distinction I can make. Honesty is the little picture. Truth's the big picture. Lord help you when they're the same thing but it's not what you want to hear.*

She walked back to Bobby, taking her place on the bench, and asked a different question, "There's a key to this story, Bobby, something that unlocks everything, but I don't have it. You knew her. Some version of you, totally unknown to me, is in this story. If anybody has that key, it's you."

"Or Pete," he added.

Sally blinked. "Is he even real?"

"More real than I ever wanted to admit, and the oddest thing about her story is that she and I would agree about Pete's character in the story and in real life, a genuinely decent man

282

who was generous toward those who did not deserve it. Pete is Pete, fact and fiction are the same. I never met him face to face...," Bobby paused and then muttered to himself, "...and that man will live forever," an uncharacteristic edge in his voice.

"Would his version of the past be the same as yours?"

"It does not matter, Sally. The story is not about him. And here is the key you want, as best I can accept for myself. The story is not about Pete. It is not even about me. It is her story. Surely about what happened between us, but not..."

"But how can you be Peyton? Do you see why I am confused?'

Bobby spoke as if he had set a trap for Sally and she had walked into it right on schedule, "This is not a memoir, Miss New York editor, it is merely a collection of fragments. You know that. You *want* to make it a memoir, but it is still fiction. Everything in it is true, assuredly in its own way, but the facts are irrelevant. She needed to make sense out of her world. Truth is, you would think that she talked all the time around me, but she was usually quiet. Oh, sometimes when she was manic she was uncontrollable, and I wish you could have seen her then. I am not Peyton, but everything that happened between him and Ellie was exactly what happened with me and Ellie. She got *that* part right. How they felt about each other, what they did."

"Bobby, you know the craziest thing about those pages? I still do not know her real name."

"Elliott, Elizabeth Elliott."

"But..."

"Yes, I did name her Ellie."

Sally was getting impatient. "Was she younger than you?'

"Yes."

"Was she your first?"

"Yes. Oh god, yes."

Sally took a quick breath and plunged into the deepest coldest part of the pool, "The first time you had sex, was it on a couch in the bookstore?" She stopped herself, almost laughing out loud, thinking *Well, Sally Graham, you have just set yourself up for more information than you might want to know*, a feeling that was quickly confirmed as Bobby answered.

"Yes, the couch in the Palmetto Bookstore after midnight. The store had been closed for over a year, and it was almost empty, and…the key I had did not work, so we broke in."

"Bobby Beaumont! You…you…*slut!*" Sally almost screamed, astounded by the fact that she was laughing at the same time, once again. *Do I laugh or do I cry?*

Bobby *did* start laughing, cut short by hacking, and then gasping, his eyes watering, his hands shaking as if he were choking, and Sally was about to help him get off the bench and on his feet, but he waved her away and exhaled, "I am fine. I was just not prepared to laugh right then. I apologize for being such an invalid more and more these days."

The moment was a bridge. Sally understood the crossing soon enough, and she would eventually wonder if Bobby ever did, before he went away. On one side of the bridge was a time when she was in love with Bobby, on the other side was the future, when she merely loved him.

Sally set aside being an editor. "Tell me the story, Bobby. Just between me and you. Tell me all the things that nobody else knows. Put yourself back in your own story."

"One last thing before I do that, Sally, about the key to the story. I told you the truth. This is Ellie's story, about her and me, but *her* story, and the saddest truth about Ellie is that she did not like herself. It took me years to understand. I loved a woman who, down deep, hated herself."

Sally looked around the empty playground again, wanting him to tell her the story, but afraid that he would leave out something. She knew this was her only chance to find out answers to all the questions she had had about him, to understand him and then perhaps understand why she fell in love with a man who was in love with someone else, who stayed in love with that woman even after they had separated. But just as Bobby was about to start, she had a jolt of recognition, blurting out another loaded question.

"This playground...," and she laughed softly again, "...this playground, is this the playground she mentions in that long list of places they had sex?"

Bobby stifled his own laugh, "Sally, you *are* a glutton for punishment, aren't you."

"*That's* the goddam merry-go-round, isn't it? " she said, pointing to a relic.

"Perhaps just a voyeur?" he said.

"You know, Bobby, at this point I don't know who or what the hell I am anymore. But this is the place, right? You and her, probably late at night, with a thousand people sleeping in the apartments around you. What else, Bobby, how much of you and her have I been walking through all these years, being right beside you and not knowing that you were probably re-living some moment from your past right when I thought you and I were alone. She was always here, wasn't she?"

"Is it a list you want? And what would it mean? How much does she owe you, or me, or some future reader? Does her story really require that you know the exact inspiration? Come on,

Sally. Does it matter that the chapel she writes about was the old synagogue that Harry Windsor had built on the thirteenth floor, and that there was no crucifix on the wall. Or that when you and I went to my mother's funeral..."

"Okay, okay, enough," she interrupted. "I'm sorry, I just wanted to understand things, that's all. But you're right, the details are irrelevant. I just wanted to understand this sort of parallel universe I've been living in with you, that's all."

Sally understood how all this worked with other writers, how every good novel came from life, and she was old enough, smart enough, to know the difference. But why had her own life led to *this* point? She wanted to tell the man next to her a secret, but she had some shred of self-respect left, so her truth remained unspoken.

Bobby, you prince, you know what I did as soon as I finally decided that I knew the truth about this story, that Ellie was real and that you were, somehow, Peyton? How pathetic am I? Pathetic enough to wish that I was her, pathetic enough to read some of those pages and imagine that it was me and you on that couch, me and you in that park back in Charleston, in that hotel back there. Goddam it, Bobby, I wanted to be her so I would know what it was like to be loved like that.

"Okay, Romeo, start from the beginning," Sally finally said, letting out a deep breath, resigning herself to the role of spectator, and editor. "No, wait, I mean, start at the end. Why did you really stop seeing each other? Something about her ending is wrong. Tell me the truth."

"The truth is not very dramatic, I am afraid," he said, pausing to rest before continuing. "She wanted to do the right thing, that was her explanation. She was miserable here at the end. We went to all sorts of doctors, but she only trusted Pete. She would go home and come back here better. I never understood it. I always knew about him, but we never met, never talked. I could not imagine that she was willing to give me up for him. It made no sense. And those pages he sent me...surely he could see that she did not love him. And then, the last time she and I talked, after my mother died and she was already living in Charleston, she told me that she was going to marry him. It made no sense. She insisted that I would be better off without her. I knew my place, but I was happy, truly happy, with the small world we had created for ourselves. Ellie made a choice, and it was not me. I was still living in a world where it was possible for her to love me all by myself. It was my delusion. I would have spent the rest of my life in that delusion, but she wanted to set me free. She thought she owed Pete more, and she wanted to set me free. She made a moral decision. In her mind, she did the right thing."

"Bobby, this makes no sense to me. She loved you. Nothing in those pages showed that she loved him more. Twenty years, you and her were in love for twenty years. It worked. That long together must have meant something. It didn't have to end."

He nodded, but Sally knew that he wasn't nodding at what she had said. Something else was on his mind at that moment. Some other conversation. She sat quietly until he came back to her.

"No, you are right. It did not have to end. I would have loved her regardless."

"Would have?" Sally asked softly, forcing him to be more precise, and telling herself, *You deserved better, Bobby, both of you. You deserved to be happy. And here I am feeling sorry that your heart was broken by another woman and you still love her. Like I'm some sort of emotional enabler. Hell, I think I even love her. Where did* that *come from?*

"I do not wish to hurt you anymore, Sally, you do believe that, do you not? I have never wanted to hurt you."

"Bobby, I'm a big girl now, really. And big girls don't cry. Right? You say you would have loved her *regardless?* Would have? You've never stopped being in love with her. Seems to me that if I can see it, you have to admit it. Neither one of us is getting any younger, and I'm pretty sure you're going away forever and I'll never see you again. Thanks very much for not admitting the obvious truth that I figured out on my own, right? So here I am doing what I do best. Years as the chosen understudy for Ellie's role, waiting for her to break a leg so I can go on stage, and, hell, she dies and I still can't get in front of the lights with you. You like that comparison? I sure think that she would. I've worked on it for weeks."

"Sally..."

"No, it's okay, Bobby. I could live with being an understudy. If you could, so could I. But, you know, there's still a question you haven't answered. You told me the truth about how she ended it, and that would have been a good enough ending for the story, telling the truth...if that is the truth. See, here's me as editor. That ending does not work. It has to be re-written, but the writer is dead, and I would not publish her story with that ending. You have to explain to me why she ended her story the way she did, or you have to give me a different ending. And is it possible that the real ending is not in those pages you got? That the real ending exists somewhere back in Charleston?"

"The truth? Why not use the truth, you ask," he sighed. "Because the truth doesn't work either. Life itself doesn't work for this story. And you have to remember. She did not write a bad ending. She simply stopped writing."

"Forget life," she said. "I'm talking about the book. *That* Ellie, and *that* Peyton, they deserve a better ending and something that flows more truthfully out of *their* story, not necessarily yours and Ellie's. She was writing a novel, not a memoir, an un-finished novel. That's how it has to be evaluated, as fiction. That makes perfect sense to me now, Bobby, and you know it does too."

"Look, all I know is that she never thought she was a good person. Perhaps she couldn't even give herself credit for doing the right thing. She had to displace some of that disappointment in herself over to another character? Sally, I have no answer for this. I am not her therapist. You listen to my version of the story. You figure it out. I am too tired."

Bobby spoke slowly and quietly, as if knowing that the story could only be told once. "The beginning was as she described it, at the bookstore. We were formally introduced then, but I had seen her weeks earlier at the Palmetto. I watched her steal a book. That was my first sight of her. I was fascinated. This girl just walked into the store, walked around, browsed, came over to my book section, and picked up a book. I was talking to Sam Simon in the back when I looked to the front and there she was. So wonderfully casual. She walked in, picked up a book, and walked out. As if the store was hers. I just looked. My only regret, which should have been a warning to me, was that I could not tell my father about her in the very beginning. And then she came back and I stopped her with a copy of *Peyton Place* in her purse. See, all the details she wrote about...true...but used differently by her. She never once in our entire relationship ever called me Peyton. He was a character that she created. Unfortunately, her step-father and uncle were real, but their names were not Peter and Paul. And, yes, I did go to her house to take her away, but I had already figured out where she lived."

He paused and then touched the scar on the left side of his face. "This...that part of her story...is true. But, no, my father did not come to the house with the police. She never saw him. Ever. But he did take care of her after I was hurt. And then..."

"Bobby, you knew she was crazy, right? You had to know that from the very beginning, surely."

"I never thought that, not the way you mean it. I just thought she was the most dazzling amazing person I had ever known. You should have known her, Sally, when she was in perfect harmony with herself. Those are the times she never wrote about. For those times alone, everything else could be forgiven. But there is one thing I need to correct about her version of our life. Do not think that I tried to keep her a secret here. That was her wish. She did not want anybody to know she existed except for me. After awhile, it was a drama in which I was her co-star, but for an empty theatre. We would be together and act as if we did not know each other. The parties were the most fun. Of course, Harry was in our small production, and Mr. Taylor too. But we were a couple only among strangers, who knew neither of us. And we did that for years. She always said she wanted to be invisible."

Sally looked away, hearing children laughing behind her. Turning, she saw nobody. *I love a man who is still in love with a crazy woman. He can live in any delusion he wants, I suppose, and I will always be on the outside.*

Okay, you're as nutty as her. Fair enough. But, seriously...you as Edgar Allan Poe at some poetry reading? That is so *not* you, Bobby Beaumont."

"Sally, consider your source. We did go to those places. We did perform. She did wear a costume. I did recite Poe, and others. But, a costume? Now, of course, I wish I had."

Bobby did not have the strength to finish his version of the story. He talked for an hour, and Sally was spellbound by the difference between his version and Ellie's version. Mostly in the small details. A fact in her story had a different context or source in his. But Sally slowly separated the two stories. One was more honest. The other was truer.

"One last thing, Sally, but about me and you," Bobby said. "I do owe you an apology. In this world now, I care about you the most. But this past year has done something to me. Perhaps merely compounded feelings that began as Ellie and I separated. And I wonder if my confusion...my anger, perhaps...is merely inevitable for people like me, at this time in a life."

"Bobby...."

He put a finger to his lips. "Indulge me."

She nodded.

"I can no longer make sense of all this, Sally. My life has come to...this end. My parents were always right. I have drifted through life. I should have done more with my life, my advantages, than I have. And when I die, my parents die with me. The books I've published are not really mine. The business I created is gone. I have disappointed you. And I did not save Ellie. When I was a young man, I thought about the future. But I did not see this moment. And now I cannot see any future. And the most damnable sentence I can pronounce on myself is

291

that I simply do not understand my own life."

Neither spoke for a few minutes. Bobby stared at the empty playground. Sally stared at the ground in front of her and thought of Ellie's effort to understand Time and Space. She closed her eyes. She was sitting on the same bench where Harry Windsor had sat and listened to Ellie scream about Bobby's mother, the same bench where Bobby and Ellie had sat countless times, the same bench where she and Bobby had sat too. Time and Space. She kept her eyes closed until the feeling passed, until she was sure that when she opened her eyes she would not see the past.

Two hours later, she went back to her apartment and packed for a trip. Bobby had told her his version of the story. She had read Ellie's version, but that version was totally unreliable. Sally still did not have the answers she wanted. There was only one other person who could add to the story, and he lived in Charleston. If there was anything else to know, she assumed, he would be the one to tell her.

Ellie and Peter

I have been thinking about your offer.

Did you tape all those calls? I hope you did. I haven't been able to write for almost a year because of her. Perhaps the other things too. But you know that. When I start to write now I get impatient. An impatient patient, bad deal for sure. So I call you and you get the first edition. Not like the old days when you got the genteel life of Miss Me, southern deb in the big fucking city. I'm coming to see you again. And I would like to listen to those tapes. You said you didn't tape me, but I don't believe you. You did, right? I'm your precious pinned butterfly under glass, Doctor PWR. Freud had somebody like me, his most famous favorite patient, or was it one of the other guys? But I'll give you credit. You always answered the phone.

She won't die. As simple as that. If I were as sick as her, I would want to die. I would want them to shoot me, like Atticus shot the dog. She won't die. The thing between her and Peyton won't die. The thing between me and Peyton is dying. Not just her fault, all those other women too. And his work. I hate this city and sometimes I hate Peyton. No, no, no, NO. I do not mean that. But sometimes I have so much energy during the day that I cannot stop moving around, and then I crash like I'm a house of cards blown to hell. As long as my body moves, I don't have to think, but then I am paralyzed and the only thing alive about me is my brain. And THEN everything is crystal clear. A body in motion is a brain at rest...makes sense to me. Did I apologize to you today? For yelling at you? If so, I take it back. You are my goddam doctor, Doctor. You are supposed to let your patient vent. It's in your goddam Hypnotic Oath. (Lame joke, who cares.) You are supposed to cure me. You know, I almost told Peyton about you, but I was madder at him than I was at you. On a list of hurtful things that I said to him, you didn't make the top ten. And what good would it do anyway? He has suffered me more in the past year than all the earlier years combined. And he still loves me. Go figure.

You know what he did last week. I was sick as a Georgia dog. Something as common as the flu. I was as common as any other sick person. You know how I hate being common. Nothing crazy, just chills and fevers and sweats and a healthy puke every few hours for good measure...and he took care of me. He stayed away from his office for TWO full days and never left me alone. He kept me warm when I was cold, kept me iced when I was burning. Two days we were alone. The phone never rang. Nobody knocked on his door. Even the regular servants were gone. The old black doorman was the only person who knew I was there, and he helped Peyton take care of me. Two days, and then I slowly got better. You want to know how bitchy I was for that two days, as I lay there dying? Peyton was holding the back of my head up with one hand and had a glass of pineapple juice in the other that he was holding for me as I sipped. Damn juice was running down my chin and I'm sure I looked like death warmed over, and I said what I was thinking...I am going to be totally pissed if I die before your mother...poison like that just comes out of my mouth and I instantly close my eyes because I am terrified of seeing his face. But not a word...not a sound from him. He takes the glass away and holds my head and lowers it back on the pillow...me still blind like a child in a closet afraid that the door is about to open and if she just does not see the monster there, then it does not see her...I feel him wipe my face with a damp cool cloth. And I feel him kiss me on my forehead. So, PWR, did I really say that awful thing about his mother out loud? Or did he forgive me by refusing to acknowledge it happened? Forgiveness I did not, do not, deserve.

And did he really say what I thought I heard, there with my baby eyes closed?

—Go to sleep, Ellie. You'll live forever.

PWR, I have this daytime wide-awake nightmare sometimes, more lately than ever before. Not when I sleep with Peyton. All is calm then. But this waking nightmare paralyzes me. Sometimes I think Peyton would be better off without me. Sometimes I think that he is not safe with me. I could never hurt you, PWR. I am sure of that, but if Peyton and I are the same person, two halves melded as one...Siamese twins (I hate this comparison, but I am lost here)...if we are the thing I always said we were, then what happens to Peyton when I die still attached to him? He is wrong. I am dying, and I am killing him.

Do I have to cure myself? Seriously, all by myself?

Stupid stupid things.

I refuse to be ugly again. I will never ever be ugly again.

Why should I worry about Peyton hating me? He should worry about me hating him. He is not who he was. I am still me. But he went away. He saved me and then he abandoned me. I do not tell him the truth. I haven't talked to him in days. Longer? He says he loves me, but I do not see it in his face anymore. I'm not him anymore. All I see in his face is a puzzle. How is it possible that he spends more time with me but I have less of him. He goes home to see her, to care for her, but does not take me? Back here, he works on books with the other her, but she does not know I exist? And the Great Lie? That when his mother dies then we will be the only two that matter? Why doesn't the other she leave? She has been here longer than the others. I know what she wants. And this city reeks. I want to smell my home again. Is this it? All there fucking is? I look at people here and want to kill them. Just to have the power to make them go away. I can't hurt anybody. I won't. I'm getting old. Older. Ancient. I can't focus in school. Has it come down to this? P&P win? And the greatest irony of all? PWR wins? It was him all along? He met me when I was ugly and he loved me anyway? I never saw me in his face. His old and stoic (?) face. I was never there. Is he all there is? If one pill makes me small and one pill makes me large...heads or tails? Go ask the bitch Alice. Late late for the inevitable date? And they think I am crazy? Me? Crazier than Harry who built a building with secret rooms and lived off the reputation of another man? Crazier than Peyton who lives in that weird building and hides me in one of those secret rooms? Rochester hiding his crazy mad wife in the attic? Crazier than that spectral accountant whose suit never changes, year after fucking year, the same suit? And it is ME who is crazy? I am surrounded by crazy people.

I am trapped here by myself, PWR...I just want to feel safe again.

Peter Stone

Like riding a bicycle, she told herself. *So what if I haven't driven in over a year.*

Sally rented a car and drove to Charleston, a ten hour trip by the map, but longer because of traffic and construction up and down I-95. She could have flown out of LaGuardia and rented a car at the Charleston airport, but a long road trip appealed to her. Time to sort and parse, *time to sit on my butt and think the big thoughts,* time to kill.

She spent the first night in a beach hotel in North Carolina, the pages read again. She spoke her favorite lines out loud to herself, trying to hear Ellie's voice. She pulled paragraphs out and copied them by hand. *She's not telling the truth, she's hiding something,* Sally told herself, *and why the hell am I trying to understand a crazy woman?*

The first week in September in Charleston was wretchedly hot and humid, and as soon as she stepped out of her rental car she had second thoughts. *You know, a phone call might have been a better idea.* But she also knew that she had already stepped through a door into somebody else's story, and the only exit was a door on the other side of the room.

Before she went to Charlotte Street, she drove past Bobby's old home, resisting the urge to go in and re-live the two times she had been there before, knowing that everything in the house would be the same. Like much of Charleston, the Beaumont mansion was frozen in time.

When she finally found Stone's house, she sat in the car, the engine running and air conditioning on, and re-read her favorite pages.

If I had any nerve, she told herself, *I'd sneak up there and peek in the windows myself, before I meet this guy.*

Stone did not give her a chance to act on her impulse. He walked out on to his front porch and waved at the woman in the car across the street. He had been expecting her.

Jesus Lord, why am I so nervous? Sally stared at the waving man, and then she made herself smile, *and calm at the same time, It's like meeting Abraham Lincoln or Robert E. Lee or anybody else who has existed all my life in some history book, somebody famous who was real, but history. I'm going back in time. And this man can't follow me back to the present. He's trapped, but I'm free.*

"Hello, Miss Graham," he said as she met him on the porch, extending his hand to her, "I'm Peter."

Sally hid her curiosity. *That can't be your real face. You're seventy years old. You can't look this young. Fifty, fifty-five maybe?*

"I appreciate you meeting with me, and I promise not to take up too much of your time."

"It's my pleasure, although I'm not sure how much help I can be. Still, you've driven a great distance, so please take as much time as you wish. Come in, come in."

Sally stepped into a shrine for Ellie, and it was that iconic confrontation that rendered her temporarily speechless. In all of her discussions with Bobby, he had never been able to show her what Ellie looked like. Inexplicably, he had no pictures. That long, and not a picture? But then she thought, *He probably has a hundred hidden away from me and the rest of the world.*

Stone's house was an Ellie gallery. More Ellie than Sally could absorb in any single glance. *My god, this, and this, and this, all this is what she looked like.*

Stone walked her through the house, pointing to a picture on a shelf of him and Ellie, other pictures of Ellie on the walls, her and friends, her at her desk, her on the beach, her as a child, and so Sally stood in Ellie's house and forgot her own list of questions.

"Sally?"

She had also forgotten about Stone. She was in *Ellie's* house now.

"Would you like to see my favorite picture of her?" he asked, but he already had a framed picture in his hand, knowing that Sally would want to see it.

Ellie was probably no more than ten years old, but she already had the adult face, a face that was interesting but not beautiful. The individual features were unremarkable, but the sum of her face was in her eyes, and those other features coalesced around those dark brown eyes and became a seduction. Sally studied that face, trying to imagine Bobby...or Peter Stone...first seeing it.

How does anybody truly *see* themselves? Was Ellie able to see her own face as Bobby must have seen it? *Surely,* Sally told herself, *somebody as self-absorbed as she was, surely they could never see how they truly looked?*

Sally sat on the couch, holding a picture of a young girl who had forty years to live, a life ahead of her that she could not imagine, and a death. The child's eyes were focused on whoever was taking the picture, staring directly at that person.

"That's a good picture of her, you would agree," Stone said, watching his guest stare at the picture.

Sally looked up at her host and smiled, forcing herself to give the picture back to him. He offered her some sweet iced tea, and when he went to the kitchen she stood and walked around Stone's house. That was when she found the piano room.

Sally had not been prepared. She stood next to the piano, remembering how she had practiced and practiced for her parents when she was growing up, never to get beyond the basics, every song a struggle. She sat on the piano bench, her hands reaching for the keys as a reflex to her memory, trying to remember a song from Gershwin about summertime, and then she saw a tiny crystal piano on the shelf across from the grand piano at which she sat. She was dizzy and about to cry all at the same time. Jealousy and voyeurism and vicarious longing let her be Ellie as *she* played the piano for Bobby. *Was it like this at all, or is it something I imagined later, why can't I make it real for sure?*

"Do you play?"

Sally jerked her head up, her fingers slamming into the keyboard, discordant notes escaping Bedlam. Her first visceral reaction was anger. *Where did you come from? Why did you have to interrupt?* But, one look at him, and she felt petty and small. She was in *his* house again. This was *his* life. *He* was the cuckolded husband, the aggrieved party, surely that was *his* burden. *She* had no right.

He stood with a glass of tea in his hand, offering her some

relief. "You just looked like you were familiar with that position, there in front of the keys. I thought you might want to play."

Sally stood and took the tea, and then admitted, "I feel very foolish coming to see you like this. I told you that I needed some help in sorting through your wife's papers."

He sat down and waited for her to continue. Sally had a thought, almost an epiphany. *This man is so…so graceful in his movements, almost a slow motion body, and I can't imagine him angry. And if I told anybody else this story they would see him as weak and pathetic. But there's something different here in person, he's the most…."*

"I should clarify something first." he said, hesitating. "I was not her husband. We never married."

Sally's face gave her away. *What the hell?*

"I never asked her to marry me, just to stay with me. I told her that I would take care of her, and she needed that. And, truth is, I was always afraid she would say no. But we were a couple, a married couple, to the rest of the world."

Sally merely nodded. *And do I tell Bobby this? And excuse me, Peter Stone, but why are you wearing a wedding ring?* But she did not ask him.

Stone looked past Sally, toward the shady expanse of the backyard that could be seen through the windows behind her, then he turned to face her, "To be truthful, I didn't anticipate this conversation with you. I just assumed that Bobby would keep the papers to himself. It was one of her last wishes, that I send that package to him. I didn't think he would show them to anyone else. I asked an attorney to send them because I preferred to have no contact with him. I'm sorry about the confusion."

And I bet he's going to tell me…

"It was between him and her, no business of mine. And, after all, it had been such a long time. I assumed it was part of the ..." and he looked for a precise word, "...part of the *reconciliation* she wanted, some sort of wrapping up. I knew she had been writing, and..."

...that he himself never looked at those pages.

"... she wanted him to read everything she had written so far, although she told me later that she wanted to write more. But she had become too weak. It was personal between them. I knew that."

Sally eased into her question, "Did you know what it was?" At the same time thinking, *Your dying wife has a package she wants you to send to her ex-lover, and you do NOT read it?*

"I assumed it was about their time together, but she had already told me a lot of the stories before then, in her last year. The papers were about their past, and that ended a long time ago. For me, she gave me a much larger collection of pages, about us, so why should I begrudge Bobby the few that he got?"

You are either a remarkable liar, or the most generous man in the universe, Sally thought. *But if you did read it, those scenes about the first time they had sex...surely, you wouldn't have sent them to Bobby. You would have burned everything. Nobody is that generous. And, Jesus God, if you're telling the truth, what would I give to read the pages she wrote for you.*

"So, Miss Graham, I'm confused. Why are you here? You said you wanted to talk about the papers, but why? Did Bobby send you?"

How much do you want to know?

Sally felt like a dishonest translator. "We're closing down our offices, clearing out files. Bobby is a bit distracted, and your wife's papers were included in a bunch of other stuff he gave me. I read them and…"

And he knows I am lying, she realized immediately. *I am so transparent.*

"Okay, the truth is this. Bobby is dying, and I want to help him sort out things, to do that *reconciliation* you talked about. I want to do for Bobby what you did for your wife."

Stone almost smiled, looking past Sally, absorbing her truth. "You care for him very much?"

All she could do was nod.

"Bobby and I might have been friends. It was not his fault. I understood that." He stopped, his hands in his lap, his thumbs tapping each other. "I'm sorry. This is probably not what you want to hear. I'm just babbling. But, as you might imagine, there aren't too many people with whom I can discuss this. So, tell me, what do you need to know to help you?"

Sally glanced over to the piano, and then back at him. "I really don't know what to ask." He looked at her but did not speak. He was right, she *did* know what to ask. All he had to do was wait. "Well, I was wondering…can I see her journals, those notes she mentioned in that material she sent. And…," this was the real test, "… is there anything else, mementos or keepsakes? Sally registered his expression, a rare flash of intensity, but she pressed ahead, "Can I see those things?"

He was now conciliatory, "If they existed, I'd be glad to share them with you. Anything related to Bobby, I'd be glad to give them to you."

"And the other journals?"

"She wanted those destroyed after her death."

Sally had never met a man like Peter Stone. Lying, or telling her the absolute truth? His body never contradicted his words.

"Those would help immensely," she said.

"She wanted them destroyed," he repeated.

"Did you?"

He half-smiled. "You must understand. I did everything she ever wanted me to do. I even accepted Bobby. And when she was dying, those last few months, she told me about other journals and asked me to destroy them. And I did that for her. In front of her. All burned. You see, I was losing her. I would have traded places with her if God had answered my prayers. I had her all to myself at the end, and she loved me more than she ever had in her entire life. In the end, I was the only one there for her. She knew that. And destroying those journals was easy."

And you keep her pictures all over this house? You worship her after death, but you never wanted to read those journals, or keep them? This makes no sense.

Sally wanted to ask him more questions, but she decided to let him talk for as long as he was willing. When he was finished, an hour later, she only had one question for him, "Did she tell you why she stopped seeing Bobby?"

He was noticeably drained of energy, his age finally apparent. "Basically, it was what she wanted."

Sally wanted to say, *But Bobby told me that it never happened the way she said,* but saying that would force her to reveal what Ellie's story actually said, and if this man had not read it, why reveal it now?

Sally waited. He almost spoke, paused, and then she thought she could see him thinking of a better answer, perhaps groping, as if he had never heard *that* question before.

"Do you think that a dying person can be trusted to tell the truth?" he finally said.

"I'd like to think that if I were dying, I would tell the truth," was her first reaction, but she was also thinking...*Not if that person is Bobby Beaumont, who is a master of the lie of omission.*

"As would I, for myself, that is," he said, as if he were imagining himself near death. "I mean, why should a dying person lie?"

Where are you going? Sally thought, but answered him only with a slow nod.

"All I can tell you is what she told me," he said. "I assumed it was the truth. But perhaps she only wanted to make me feel good, there at the end?"

You are alone on this stage, Peter.

"It was a week after his mother died."

Chronology, chronology, Sally told herself. *Bobby's mother died...ten years ago? I should remember this. I was there. Bruce said that Bobby changed right around when I was hired.*

"She went to his mother's funeral. It was the last time they ever saw each other."

"They had broken up before that, before the funeral, right?" Sally was struggling to keep track of sequences, and she was feeling a chill somewhere that was creeping around her, through her.

"No, it was after the funeral, the reception at his house. You know, she told me all this in her last few months, not a good time for her, so she might have been mixing up places and times." He had noticed a change in Sally's face, her color draining. "See, the thing about Ellie that I knew, and I hope Bobby knew too, was how she *wanted* to be good. In the beginning, Bobby was... *allowed,* her word...to see others when they were apart. She had me. It was her trade-off. She knew that Bobby had never been happy with just part of her. But they would not give each other up."

He stopped talking, furrowing his brows in concentration, trying to be precise.

"It was one of her last clear moments, telling me about seeing Bobby at his mother's funeral with some woman from Savannah. She told me…"

Sally stopped listening, her chest hurting, her hands squeezing her purse. She screamed at her memory. *You have to show me. You have to show me where she was that day. Bring it back. Why did I miss her?*

"Miss Graham, are you okay?"

Sally blinked and tried to remember where she was at that present moment. *Who was this man?*

"Ellie told me how the woman looked at Bobby, and she said it more than once, so I know she meant it." Stone's voice became Ellie, *It was a look I would see in his face when he looked at me, how much one person could love another. I had seen it in his face, but he didn't see it in that woman's face because all he could see was me.*

"I don't think that I need to…"

"No, you wanted to know why they broke up. It was, Ellie told me, her last chance to be good. She had to force Bobby away, so he could find somebody who would be totally his, somebody he would not have to share. I know this doesn't make me look good, but I hated Bobby Beaumont more then than I ever had before. She gave him up because she cared too much for him to keep him tied to her forever. How was I supposed to feel? That was my first selfish and low thought, and she knew it when she told me, but it went away, my resentment. I eventually understood. She could have kept both of us, but she picked me. I was the only one that mattered. At the end, I was there with her, not him."

Sally wanted out of that house, but she was paralyzed. She wanted to tell somebody, but the man in front of her was surely the wrong person. *Sure, she gave him up, just like Bobby told me. He and Peter are both right. But he never gave...her...up. She wanted him to have me. For chrissakes, Bobby, it was supposed to be me. She wanted you to be happy with me. It was possible, I knew it. I was right. I was right. I was right all along.*

She looked around the room. Ellie was everywhere.

"Was that what you wanted to know?" he said quietly.

"The truth is, I don't know where to go from here," Sally finally said. "Her last pages do not say what you told me. And I can't reconcile what she told you with what she wrote in the material she sent to Bobby."

He tilted his head to one side, then looked down before looking back up to say, "All I know is what she told me."

Sally sat back, and neither spoke.

All I know is what Bobby told me. All I know is what you told me. All I know is what she wrote. A story told by three people. And something is wrong with the ending. That's all I know.

She finally stood and offered her hand to him, to help him up. Then she made one final request. "Can I just look around this room for awhile by myself? Study the pictures. Think a little bit...by myself."

He left her alone, and Sally went straight back to the piano. She sat down on the leather-covered bench and moved her hands across the keys without touching them.

This is the most silent room I've ever been in, except for Bobby's apartment. Was it this way when she was here? She looked at the keyboard in front of her, leaning down to study it. *If Bobby and Peyton are the same person, all I have to do is become Ellie. Then I can finish the story. Make it make sense. Peyton and Bobby and Ellie...and me. That's all I have to do. Become Ellie. If Bobby is Peyton, why can't I be Ellie?*

The drive back to New York was quicker than the drive to Charleston, even though there was no hurry. Windsor House was gone, and the Windsor Building was going in a few days. Bobby's people, herself included, were scattering to other houses. The Germans had bought the name and were about to destroy the body.

Sally drove her rented car north, leaving the South and not looking back. As she passed Baltimore, she checked her cell phone for messages. Too many, and none from Bobby. She had much work to do for her new publisher, loose ends to tie up for Windsor, but those could wait a few days. She had a party to plan, one last party. Bring the past to the present, and say good-bye to Bobby.

Back in her condo, Sally left a message on her phone answering machine and an automatic reply on her email: *I am out of my office until September twelfth. I will get back to you as soon as I return.* She spent a day and a night re-reading the Ellie story, and then she wrote a new ending. It was easier than she had anticipated. Then, the day before the party, she thought about Ellie's first line. *I kissed a page for him.* A chain of moments leading to an unplanned conclusion. A first line recalled, the memory of a piano in Charleston, Sally looked at herself in the bathroom mirror, but she saw someone else's face. *As soon as I find my lipstick, I need to add one last thing to the ending we wrote. And then, you and I, dear, are going to Harry Winston's and buy a gift for somebody we both love.*

The Last Party

As much as she loved New York, Sally lived in New Jersey, directly across the river, in a tenth floor condo that had an unobstructed view of the skyline across the river. Her housing history matched her income history. Studio apartment in the Village, a one bedroom in Soho, half of a Brooklyn duplex, a townhouse apartment near Gramercy Park. A steady forty percent of whatever income she had at that stage in her life. But as soon as she went to work for Windsor she finally figured out that everywhere she lived had served one basic purpose: a place to sleep. She worked long hours and ate out almost every night. She went to work early in the morning and went to bed late at night. In between, wherever she lived was empty. She had a cat once, but she gave it away to a couple who actually had time to enjoy it. Then she went to a party in the building that would eventually become her home. The decision to move was easy. The two bedroom units were huge by New York standards, but the best feature was the enclosed balcony that ran the length of the condo, space enough for a party all by itself. It was the view that sold her. She was in the City all day, always looking up it seemed. And nowhere she had lived in the City had given her this New Jersey perspective. On a Sunday afternoon, the panorama included every icon, from the Chrysler Building and Empire State Building all the way down to the World Trade Center. But it was the nights that mattered. She would come back and for the last few minutes before she went to bed she would look at the lights. For the full moon once a month, Sally would sit for hours.

She wanted Windsor's last party to be special. She was reminded by the Germans that, technically, it was not the last Windsor party, but she never heard *that* from anybody who actually worked at Windsor, past or present, and they were the majority of guests this night, along with a few Windsor writers who lived in the City. *And, besides, the German bastards aren't invited.* She insisted that the party be at her place, over-riding any suggestion for a more central location. Sully Semken had called her *Nurse Ratched*, but he still made sure everyone else made plans to be there. It was a farewell to the Windsor they had known, and a bon voyage party for Bobby. He was booked on the Queen Mary II for a morning departure. He insisted that he did not want to be in town when the Windsor Building came down. But he had promised that as soon as he returned he would host his own welcome back party at his new apartment, its location to be kept a secret until then. An Atlantic voyage, a separate Mediterranean circuit, and then some privacy. *All I need*, he insisted, *to get back in shape and start over. And I plan to re-read all the books I read when I was too young to appreciate them the first time.*

Sally had some surprises for Bobby, and the others would be bringing their own tokens for him. Her public surprise was a collection of letters from independent booksellers across the country who had worked with Windsor over the years. *Thank you* notes, testimonials about books for which Bobby had personally called them to ask their support and which they turned into bestsellers. Dozens of them, still fighting the good fight, and more poignant letters from independents who had gone out of business, having lost their own local wars. Sally was not as sentimental about them as Bobby was, but she was especially touched by the gracious note from Mitch Kaplan. He and Bobby had met when Windsor House was born, and Bobby made sure that all first-time Windsor writers began their tours at Kaplan's *Books and Books* in Coral Gables.

In Sally's view, the chains had been just as good for Windsor as the independents, but she understood his affection. In the beginning, he was one of them and he never forgot. She had called a hundred independents and asked them to send a letter, but she insisted that the letter had to be on the store letterhead stationery, and even those who were out of business had managed to find an old sample. She took them all and had Sully design a special scrapbook for the collection.

Sally had also issued another request to all the future guests: *Can we just lighten up for the night? It's a party, for chrissake. I would really appreciate it if we would just gossip about writers and editors or agents we hate, and it would be great if somebody would actually get drunk and punch somebody else's lights out, do a Mailer/ Vidal cat-fight thing, but in a non-litigational way, please. If I hear anybody moaning about how the business is going to hell in a fucking hand-basket, I will personally throw them off my balcony. No talk about asshole reviewers or the lack of any reviews, no talk about more books being printed and fewer being sold, no talk about e-books or self-published books or remaindered books or returned books or advances not being earned. Mention Amazon and you get thrown off my balcony. Not a word about how television is killing the book business. No talk about conglomerates squeezing blood out of our turnips, no talk about the good old days of five martini lunches and publishing being exempt from the law of supply and demand. No talk of how we are poor misunderstood flowers in a weedy world. This is a party for Bobby. It is not a fucking wake. I want gossip about anybody who is not invited, and I want you to make Bobby feel good.*

Bruce Tucker's favorite line?...*poor misunderstood flowers in a weedy world.* "Sally, I am putting that on your tombstone: *She was a poor misunderstood flower in a weedy world.*"

Sally laughed through the phone, "And on yours I'm going to make sure it says: *Here Lies Bruce: He Never Read a Shitty Book He Couldn't Sell.*"

Bobby was the guest of honor, and he arrived last. It was not a surprise party, but he was still surprised by how many old and familiar faces greeted him when he entered. All his former assistant editors, all the women who went from being his second to being the first chair at other houses. His editor friends from other houses were there, as were a few agents who consistently found dazzling first-time authors for Windsor, men and women whose judgment anticipated Bobby's. The biggest surprise for Sally was that Mr. Taylor accepted her invitation. She had arranged for a town-car to spirit him across the river, and he was proud to tell her that *it was the first time I ever rode in the back with a driver up front, taxi-cabs excluded, of course.* Mr. Taylor was the oldest man in the room, and he was dressed, as he would say, *in my burial suit, black like me, but saved for special times like this too.*

Sally was the frenetic host for the first hour, mingling and steering, until Sully Semken nudged her from behind and whispered, "Sally-pants, the alcohol is kicking in. People are starting to slur. You can relax." She scanned the room. *My lord, and I haven't even had my first glass of wine.* She turned to speak to Sully, but he was over talking to Bruce about cover art. Bruce and his wife were the loveliest couple at the party, but Sally had expected that. *Some people,* she knew, *just look good together.*

She had chosen the guests for Bobby's sake. If it had merely been her party, many people in the room this night would not be there. Ashley Bancroft, for one, for whom Bobby evidently still held some affection despite her leaving Windsor. Ashley was ten years older than when Sally had first met her, three books added to her *resume,* divorced and re-married, but with another man this night, a man she insisted that Bobby meet. Sally had opened the door and acted sincerely pleased to see Ashley, but Ashley's hug was not returned.

Ashley's bad karma was erased by the next guest, Whitney Randall, the woman that Sally had replaced. Whitney and Sally had become close friends over the years, more so than any of Bobby's other former assistants. Whitney swept in the door and hugged Sally, waving at faces she recognized, but she lingered at the door long enough to tell Sally, "You and me have to talk. I want to hear all about your new job, and you promised to tell me a secret. I'm dying to hear it."

I should have figured this out a long time ago, Sally told herself as the party went past the two-hour mark, *these things can be a lot of fun if you're the only person not drinking.* She wandered from group to group, stopping occasionally to make sure she knew where Bobby was, seeing him and sadly noting how frail and small he looked compared to everyone else. He would wave at her with a smile when he saw her looking, knowing what she was doing, aware that she was his nurse for the night. She drifted in and out of other people's conversations.

"...How could Gore lose to that idiot..."

"...Rudy wants to be Mayor forever..."

"...You know anything about the new Franzen book?...."

"...*Black House* can be a piece of shit, but who cares, I wish we had..."

"...looks great in that white dress, even for a woman her age...oh, hello Sally..."

"...I will miss Bill...."

"...Can you believe it, Steve Malloy is here. If you had told me..."

"...Did you hear Bruce's idea about readings? Get them in bars and coffee shops and hotels and places other than bookstores...who's *that* desperate?... and his idea about video trailers on the web!!...where did that come from?"

"...the best ones are leaving, even...oh, hello Sally...great party..."

"...yes, I heard that too...right there in his office...his wife damn near..."

Variations on themes that she had heard many times, but she was still not bored after all the years she had been in the business. Sally surprised herself. *I'm beginning to like some of the people here that I have never liked. Go figure. Except for that bitch Ashley. I should stay sober at the next party too.*

At eleven o'clock, toasts were made and maudlin Bobby

stories exchanged. Bobby was given his scrapbook and not an eye was dry, even Mr. Taylor's. Through it all, Bobby remained the most gracious person in the room. As her guests started drifting away, saying good-bye to Bobby as they retrieved coats and scarves, Sally sometimes winced to see how tightly Bobby was embraced as a farewell. *My god, not so hard, can't you see how sick he is.*

Standing off to one side, watching the party dwindle, Sally saw Whitney Randall slipping toward her. She knew what Whitney wanted to know.

"Sally, the scar. You said you knew how he got it. I'm very impressed, but not surprised. We all knew that if he ever told anybody, it would be you. So, tell me."

"You'll be disappointed. He had too much to drink a long time ago, tripped into a glass door and was lucky he didn't bleed to death. Not mysterious at all. But he was always embarrassed about the fall, so he let the rest of us spin stories about the scar." Sally lied convincingly, keeping Bobby's secret.

Whitney *was* disappointed. "Really? That's it? Why would he keep that a secret?"

"Well, you know how he is," Sally replied. "He likes his privacy, and his *mystique*."

Whitney looked at her, smiling as she arched her eyebrows, "And his secrets. But you know that too."

It had been a good party. A few had grumbled about Sally's no smoking rule, but even Bobby had obeyed it. Nobody had gotten into a fight, to Sally's disappointment, but she was satisfied enough that Ashley Bancroft and her date did not leave together. Close to midnight, the publishing world was reduced to Sally and Bobby, Sully, Bruce and his wife, and Mr. Taylor.

Sully and the Tuckers had come together and would leave together, but not before Sully and Bruce and Bobby huddled by themselves in the corner, whispering and laughing and tapping each other's arms and chests, twenty years of intimacy between the three men who had made Windsor a success. Bruce's wife was standing with Sally, their arms entwined, and the two women did not speak as they watched the men. When Bruce finally put his massive arms around Bobby for the last time, Sally, knowing that she could not stop from crying, whispered to his wife, "I can't watch this," and she walked out to the balcony to look at New York. The moon was full.

The party was over, and the most surprising thing to Sally was who remained. Bobby, she expected, because he had told her that he had a present for her. But, Mr. Taylor? Sally had seen him almost everyday for over ten years, and he had been at Windsor for twenty, but neither she or anybody else had ever heard him say much more than *hello* and *good by* and *let me help you with that*. But there he was in her living room, walking around and picking up dishes and trash to take to the kitchen, still in his black suit, actually humming to himself, seemingly oblivious to Sally and Bobby.

"I told him that he could ride back with me in the car picking me up," Bobby said, leading her to the balcony. "After it drops me off at the Plaza, it will take him to his hotel."

Sally sighed, "So I guess we'll say good-bye here then? You know, I *could* take you back to your hotel."

Bobby said, "In the car you do not own?"

"Oh, Bobby, I mean…"

"No, no, this is better. You know me, prince of the symbolic gestures…well, perhaps you do not know *that* me…but I do like this circle I have drawn. Mr. Taylor took me to my first hotel in New York. He should accompany me to my last."

"Bobby, you're not going to do something dumb, are you, like jump out a window or jump overboard somewhere in the middle of the Atlantic. Right? Tell me that. Promise me that you are coming back, okay? Promise me that you will see me again. You promise me that, or I will not let you leave my place. You and Mr. Taylor will live with me forever. So, you promise?"

Bobby looked at her, and then across the river to the City. "Absolutely, I promise. You have my word on it."

Sally trembled, stifling a cry, but she believed him, she had to believe him for now, and she let out a breath she had been holding for months. "Well, okay, Mr. Prince, where's my present?" They were sitting on the balcony, at a forty-five degree angle from each other, so they could see each other and the New York skyline in the same glance. It was a mild and clear moonlit night. "I threw the damn party. And you promised me a present."

Bobby turned toward the living room and waved to get Mr. Taylor's attention, then he turned back to Sally, "I gave it to him, since he was here, and asked him to add something to it. Close your eyes."

"You are *such* a romantic, Bobby," she said, calmly happy, and she closed her eyes. When she opened them again, she found a tray on a small table that had been set between her and Bobby. On the tray was a stack of Graham Crackers and two glasses of milk.

Sally almost gasped, but said to herself, "Oh, Bobby, you *are* a romantic."

Small talk and gossip, plans for her future, Steve Malloy's

memoir, their mutual escape from the Germans, for an hour they shared Graham Crackers and milk, and their past. Sally knew that Bobby needed to rest, but she did not want to let him go just yet. And, besides, he seemed to have more energy now than he had had for a long time.

"And my present?" he finally said.

She went to her bedroom to retrieve his gifts. Back on the balcony, she sat across from him, as nervous as a child.

"You get two things. I only had time to wrap one, but the other…" she said, handing him a manila envelope, "…the other, this, you can look at here or wait until you get on the ship tomorrow."

Bobby was curious, she could see it in his face, but he did not speak.

"But this one," she said, still holding a present gift-wrapped in red, "this one you cannot open in front of me."

Because the look on your face will break my heart, and I can't do that to myself. As much as I love you, I can't share that moment with you.

Bobby held up the manila envelope, "I can open this?"

She nodded, but then as he was about to pull the pages out of the envelope she stopped him, preparing to give the best performance of her life, "Oh, god, Bobby, I have to warn you. It's…" and she braced herself, "…it's the ending to her story. I went to see Peter Stone."

Sally had never seen a look on Bobby's face to match how he looked at this moment. She had *finally* surprised him.

"I made him let me see her other papers, the stuff he did not send you. How could he resist my charm? And I found what I was looking for…the last few pages she ever wrote. The end of her story. And I stole them when he was not looking."

He slid the sheets back into the envelope, paused, looked back at her, shook his head as if clearing it, and then took them out again. "I think I need more light," he said.

She pointed with her head to the living room, and then she sat back to look at the moon as Bobby rose to go inside. Then she waited.

A few pages, perhaps five minutes reading at the most, that was all it should have taken, but it was half an hour before she heard his voice again. "Sally, it is time to go. Mr. Taylor and I have a car waiting downstairs."

She did not want to ask him about the ending. She wanted him to volunteer his opinion without her asking. That was her new rule. She would not petition the prince for his opinion.

He came back to the balcony and sat down beside her again. "I need to leave soon. I have a long journey planned."

She did not respond.

"You want to know about the ending," he finally said, but she still did not respond. "Sally, I wish you had known her," was his most sincere feeling at that moment, but he immediately wondered if it was the wrong thing to say. "Sally?"

You wish I had known her? Bobby, did you read what I wrote? How much better do I need to know her? Sally remained silent.

"It was perfect," Bobby finally admitted.

Sally knew what was coming next.

"And you must promise me to publish her story just as it was written, but with this perfect ending. I think she would have liked that. It is how it should have ended."

"I can't do that," she said, looking at his face go from pleased to perplexed. It was his turn to remain silent. "I *will* make you a solemn promise. I *will* publish her story. I *will* include the new ending. But I won't do it as long as Peter Stone is alive. Nobody would understand why he did what he did, and they would see him as weak. But he's not. I know that. You know that. He doesn't deserve to be hurt any more, and I won't do that to him. And neither would you."

Bobby stood and walked to the balcony railing, grasping it with both hands and leaning forward toward the lights across the river. Sally then rose and stood beside him. Neither looked at the other, neither spoke.

"I suppose you are right," he finally said. "And, of course, I assumed I would never see it in print anyway. But you will do it, right?"

"I promised, Bobby, I promised you."

"Yes, you did, and I know you will keep that promise, but you do realize, of course, that he will probably live forever, outlasting all of us," he said, "so you might want to prepare to wait a long time."

Sally shoved his arm gently, "Be nice, Bobby."

"Yes, I must be an adult," he sighed.

Sally noticed how quiet it was as she waited for him to speak again. She did not turn around, but she sensed that Mr. Taylor was waiting patiently for her and Bobby to resolve their lives.

"You told me it was her story," she said quietly. "And true, and I wondered why she chose not to use your real life to create Peyton, but I figured it out. All I had to do was think like her."

Bobby did not look at her as he spoke, "She was protecting me. She knew that *I* would know it was me, and that is all that counted, but nobody else would ever know. She was wrong, of course. She thought it would still be our secret...*ours*... the two of us. She wrote the story for me, not for publication. But I do want others to know her story too." He took in a deep breath, shaking his head in denial, "Even though it never happened. Not that way. All along, I suppose, you have been dealing with fiction."

Sally was disappointed. Bobby would never tell her the whole truth, but she still wanted him to understand her. "See, this is what I think, right or wrong, what I choose to think. The ending you had in those original pages was not the ending she intended to write. There was more to say, but she ran out of time. And we'll never know all the rest, everything in between, but she never stopped being in love with you. But she got sick and when her time was running short, I am sure, she wrote these last few pages."

Sally waited for him to talk, but he remained silent, looking away from her, pausing before he spoke again. "And here's what you need to understand…I know that she disguised the story to protect my public life. And you're right, you should not publish it while her husband is alive because he deserves to be protected too, I suppose."

Sally held back one last thought, something she understood but Bobby never would. *Dammit, Bobby, I wrote the ending for you and me too, not just her. But you'll never know. The two of you, Stone and you, loved the same woman. And I understand that. But if you want to believe that she wrote her story the way she did to 'protect' you, then I'll let you keep that delusion. The story is about her, Bobby, not the two of you. You and Stone were always supporting actors in a story about a woman whose life revolved around… herself. Her only redeeming quality was insanity.*

Bobby finally turned toward her and smiled sadly, saying,

"And people ask me why I like you."

Sally reached over and took his hand. She edged closer to him, still side by side, their shoulders now touching. From behind them came a voice, "Mr. Beaumont, it's time for us to go."

The Lincoln's driver was holding the back door open when the three of them got downstairs. Mr. Taylor got in first, and Bobby told the driver to wait. He stepped back to Sally and took her arm in his and led her back to the front door of her building. "You are to take care of yourself, Sally. And you must keep track of Sully and Bruce for me."

"You'll write me, you hear me, and I'll be pissed if all I get are some post cards from Europe. You write real letters, and get somebody to take a picture of you next to some damn leaning tower or in a gondola or something touristy like that," she said, doing her best to smile.

"Yes, ma'am," he said.

"You promise?"

"I do promise."

We're the same height, Bobby, how come that was never obvious to me before now?

He stepped away, saying, "And thank you for finding that ending. It was a perfect gift."

"Good-bye, Bobby."

"Good-bye, Sally."

He got in the town-car, and the driver closed the door behind him. Sally walked to the curb as the Lincoln began to drive away. Through the rear window, she saw Mr. Taylor hand an envelope to Bobby, and then she saw Bobby turn around and wave at her. She waved back, thinking softly to herself, *Oh, Bobby, if you think that the new ending was a perfect gift, how will you feel about the other one?*

Home Again

The Lincoln took Bobby to the Plaza, where he had been staying as the Windsor Building was being gutted. After shaking hands with Mr. Taylor one last time and wishing him well on his journey back to New Orleans, he went inside and checked out, telling the clerk that he had made arrangements for his belongings to be picked up in the morning and shipped to his home in Charleston. "I have also arranged for a cab to get me now, but I want to wait by the fountain outside," he told the clerk. "Would you please make sure he comes to get me there. I might miss him."

Thirty minutes later, the cab dropped Bobby off three blocks away from the Windsor Building. The Korean cabbie was concerned, "You sure you want to get out here...now? I should wait for you?"

Bobby assured him, "No, no, I will be fine. I know this area quite well." A twenty-dollar tip in his pocket, the cabbie drove off, and Bobby walked to the Windsor Building. When he turned the final corner, he stopped to look at the dark façade. The electricity had been cut off, and the building would be black inside. He then stepped under the yellow tape blocking the entrance gate of the chain link fence that surrounded the building, found the pad lock, unlocked it, stepped inside, shut the gate behind him, and then reached through the links to close the pad-lock again. Up the steps to the front of the building itself, he unlocked that door, stepped into the dark and closed the door behind him. He was exhausted, but he quickly found the folding chair behind the front counter that he had left for himself weeks earlier and sat down to rest. The hardest part of his journey was still to come.

He could have slept in the empty lobby until morning and waited for that light before he proceeded, but he did not want to chance any of the demolition crew arriving earlier than he expected. So he rested for a half hour, then he felt his way in the dark lobby toward a low cabinet where he had left a bag. Taking the flashlight out of the bag, he was ready to begin his ascent to the thirteenth floor. Stepping into the stairwell, the beam of his flashlight bouncing off the walls, Bobby told himself: *Well, if this does not kill me, nothing will.*

He started climbing stairs. The first three were no problem, but he had to stop on the fifth and rest again. He sat on a step and leaned against the wall, forgetting to turn off his flashlight as he dozed off. When he woke up, the light was noticeably dimmer. *I have got to hurry. Harry is waiting for me.*

Another four flights, or was it five, more rest, and he worried that he might miss the thirteenth floor stairwell door. And then he had a flash of panic. *Did I bring that key too, the one that Harry gave me a long time ago? When was it? He said nobody except him and me and his Accountant had one. But he would laugh and say that the Accountant would not walk up a single flight of stairs even if it meant meeting Moses himself, Harry said that.* Bobby found the key in his pocket and started climbing again.

The flashlight beam was dimmer, and his lungs were contradicting themselves, constricting in ice and expanding in flames. Or was it his heart? *This is a foolish drama, Bobby Beaumont,* he told himself. *You have taken Dylan Thomas too much to heart. Go ahead, Bobby, go gentle. Do it, just go gentle.*

Almost to the thirteenth floor, Bobby realized that he had left his bag somewhere below. He had set it down and forgotten it. He could wait until morning, he thought, but then he realized that the stairwells got no sunlight anyway. He would still have to use the flashlight, and he had to do it now or else he would be too exhausted to come back. He gripped a handrail and let the faltering beam lead him down two flights, but he was lucky. It was right there on the landing at the tenth floor. Sally's presents were in the bag, and his drugs. He wanted to re-read the ending, and open her other gift, but only at the last moment.

He climbed back to the thirteenth floor, making sure that he saw the number 12 on the floor below it. That was the only sure sign. The door to the fourteenth floor was marked 13. The door to the real thirteenth floor, Harry Windsor's home, was marked: *Utility Room 12ᵗʰ Floor.*

Bobby put the key in the lock, leaned his head against the door, and waited for his lungs and heart to slow down. He had forty hours until the demolition. Time to rest and get ready, but he had to get to his apartment soon. *Second Sunday in September. Second Sunday in September.* Harry Windsor had died on the second Sunday in September, 1985, and his last words, according to a male night nurse who claimed to have actually heard them, were not profound nor were they tender, but Bobby believed the nurse because he could hear Windsor say, *That goddam Reagan is going to totally fuck this up for all of us. Mark my words this second Sunday of September, young man, that chump actor is an idiot.* Last words? At least Harry Windsor had an audience. Bobby knew that Harry might appreciate it if he died on the same day years later. Bobby, however, had his own schedule in mind. Harry would have to wait until Tuesday.

Where the hell have you been, Bobby?

Bobby woke up quickly. Sunlight was pouring through his apartment windows. Monday morning. The Windsor was a tomb. He liked the comparison. A building with no electricity or running water. No pulse to be felt or heard. In the weeks before this moment, he had calculated the things that could go wrong with his plan. The worst thing would be to have been discovered by the demolition crew, or for them to have discovered all the rooms and attics that were not on the original blueprints or marked by obvious doors and windows. It had been essential for him to get back into the building at least twenty-four hours before the actual demolition, hiding during the day, especially in the hours before the switches were pulled, when the crew would go back through the building one last time making sure their safety record would remain unblemished. Now, himself safely back inside, all he had to do was be alert for any unscheduled intrusions. He had a copy of the demolition company's timetable and countdown procedures. But he was more tired than he had anticipated.

Harry Windsor wanted to take full credit for anticipating Bobby's dilemma. *Sooner or later, we all need a place to hide. Just like Anne Frank. I knew the Germans were coming a long time ago.*

Just like Anne Frank. She taught me a lesson. Your people don't know these things. We do. Just like Anne Frank.

Bobby had listened politely, but he had pointed out, *Harry, you built this place before anybody had ever heard of Anne Frank, before the war itself.*

And this makes me wrong?

Bobby woke up again. The morning sun was barely visible, but he was prepared. He had hidden candles in his vacated apartment, and a wind-up clock. He had a jug of water, a bottle of wine, and his pills. A candle in hand, he went looking for Harry Windsor, but all he found was his voice.

You keep asking where I'm going, Bobby. As if I was going somewhere else. You think all this will disappear because they blow it up… about all the goddam krauts are good for, blowing things up… no, no… this place stays and I stay with it. And, no, I don't need your company, as much as I like you. I've got company. This is not the place for you. You think it is, but you're wrong. Hell, you made it famous, you and your books, but this is not your home. And home is where you're going.

Bobby was glad that Sally and the others could not see him now. He knew how preposterous he looked, a human skeleton in a cadaverous building, talking to an invisible Jew.

The alarm sounded again. He had gone back to sleep. He woke up again. Tuesday morning, the sun was up. He had to hurry. He packed his bag, careful to keep the manila envelope next to the red-wrapped gift. He splashed his face with what was left of the bottled water. He swallowed the pills, then the wine. And then he opened the door to what he expected would be a dark hallway. Just as he stepped through, he heard a crackling pop, and then an electric sizzle, like lightning in the sky, followed by rolling thunder in the distance, and then silence.

The sound of someone snapping his fingers. A sudden illumination of the hallway, and Bobby was temporarily blinded. Every lamp along the wall was burning brightly all at once, and, his sight slowly restored, there in front of him, wearing a black fedora, was Harry Windsor.

I told the bastards that I wanted this hallway lit all the time. I pay my bills. I want light. Eternal goddam light.

Bobby blinked and walked toward Windsor.

You're gonna get a reputation, Bobby, not wearing your shoes at the office.

The two men walked the hallway. *Are we alone?* Bobby asked, hearing footsteps behind them but seeing nothing when he turned around quickly. He turned to Windsor again.

The older man offered him a cigar, laughing, *Fuck the Surgeon General, eh?*

Bobby inhaled tentatively, some vestige of a memory about how painful smoking had become for him near the end, but this was different.

You like? Windsor asked.

It is like the first time I smoked, a long time ago. The same aroma, the taste. I can remember it exactly.

Well, keep that stogie and make it last. I only had one made.

You have always been here, always, am I correct, Harry?

In the beginning was the Word, and Harry Windsor, I always say, but none of you gen-teels think that's funny. You people are so dry.

When did you start doing stand-up comedy, Harry?

Bobby, I've always been a funny man. It just took you a few decades to become my ideal audience. So, young man, all I want to know is this…where the hell did you get a key to that fence lock downstairs? You were always methodical, just like my friend Harry Houdini, but I still wonder…

You never knew Harry Houdini. And I even have my doubts about Harry Winston too.

The key… Mr. Cynic… the key?

I had somebody cut off the original lock a few days ago and replace it with a identical new one, so I had the keys. I am sure the demolition people had to cut it off this morning, not having time to ponder its significance.

Let me guess… it was that Taylor man. My money's on him. Right or wrong?

Right, of course. Remember, he was the first person I hired. I trust him. As you trust your Accountant.

With that word, Windsor was gone. Bobby blinked. The hallway was still blazing. He walked toward the end, wondering if Harry Windsor was around the corner. Just as he was about to turn, he heard footsteps and a different voice behind him.

This is where we part company, Mr. Beaumont, but Harry wanted me to make sure that you knew that he was very proud of you, and what you did for his name.

It was the Accountant, his brown pinstriped suit still looking like it just came off the rack.

I do not understand, Bobby said.

That's why you hire an accountant. To keep your books balanced, pay your bills and your taxes, so you can have time to think the big thoughts. To understand things. Harry needed the best in the world, still does, but you don't. Good-bye, Mr. Beaumont.

Bobby turned the corner and stepped into the wide red-carpeted hallway of his parents' home in Charleston. Ahead of him was his father. Forrest Beaumont had a drink in each hand, one half full, the other full glass raised toward his son.

You must hurry, son. Your mother is waiting. Drink this, and then we will dress for dinner. Ruby has prepared a wonderful supper, and she made sweet tea just for you.

Bobby's heart swelled with joy, and a peace he had not felt since he left Charleston. He took the drink from his father and walked beside him. *I am very tired*, he said. Still, he was compelled to ask a question. *Did you always know, even before I told you?*

About the woman? His father said, without reproach.

Yes, about Ellie. I never got away from the feeling that you and mother would be so disappointed in me, and then, to our amazement, hers and mine, it lasted so long. I felt I had to keep it from you, and... even after you told me about how you were taking care of her... there never came a good time to really talk to you, and New York became another home for her and me, and you died, and...

And you should rest, Bobby. We will talk. But I do need to clarify one misunderstanding of yours. You think that she and I never met, but we did. Just as she described it, as your life ebbed. I was there, and she became mine as well as yours.

I am going to see her again, am I not? Surely, now, finally.

His father tilted his head slowly, and then said, *Perhaps in the future. On one of our walks. The streets have many surprises here in Charleston. Until that might happen, you will only have what the other woman gave you, there in your bag, but it will be enough until then.*

Sally? Of course, her gift.

Bobby reached into his bag and pulled out the manila envelope and showed it to his father, who said, *I know the story, and the ending is as it should have been. She cared for you very much.* Bobby reached back into his bag again and slowly pulled out the other gift. Inside the cardboard box, wrapped in red tissue paper, with the weight of a heavy book, was a music box shaped like a grand piano, as big as his hand. Ivory keys and a dark teak body, with a diamond border along the keyboard. He wondered where Sally had found it, but then he saw the Harry Winston logo on the cardboard box. Bobby looked up at his smiling father again. He lifted the glistening lid of the piano, and the two men heard music.

Ellie and Bobby and Home

Bobby, one of us has to stop being so stubborn. I suppose I'm to blame, and for that I apologize. I should have realized that, as much as everyone else thinks that I am a drama queen (you said that too), you are just as bad. I assigned you a role...was it jilted lover or scorned lover? And you ran with it. But, please... me, I was crazy. You have no excuse. Grief explains you...but not forever. I could have told you about my own diagnosis, but you were dealing with your mother's death. I was dying, Bobby, God's final trick on me. When I left you in New York, the only thing sick about me was my head. Pete took care of that. I mean, he sort of took care of that. He put me back on my feet. (Remember how I would not get out of bed for that last few months I was around you?) He told me that he would take care of me. And he did. You owe him for that. He took care of me even though he knew where it would eventually lead. And just as the cosmos aligned itself as I always said it would...a week before your mother died I sat with Pete in another doctor's office as he told me that I should have my breasts removed as soon as possible. And even then...he was so calm about it...he said there was no guarantee. I actually laughed in his face...No guarantee? Hot flash, Doctor Calm, the only thing anybody is guaranteed is that we are all going to die. Yes, once again, I was not a good patient.

No...the calm doctor said...I mean there is no guarantee you will live for more than a few more years.

You want to understand grief, Bobby, you should have seen Pete's face. Me, I was angry. At the calm doctor, at God, at P&P for robbing me, and at myself. All I thought of that moment was wanting to see you again. At least one last time.

You're out of parents, Bobby. Seems like our grand reunions always require somebody else's death. Ain't nobody left but us.

I wanted to see you before they started cutting on me, peeling away my diseased flesh piece by inch, and then going deeper. And you came back to Charleston. How awful had I been to you before I left New York? I honestly do not remember. I must have given the best performance of my life, because you obviously took me too seriously. In your mind, I must have cut the cord and burned it. You never contacted me about coming back. But I went to your house after your mother's funeral all set to apologize, and to tell you about my imminent surgery...but I changed my mind and lied to you. Why is that, Bobby? Why could I not share that with you? Pete gives me too much credit for goodness, but he makes sense. How unfair would it have been for me to burden you at that moment with additional bad news? Trust me, martyrdom is not my strong suit.

I stepped through the front door and there you were...and I turned to mush again. How is it all connected? Turn around and your entire life is right there behind you, every version of yourself trailing you, like some stupid modern art painting, me descending a staircase (You and I saw that together? Where?) I saw us again, Bobby, that morning you took me to your house after we did it at the bookstore. Morning light and silence. Just me and you in that house. A hundred old adults there to grieve for your mother, but we were sex-drenched teenagers again, and then the other moment returned. I stood in that doorway of your dead mother's house, seeing you before you saw me, and then I saw myself run past me out the door, leaving you behind as I returned to the hell of my dead mother's house. But, see, yes, I have a point here, something I understand now, and why it is time for us to see each other again. We had no "distance" then. No big picture. Nothing but fragments of our lives (photos out of order, most missing?) but not a picture.

And you saw me. (Wasn't that perfect?) I understood that your mourning ritual had protocols...guests must be received, condolences accepted, embraces and handshakes of communion. I was in no hurry.

You took my hand in greeting and whispered.

—We will talk soon.

I was used to waiting. I turned and that is when I saw her, the woman from New York, your favorite assistant, the one who would never leave, wine glass in hand, walking toward you as I was walking away. She must have seen me, right? But she was looking only at you.

Okay, I guess I do have martyr potential. Sentimentality warning...that woman did not see me because she only had eyes for you. Cue the cliché, I know. I saw a woman in love with you. Remember, I am an expert in loving you. I was also, I was sure at that moment, a dead woman walking. I knew, contrary to what you had assured me, I was going to die long before you. (Pete tells me that those sorts of "moments of absolute clarity" are real. But I figured out all by myself that they can also be absolutely really wrong.)

I looked at you and her, your back to me, but she was...and I say this just for you, Mr. Editor...an open book. Bobby, I let her have you. When you and I finally found time to talk privately, I had measured the words I needed to say. I told you that I was a different person, that I was cured, that I was going to marry Pete. I was a better surgeon on you than the one who cut me later.

And I was a fool.

And now I see it. I found the distance. Life makes sense, Bobby, but not up close. I don't remember the first time I heard the song, and the lyrics did not really fit me and you, except for something about...from a distance there is harmony. I listened over and over, all about harmony and hope of hopes and love of loves. We'll keep the song title, but we'll write new lyrics.

I did not die, Bobby. I was cut and bled and I waited for the end, but I did not die. I fooled God himself. I waited for you to marry that woman, you knowing that I was gone forever, but you did not. Pete did want me to marry him, but I did not accept. Those refusals were there from the first moment we met, us not settling for anyone else, but we would only see them...from a distance. Time became Distance, and from that distance I understood us, me and you, Bobby. We owe the world an apology, and there will be time for that too. But you need to come home soon. We need to walk in White Point Garden again. We need to visit Peter and Paul at St. John the Baptist.

Hell, we can even go to St. Phillips and talk to the dead. We need to go to your house and talk to the ghosts there. Most of all, we need to find that magic mirror. We will look at each other's faces and see our children. And see ourselves. We'll go to sleep together on that couch and then we'll wake up and live forever, just like you promised. Come home, Bobby. I'm waiting for you.

Acknowledgements

For his continued support (an outsider might describe that support as long-suffering), Steve Semken at Ice Cube Press. I am lucky to know him.

Tim Conroy was an invaluable source of information about Charleston geography and history. He was always gracious as I asked a lot of questions about how to describe the hometown of Ellie and Bobby. Helping Tim was Linda Bennett at the Charleston Public Library, and she gets my thanks too.

Providing essential medical details for the story, sometimes a single word made a big difference, were Susan Lambert and Jeannine Ayres.

I needed information about Harry Chapin's last appearance in New York City. Howard Fields was my go-to guy. For a lot of New York City history in general and the Seventies in particular, Alan Roberts never failed me.

I asked Beverly Willett for a long description of a home in Savannah. It was so good that I included it verbatim.

In Iowa City, Brady McDonald generously allowed me to use his Basta Restaurant for the cover photo-shoot. Howard Horan was my photographer again. My main models were Anna Goodsell and Ross Vander Peut.

Finally, if patience and good humor are virtues, my wife and children are saints.

A GOOD MAN (2009)

Harry Forster Ducharme is at the end of his rope. Booze and bad decisions have taken him from the A-list of talk-radio fame down to a tiny cinder-block station, WWHD in St. Augustine, Florida. He talks mostly to himself from 10 p.m. to 2 a.m., not sure anybody is listening, reading books and poetry that he likes, not caring if anyone agrees with him, playing golden-oldies from the Sixties, and wondering how he got there.

Then, as a hurricane pounds north Florida, with WWHD broadcasting to a town without electricity, Harry gets a visitor just as the eye of the hurricane passes over. An old black man who calls himself The Prophet wants to borrow a Walt Whitman poem that Harry read the night before. He wants "A Noiseless Patient Spider" to be the core of his next sermon, in which he announces the imminent arrival of a New Child of God. Harry is a bit skeptical.

The story weaves back and forth in time, revealing the history of an orphan named Harry Ducharme. From Iowa farm to Florida beach, Harry is finally surrounded by men and women with their own burdens to carry. Captain Jack Tunnel is the morning host, more rightwing than Rush, with a cranky co-host parrot named Jimmy Buffett, but also with a gentle secret life. Nora James is the mysterious "cooking woman" who broadcasts from her home kitchen, but whom nobody has ever seen. Nora cooks on-air and discusses women's issues. Harry spends his first year in town trying to find her, only to discover that Nora's whereabouts are a communal secret, revealed only to a select few. Carlos Friedmann has the 2–6 a.m. slot, a fourth-generation Jewish Cuban who cannot speak Spanish, but whose forte is to broadcast fake interviews with Fidel Castro. Friedmann's great desire is to kill and cook the parrot Jimmy Buffett.

Harry had arrived in St. Augustine in November of 2000. Living in America's oldest city, Harry reveals profound insights into American politics and history throughout A Good Man. Eventually, his role in the New Child's arrival becomes intertwined with contemporary politics, Iraq, 9/11, old-time religion, and classic literature from writers like Flannery O'Connor and Emily Dickinson, as well as the music of Harry Chapin.

A Good Man opens with the first sighting of The Prophet and ends on Election night-2008 in Florida with the revelation of the New Child. Or perhaps not. Still, Harry is there, in the parking lot of a Jacksonville football stadium, surrounded by thousands of pilgrims, as witness to and participant in one final act of death and redemption that might be a sign of the beginning, or the end.

Praise for A GOOD MAN

"Larry Baker's **A Good Man** updates the world of Flannery
O'Connor s characters through the Bush years and into the
age of Obama. Fans of O'Connor s fiction will be intrigued
by Baker s imaginative reunion, in the home of the fountain
of youth, of Bevel Summers with a very grown-up Harry from
O'Connor s The River. Without imitating O'Connor, Baker
does serious honor to her legacy." —Marshall Bruce Gentry,
Editor, *Flannery O'Connor Review*, Georgia College & State
University.

"In Harry Ducharme, the hero of **A Good Man**, Larry Baker
has created a main character as memorable and complex as John
Updike's Rabbit Angstrom or Richard Ford's Frank Bascombe.
Not since Robert Stone's A Hall of Mirrors have we been
this privy to the troubled soul of a disc jockey. Fans of Baker s
previous novels won t be disappointed while readers new to his
work will be bowled over." —John McNally, author, *Ghosts of
Chicago* and *The Book of Ralph*.

THE FLAMINGO RISING (1997)

In this touching, hilarious novel of the heart and mind, of dreams and memory, of desire and first love, Abe Lee comes of age in the 1960s, living with his unforgettable family at the Flamingo Drive-In Theatre on a scrubby patch of coast between Jacksonville and St. Augustine, Florida. There, some of America's last sweet moments of innocence are unfolding.

For Abe's father, Hubert, there's nothing better than presenting larger-than-life Hollywood fantasies on his vast silver screen. Nothing, that is, except gleefully sparring with Turner West—a funeral home operator who doesn't much appreciate the noise and merriment from the drive-in next door. Within the lively orbit of this ongoing feud is Abe's mother, Edna Marie, whose calm radiance conceals deep secrets; his sister, Louise, who blossoms almost too quickly into a stunning, willful young woman; and Judge Lester, a clumsy man on the ground who turns graceful when he takes to the sky, towing the Flamingo banner behind his small plane. Then Abe falls for Turner's beautiful daughter Grace. That's when, long before the Fourth of July festivities, the fireworks really begin.

Praise for **THE FLAMINGO RISING**

"A first novel that dares mix the Icarus, Oedipus and Earhart myths, risks a Romeo and Juliet update, plunders Dante, references the Bible, rewrites movie history and inside-outs the American past. Yet Baker's book is far from pretentious. It's one of the more endearingly adept debuts to come along in a while....A novel that is as fully realized as it is inventive, humorous, and heart-aching."—*Los Angeles Times*

"What could be more all-American than a longstanding family feud between an earnest funeral director and the visionary, grandly egotistical owner of a drive-in movie theater in Florida called the Flamingo? Especially when the owner's son, who narrates the tale, is an adopted Korean boy named Abe. And the owner's daughter, Louise, also Korean, overcomes a slight limp to become a famous movie star. And the son falls for the daughter of the funeral director in one more classically star-crossed romance. And, what's more, in the pre-Civil Rights Sixties, the hired hand who helps keep a lid on the boiling tensions is a wily black man. Young Abe Lee's narration is partly a tender coming-of-age tale, partly an astute view of a family coming painfully apart. Everything goes up in smoke at the end, including Louise's crazy, beloved dog, Frank, whose imprisonment in a tower above the family quarters is a painful reminder that everyone else in this story is also boxed in, but not everyone breaks free. Highly recommended." Barbara Hoffert, *Library Journal*

ATHENS, AMERICA (2005)

Athens is the best of small college towns: affluent, cultured, tolerant, safe, and insulated from a world that seems to lack all those advantages. But at the beginning of a long dry summer, Athens sheds its communal innocence as two teenagers are killed in a police chase gone bad.

Joe Holly, burned out city councilman is suddenly in the middle of a public crisis as the Athens police department is accused of negligence in the death of a drug-dealing thug and Becky Hamilton. As his campaign for re-election nears the first Tuesday in November, he finally understands his own limitations and the choice he must make. As he says early, "This is a story about my family and my town, and how I lost one."

Jack Hamilton and his wife Marcie refuse to participate in the public drama that their daughter's death has inspired. Their private grief has its own spiral, and all they want is to be left alone. But with the help of their daughter's own words and the lyrics from a forgotten Harry Chapin song, they eventually find peace. **ATHENS, AMERICA** is the story of two men dealing with public tragedy and private grief. And the lesson for a reader is from Joe Holly, who amends Tip O'Neill's famous axiom "All politics is local." For Holly, "All local politics is personal."

Praise for **ATHENS, AMERICA**

"Larry Baker's immense knowledge of local politics comes from his own experience, and that knowledge is put to dramatic effect in **ATHENS, AMERICA.** But **ATHENS** is more than a political novel. It's also a highly moral and humane story, with a narrator who is both astute and forgiving of human foibles. And, ultimately, while being a story about a certain kind of American, it's also a very tender love story. I hope it sells a million copies."—Haven Kimmel, author of *Something Rising* and *The Solace of Leaving Early*

"I read this extraordinary book in two enormous gulps while on the set in Vancouver. **ATHENS** has it all. Like a multi-layered world carved on ivory by the most skilled of Chinese artisans, Larry Baker has replicated our complicated, contentious, duplicitous, stupid, and deeply moving America. You'll see your town in this powerful story, and how you see yourself after reading it may be determined by who you are in your own community." —Peter Coyote, actor and author of *Sleeping Where I Fall*

"How do you find the soul of a town? You look deep into the souls of its people, as Larry Baker has done so compellingly in *ATHENS, AMERICA.* Two families, one very public, one very private, each struggling with tragedy — in particular, that most unspeakable grief, the loss of a child. Add a community riven by controversy and grappling with its changing sense of itself, and a mythic deer whose presence lurks at the fringes of every twist and turn, and you have one mighty fine story, told by one of the best storytellers I've come across in a long time. If this book doesn't move you, check to see if you still have a pulse."—-Robert Inman, author of *Captain Saturday* and *Home Fires Burning*

THE EDUCATION OF NANCY ADAMS (2014)

Nancy Adams is a childless widow who has spent the previous four years slowly spending her dead husband's estate and drinking too much. Afraid of becoming the town's official spinster and overall spook, she finally accepts her first real full-time job ever, as a history teacher at the Florida high school from which she graduated almost twenty years earlier.

The principal who offers her the job, Russell Parsons, was her history teacher when she was a student. They had an intense, but platonic, relationship then, but he was too old for her and about to get married. He is now 47, she is 37, so age is not a factor anymore, and he is married to a woman that everyone in town hates and they assume he must be unhappy. Nancy thus sees an opportunity to start her life over with her first love. She is wrong.

Looming in the back of Nancy's mind is the intellectual ghost of Henry Adams, the Harvard historian whose *Education* was required reading for her in college. Her own education sends her back to him, requiring her to first acknowledge her debt to him before she eventually becomes his teacher.

Other key characters include: Dell Rose, the basketball coach who most people believe is sleeping with any and all living females of any age or color. Dell is charismatic, charming, absolutely politically incorrect, but eventually becomes heroic at the end. Agnes Rose is Dell's mother and also a teacher at the same school, a wonderful teacher who has a hard time reconciling her strong religious beliefs with her favorite son's behavior. Donna Parton is the school counselor, a witty woman who knows everything about everybody. Fred Stein is an over-achieving senior who becomes Nancy's favorite student. April Bourne is headed for valedictorian, super intelligent but also malicious and unprincipled.

Finally, Dana O'Connor, the eighteen-year old unwed mother who is brilliant and mysterious. Dana was headed for the valedictorian honor until she had to drop out of school to have her baby. Back now, child in tow, Dana is being allowed to make up all the courses she missed in addition to her regular class-load. Russell Parsons is letting her do this, fueling rumors about him and her, rumors that April exploits. Nancy slowly uncovers the "truth" about Dana and Russell, but it is not what people think.

Praise for **THE EDUCATION OF NANCY ADAMS**

"First of all, I finished Nancy and continued to love it. It really was very hard to put down… I'm no critic, just a reporter who's done a lot on books and publishing for NPR and an enthusiastic reader of good books. The writing was vital and under-lineable without being intrusively writerly…" Martha Woodroof, WMRA Public Radio, author of *Small Blessings*.

"There's much to love about **The Education of Nancy Adams**, especially Nancy herself, widowed, childless, unemployed, approaching 40 – and wielding a gun – when the story opens. Life seems to have passed her by, but it's actually just beginning. Under Larry Baker's masterful pen, you are immediately transported back to high school with the once student, Nancy, now suddenly among the teachers. Baker's cast of characters, weird and distinctly Southern at times, are nonetheless a microcosm of people we all know, real but by no means stereotypical. Among them you will meet yourself either as you are, imagine yourself to be or aspire to become. There is of course no Nancy without the people she's about to both teach and learn from. And others are not always what they seem. As you begin to know more of who they are, you will also begin to know more of yourself. A compelling – and often funny – read from start to finish, Larry Baker now has a permanent place on my short list of favorite novelists." Beverly Willett, essayist and columnist, *Salon* and *Huffington Post*.

LOVE AND OTHER DELUSIONS (2012)

In Alice's world, it all made sense. She told her husband: "I stopped cheating on you when I started sleeping with Danny." Her husband finally understood, but too late.

Alice Marcher is dying, but she is still trying to understand her life. She was thirty when she met Danny Shay. He was eighteen. Two years later, they were sleeping together. Twenty years later, they parted. Alice insisted: "It lasted so long, so it must have meant something, right? We weren't a cliche', were we?"

Katherine Arnett is Alice's audience, or therapist, or ghost. Only when Alice dies is Katherine's true identity revealed. The two women share a final moment in a room with a man who simply asks: "Who are you?" Only one woman knows the answer.

"A story came back to her as she died, fiction as real as her own life, and she herself finally understood it. A beast in a jungle had always been there for her, all those years with Danny. Her own incarnation of that beast, its breath finally upon her throat, had finally turned on her. She had done a very bad thing, falling in love with Danny, and the beast had always been waiting. "

Peter Bartram is Alice's husband. He has always known.

Praise for **LOVE AND OTHER DELUSIONS**

"Some art just points us at the direction it wants to take us. Other art takes us gently by the hand to lead us towards its goal. Larry Baker's art in "Love and Other Delusions" does a bit of both, but most of the time it engages us more fully, in an deeply intellectual wrestling match with matters of the heart, if not the soul. And at its best, and for I what I suspect will be the case for many readers, the heart involved is our own.

Baker's gift then is that he creates not only a story of Alice, Danny, Kathy and Peter, but a story of ourselves. Like our players in the play, our lives are sticky—no—doughy. Doughy with thorns. And we recognize the places where the characters find themselves, both geographically and emotionally. We also recognize their decisions, and even if we don't necessarily agree with them, we can empathize. Baker writes well enough that their pain is our pain, their joy ours.

There is another element to Baker's work that I just now recognize in at least one of his other books—"A Good Man," and that element how he weaves in and out of clarity and opacity. The clarity is in the richness of description, of characterization, and of language. And just when you start to think you know what is going on, boundaries become fuzzy, nearly opaque. Time becomes a character, and characters blend in and out of each other, and its difficult to tell who is who, and when and where we are. And when "Love and other Delusions" is at its very best, we ARE Alice, or maybe another character, because those of us who are old enough to have been around the block a time or two and have taken and or given our share of lumps, share her story. Or his story. Or at least a part of it. Maybe we are her story.

And we may not like it. But we know we aren't alone.

And with respect to love, is it indeed the delusion Baker asserts? The cynic says of course it is. No question. The romantic replies, maybe. But what better do you have to offer? Most of us will take love when we can get it. As did Alice."—-Robert Leonard, KNIA/KRLS Radio

Larry Baker

Larry Baker's wife would insist that the use of "career" in conjunction with his life is a bit misleading. While acknowledging her opinion, however, Larry would still insist that he has done a few things in his life that might constitute real work.

Prior to getting his PhD in 1986, Larry was, in no particular order in a list not meant to be comprehensive: a Pizza Inn manager, Pinkerton security guard, emcee at a strip club, ad salesman, sports reporter, and hotel desk clerk. Most importantly, he owned and operated movie theatres throughout Oklahoma and Texas for fifteen years.

With a PhD in English, he began teaching composition and literature on the college level in 1986, but he soon discovered that he was an overly critical comp teacher and an overly opinionated lit teacher. Thus, he went back to graduate school and earned post-doctorate credit in history, being certified to teach basic American History courses at the community college level. He was very happy. He was known for entertaining and enlightening lectures, and he was an easy grader. Students loved him. Most students did. At least, some.

Although he had been publishing short stories since he was a teenager, he was fifty before his first novel, **THE FLAMINGO RISING** (Knopf-1997), was published. **FLAMINGO** was one of three finalists for the Barnes and Noble "Great New Voices" award for 1997, a *Los Angeles Times* "Top 100" book for 1997, and chosen by the *Iowa Center for the Book* to represent Iowa at the 2010 National Book Festival in Washington. It was also adapted for a Hallmark tv movie in 2001. With those pro-family credentials established, **FLAMINGO** was also included on the American Library Association's "Banned Books" list for 2011.

After moving to Iowa City, Larry was soon involved in local politics. He was elected twice (yes, people voted for him) to the City Council. From that experience came his second novel, **ATHENS/ AMERICA** (2005), a book that managed to agitate the dots of many people in Iowa City. Shortly after **ATHENS** was published, Larry ran for another term on the Council. He came in fifth

His third novel, **A GOOD MAN** (2009), was nominated for "Book of the Year" by the *Southeast Independent Booksellers Association* in 2010.

His fourth novel, **LOVE AND OTHER DELUSIONS** (2012), was a dramatic departure for Baker in style and theme. As he said, "This is definitely not Hallmark material." Love, Sex, and Death.

THE EDUCATION OF NANCY ADAMS was released in April of 2014. Early buzz about that book was enough to get Larry selected as the "Writer on Tour" by the *Florida Literary Arts Council* in 2014 and 2015.

Larry was included on the *Iowa Literary Walk of Fame* in 2010; joining other writers such as John Irving, Marilynne Robinson, Kurt Vonnegut, and Flannery O'Connor, et al.

Everything considered, Larry thinks his parents would be proud of him, and surprised. His wife is still skeptical.

He can be reached at icwriter@gmail.com